NADINE DORRIES

Ruby Flynn

HEAD
ZEUS

First published in the UK in 2015 by Head of Zeus Ltd

9 7 5 3 1 2 4 6 8

A catalogue record for this book is available from the
British Library.

ISBN (HB) 9781784082185
ISBN (XTPB) 9781784082192
ISBN (eBook) 9781784082178

Typeset by Ben Cracknell Studios, Norwich

Printed and bound in Germany
by GGP Media GmbH, Pössneck

Head of Zeus Ltd
Clerkenwell House
45–47 Clerkenwell Green
London EC1R 0HT
WWW.HEADOFZEUS.COM

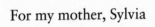

For my mother, Sylvia

Chapter one

Doohoma Head, Mayo, the last day in February, 1947

'Con, I have them, I can see the girl. She's on the back of the cart.'

Con O'Malley lifted his head and faced his assistant, Thomas; the ferocity of the almost horizontal west-coast sleet from the Atlantic slapped him straight in the face. It was so cold and hard, the sting almost made him shout out loud. He took a deep breath, shaded his eyes with his hands and squinted up towards one of the most desolate and tragic sights he had ever seen.

'I can see her, but not the lad. She doesn't look good now.'

Thomas was almost twenty feet above Con, who bent his head against the force of the driving sleet and slowly made his way up the steeply sloping hill. Even this close to the sea and in such ferocious wind, the snow stood deep and both men found the going treacherous and bitterly cold in their inadequate rubber boots. Even though his wife had made him wear two pairs of her own knitted socks before he set out, Con's feet were so frozen, he could not tell where they ended and the snow began.

Thomas had begun to sink into the snowy bog and was nearly up to his knees as he waited for Con to cover the ground.

'Good Lord, give me breath,' said Con, resting just a couple of feet below Thomas while he waited for God to deliver. He lifted his face once again into the sleet to try to catch another sight of the girl and was whipped across the face by tines of ice carried on the wind.

'Who knows how old she is, what with being fed so little. Jesus, she has only a shawl and rags on her, she must be soaked and frozen through. There's nothing on her feet, Thomas.'

It was an hour since Con and Thomas had entered the cottage below them. Con's yellow vomit was still clearly visible at the front door, not yet totally covered in snowfall. The mother was indeed dead, as they had feared, but Con had not expected that the father, who they knew had died days earlier, would still be indoors. The mud floor of the cottage was soft in parts, from urine and vomit, and the smell had been acrid and overpowering. There was no food, no fuel, nothing in the cottage that would sustain body or soul, just the overpowering stench of death seeping from the two bodies lying side by side on a straw mattress.

'How long have those kids been living like this?' said Thomas as they stood outside the cottage door, recovering from what they had just seen.

'God alone knows, looks to me like maybe they had the idea to go out and cut the turf for heat. But it would be no use to them, not having been dried out.'

Being the town clerk in one of the wildest and most rural parts of Ireland, Con O'Malley thought he was beyond being shocked by how people in these parts scratched a living. As the government administrator for the area, his job consisted of everything from making sure local taxes were paid to lending a hand at harvests, and anything in between. And that was before the winter of '47 bore down upon them with the worst conditions anyone alive had witnessed, or any storyteller could recall.

Down on the bottom road, the drifts stood fifteen feet high. He had sent a search party out only yesterday to check on some of the more remote farm dwellings, but they had been unsuccessful, forced back by the weather.

Those locals and farmers who could travel met by the fire in the Doohoma Inn each night, to exchange information about the worsening conditions.

'Two brothers have been found frozen to death in Geesala. Indoors they were with their cow, but that never saved them. They were dead by the time they were found and the cow nearly was too,' said the publican. '"Tis the cold that does it, not the hunger. For those who store it with no good cover, the turf is frozen wet and won't burn.'

The men blessed themselves as silence fell for a while.

'They say 'tis hundreds, so it is, four hundred or more that have been killed, 'tis as bad as the famine.'

Now, in the harsh light of the day, Con turned and looked back down the cliff to the low white, single-roomed cottage, which was, or rather had been, the home of the children they were searching for. It stood alone. Isolated. The gable end proudly faced down towards the sea, protecting those who had lived inside from the force of the gales. Con had driven along the coast road and noticed the home in the far distance during better days. Take me on if you dare, the cottage had seemed to shout to the Atlantic squalls as a thin plume of smoke struggled from a lone central chimney, take me on if you dare.

No fireside smoke defied the elements today. The cottage, or at least its inhabitants had been well and truly taken on and they had lost. If the men had only walked in this direction when they first arrived at the house, up the cliff, rather than back down towards the sea, they would have found the children much earlier. There was a boy too, a little older, they understood.

'The lad must surely be near the girl, Thomas? I doubt they would have separated now in this weather.'

Con swore under his breath as the snow soaked through his socks.

He had been woken by the village priest's housekeeper, Mrs O'Toole, not two hours since, although it felt like a lifetime already. She had imparted her news and a direct request for help, from the priest.

'Mrs Flynn has the consumption. The daddy died on Sunday and Father has given the last rites to the mammy. He thinks she may have gone by now but he is in Castlebar today. They have a big mass up there for those who have lost their livestock. The nuns at the convent school outside Belmullet are expecting to take the children in when the mammy is gone, but someone needs to go up there and fetch them down. The journey is terrible. I've never seen snow like it in me life, so deep it is and the bog is as bad up on the top just now as it is at the bottom.'

Mrs O'Toole furtively scanned the O'Malleys' kitchen. A home she had not stepped into before and one she knew she might never be invited into again. Her eyes darted from the range to the press, from the fire to the curtains. She took in the newspapers laid on the floor and the books piled high on the bookcase. She wrinkled her nose at the pipe laid on the hearth and almost had to stop herself from wondering, out loud, what it was that remained in the glass on the floor by the chair.

Con's English wife, Susan, not long arrived from Liverpool, was in the kitchen, still in her nightdress.

A look of satisfaction crossed Mrs O'Toole's face. 'The cut of her,' she would say to her husband later, 'as she swanked around, with no notion of shame. Come from Liverpool, so she has and brought the fast ways with her, I would be saying.'

That would do nicely. A glass on the floor that had obviously once contained strong alcohol, a woman verging on the brink of nakedness and the threshold of eternal shame, wearing a pink nylon nightdress in the kitchen without so much as a pinny to cover her modesty, or the babby in her belly, was plenty to be going on with. No woman of religion carried on like that.

'Father said someone needs to check the cottage. If the mother's dead an' all, and I would be saying that she must be by now, then the children need taking to the nuns. You know the Flynns, they have no family or friends, living up on that cliff alone. They were always too proud and full of themselves.

Neither mountain nor country people. She was supposed to be from a fine heritage altogether, she was, but Flynn, he was just a fisherman like the rest. How they have managed since he lost the boat, with no catch to feed them God alone knows. There is only turf and bog up there.'

Con nodded and edged Mrs O'Toole gently towards the door. 'I'll away to Thomas and we will make our way up there now, Mrs O'Toole. Tell the priest that if he's given Mrs Flynn the sacrament and informed the nuns, he has done his job. You can leave it to Thomas and myself now.'

As the kitchen door closed, Con sighed and turned to Susan. Until December, she had taught at the only school for miles around.

'Those children have never been to the school, Con, ever,' she said. 'They would have needed to leave home when it was still dark to walk to the school and they would no sooner have got to us than it would have been time for them to walk back again.'

Con placed his boots in front of the range to warm. 'Aye, it was always the way. There are plenty of families like the Flynns and God knows, if this government doesn't act after this winter and do something to help the country people, there will be blood on the streets so there will.'

Susan carefully laid out two pairs of socks on top of the boots. 'I went up there once in the car and Mrs Flynn, she was grateful to me, she was, but I could see there was no sense in trying. She was well spoken and very well educated though, she made sure I knew that, showed me the books on her bookshelf. One of which was *The Iliad* no less, which really surprised me.

She told me she could provide her children with as good an education as any school and I believed her. She made me feel, oh I don't know, less well-bred than she was. She was very striking to look at, I remember that, and she had lovely green eyes, but, apart from the books, she was as poor a woman as the next around here. They had less than nothing and the books, well they couldn't eat them.'

Susan paused and watched Con, who had sat down in the fireside chair and was now pulling on his socks and extra layers. She nodded towards the whiskey glass and held out her hand. Her pregnant belly made bending down impossible. As she walked to the tap and began rinsing the glass, she continued.

'This didn't go unnoticed by the nosy beak.' Susan held the glass up to the light to check that it was spotless, before she dried it to squeaky clean with the Irish linen tea towel.

Con appeared deep in thought and lifted his coat down from the peg on the back of the kitchen door.

'There are still too many kids around just like the Flynns,' he replied. 'I see them, teeming over the fields, some in their bare feet each morning heading for school. Something has to be done, Susan. This storm, it has to be a wake-up call.'

Susan wrapped her arms around her caring husband. 'Be careful up on that cliff,' she said. 'You will have your own child to look after very shortly: we both want you back, safe and sound.'

With a heavy heart and a deep and tender farewell kiss for Susan, Con headed out into the foulest weather he had ever stepped into.

*

Now, as Con and Thomas edged their way up the steep and slippery slope, taking small but sure steps towards the cart, through the white blizzard, they spotted the desolate form of the dark grey donkey, standing with his muzzle almost on the ground. He was covered by snow, inches deep. The wind sliced away the top flakes from the ridge on his back, and as they drew near Con saw that the girl remained motionless.

They both spotted the boy at the same time. Sitting in the snow, sheltering under the cart, clutching at two scragged lumps of wet turf in his blue hands. He was frozen dead. The donkey gave the impression of providing shelter, as though trying to protect the boy from the ferocious wind and swirling icy snow. Con looked into the eyes of the forlorn animal and met despair.

'I'll carry the girl, Thomas,' said Con. He had to shout to be heard, but still, his voice was heavy and almost lost into the air. 'You put the boy on the wagon and lead the donkey down, if you can, we will follow on behind. It will be easier going down than it was coming up.' Con prayed that he was right.

As he walked across to the girl, he noted that at least she was obviously still alive. She had raised her head as they approached but she appeared incapable of little else. Her long, wet and matted hair had frozen almost solid to her face and Con thought that no matter how terrified she might be of two strange men, she would be too cold to run. She wore a black knitted shawl that covered her head, and she had wrapped it around her body. Now she clung to it as though it were life itself. It was possibly the only thing that had saved her.

'Come here, colleen,' whispered Con, as he lifted the girl up and slipped her straight inside the warmth of his coat.

'Jesus, Holy Mother, she weighs no more than a baby,' he said, as he fastened the buttons and pulled his scarf across the front and around the back of her head.

As they walked down the cliff, the girl did not make a sound. Not one whimper of cold or hunger. As they passed the doorway of her family home, Con felt her body stiffen. Her eyes, suddenly alive, turned and stared up at Con, huge dark emerald green craters, deep in her hollowed-out face. They blazed at him and for a second, Con was startled by their clarity and brightness. He had never seen eyes as green. Con knew what she wanted to say. He knew what her thoughts and questions would be. *My mammy and daddy, we have to get them, we cannot leave them, stop.* Con avoided her gaze and pulled on the side of the cart to help Thomas move the wheels out of the ruts left by the cut turf. It was a relief that the girl did not speak. He could tell her nothing she would want to hear.

Thomas turned to face back towards the road, holding his hand across his nose and mouth to keep out the sleet. The wind had increased in volume and Con could barely tell what he was saying.

'How can we be sure that there are only the two of them? Are they the only ones? God knows, there will be others on these hills in exactly the same position.'

Con shifted the weight of the girl up inside his coat and used his arms to support her. His heart tightened in his chest as he saw the tears running down her cheek. They were not tears caused by sleet or snow, but were hot tears of pain.

'Do you have a name, colleen?' Con said as gently as he could into the side of her face, so that she could hear him. 'What is your name?' But she did not reply.

He tried to reassure her. 'We are taking you into the village, first to my house and my wife, Susan, for some food and warmer clothes and then on to the convent.'

Con knew the look that passed over her face had been one of relief and that she understood some of what he was saying. She knew her parents were both dead. Neither he nor Susan would have the job of breaking that news to her. She knew. She might have been in pain from the cold and from whatever she had witnessed but she was glad to be alive, that much he could tell. Her eyes might be focused on the form of her dead brother lying under her wet shawl on the back of the wagon, frozen solid into the crouching position they had found him in, still clutching the turf. She might desperately glance back towards where both parents had died while she sat by their side, wiping the vomit from their deathly pale, waxen-like faces, crying for someone to help. She might be herself frozen to within an hour of her own death, but Con knew that in the midst of her torment, a flame of hope had lit somewhere within this child. It burned behind her eyes and she was thankful to have been saved and to be in his arms.

'What's your name, colleen?' Con whispered into her ear again and this time, her voice answered with such a force and pride, that she took him totally by surprise.

'Ruby, I am. I am Ruby Flynn.'

And they were the last words she spoke for almost a year.

Chapter two

Belmullet, Fenningale Convent of the Blessed Heart

'Heavens above, what have we here,' the reverend mother exclaimed, as she opened the door to Con. He stood on the doorstep, protecting the undersized bundle in his arms from the snow. Ruby must have been all of twelve, but felt more like a small eight-year-old. He could feel her heart beating against his, like a frightened bird. He had almost been convinced that they wouldn't make it, but the road from Doohoma and on through Bangor Erris had been freshly cleared and made passable, not by the council, but by the efforts of local farmers and the residents of the small village who had an urgent need to reach each other after weeks of isolation, in order to exchange food and help, turf and milk for porter and jam. Animals must be transported, phone calls made once the cables were repaired and letters posted to concerned relatives in places as far-flung and as exotic as Liverpool, Watford, London and New York. Cash-stuffed envelopes waited to be collected from the post office by those whose relatives abroad had been able to spare it. Many depended upon the charity of local neighbours, shop owners and friends. People could not live for long if they were alone, snowed up indoors.

'It could have been much worse, Reverend Mother,' Con said, with a knowing look. 'She's dry now. I took her home with myself. My wife sorted her out and put a jumper of her own over her. She's in a bad way now, though, and no mistake. We had thought of keeping her for a while, but Mrs O'Toole said that the priest had contacted you and you were expecting her. If my wife had not been due any day, we'd have had no hesitation.'

The reverend mother looked less than pleased.

'That's as may be Mr O'Malley, but we are struggling ourselves with this storm. We have taken in half a dozen orphans this week alone. I have no more beds or blankets. We live off what we grow and make. You would have been as well to keep her. I am honour bound to spend the money I take for fees on the school alone. On educating the young girls sent to us. Girls who have passed the entrance exam. Their parents don't pay to educate half of Mayo, just because it snows. It is all very difficult. How are we supposed to manage? How many more can we take? It is desperate crowded in here right now, so it is.'

Con looked the reverend mother square in the eye.

'Would you like me to return home and fetch the blankets from my own bed, Mother?'

The reverend mother was instantly shamed, her lack of charity highlighted in just a few well-chosen words. Moments later, they were standing in her study, in front of the roaring fire. Con pointedly inspected the splendour of the study.

''Tis a mighty grand vase you have here, Mother.'

Con nodded towards a large red and gold vase, which stood in the centre of a round table.

But if the reverend mother had noticed the irony in his voice, she gave no sign of it.

'Isn't it just the most beautiful thing?' she trilled enthusiastically, moving closer to admire it with him, as though seeing it for the first time. 'Father Michael carried it all the way home from Chicago himself, you know. It was given to him by a firm of Irish builders, a very well-to-do family. He gave them communion in their own private chapel. Can you imagine that? Before he died, God rest his soul, he asked us to keep it safe for him. I don't mind admitting, it brightens up my day. There is not one person enters into this study who doesn't admire it.'

As she rattled on, Con's gaze took in the rest of the room. The pictures on the wall, fine china, the brass lamp on the desk and the ornate fender around the fire. The room was packed with beautiful things. Silver on the windowsill, a gold knife on the mahogany desk. As he looked down, he noticed that Ruby was copying him. She, too, studied the room. He had expected her to be intimidated and he felt strangely moved that she stood up straight, with her hands rigid by her sides, almost proud and yet, God knew, the child had nothing on this earth to feel proud about. Her gaze rested, just as his had done, first on the vase on the table, then on the paintings, the windowsill and finally on the brass fender around the fire.

She's mimicking me, he thought to himself, as a faint smile touched his lips. She doesn't know what to do or how to behave, so she is mimicking what I do, God bless her.

'Will she be fully educated, Mother?' The expression on Con's face said clearly that he would not be fobbed off with prattle of vases and rich American benefactors.

The reverend mother felt slightly uncomfortable.

'Of course she will. We will do all we can for these unfortunate storm orphans, but please don't bring me any more children to look after. There are practical limitations to what we can achieve here. You haven't brought me this girl just for one day, as you well know. She will be here until we can place her into service. But, goodness knows, some of these children we have taken in from the bogs are as good as feral. Now, please sit yourself down, while I ask Sister Francis to fetch some tea and brack, then you can tell us all you know.'

Ruby stood next to the chair on which Con was now sitting. He had slipped his hand into hers, to reassure her, and now she stood still clinging onto him, scared to let him go. She was exhausted and the heat from the fire thawed her bones and stung her eyes, while the lack of sleep made her feel drowsy. She looked at the turf stacked up in the wicker basket and her heart constricted with pain. They would only have needed a few sods, she and her brother, to warm up their ma and da. The snow still fell heavily, but here in Belmullet, the wind was nowhere near as fierce as it had been in Doohoma.

The trees outside were thick with the snow, their branches creaking and groaning under the weight of it. She had spent every day of her life with the noise of the ocean breaking on the sands and pounding in her ears. Now, her ears tingled as they adjusted to the unfamiliar sound of voices in deep discussion. The kind man and the reverend mother were talking about her. Their words reverberated in her brain.

Her mammy's dead. Her daddy's dead. Her brother's dead. They are all dead.

'We are full to the rushes here. The last thing we need is another child. We cannot manage with those we have, can we, Sister Francis? Overrun we are.'

Sister Francis, who had brought in the tea, caught Ruby's eye and gave her a sympathetic smile. No one offered Ruby a drink.

They didn't want her. She was not welcome. Her face burned hot with shame. The man, Con, had taken her from a cold hell to his own fireside. His soothing. His wife. She had sat on the pregnant woman's knee and felt a new life kicking her in the back, as her frozen hair was rubbed with a hot towel. She felt the burning then too, and had wanted to turn around and kick the unborn baby back. Over and over.

'He's off again,' the wife had said to Con, with a knowing smile. He smiled back as he placed his hand on his wife's shoulder and even though Ruby was sitting there on the knee of his wife, for that moment, she did not exist.

For almost a week, she had squatted on the earth floor by her mammy's side and done her very best. Every word her mammy had cried out was burned into her memory. During interludes, when her mother recognized Ruby and spoke, she had stared into her eyes, desperately wanting her mother to say something that would help, to make the cottage warm or to tell her where to find food. The words were still there, sitting in her gut, gnawing at her, telling her she was Ruby Flynn and that no man or woman on this earth was better than she.

'You have family, Ruby. Find my family,' her mother had croaked.

Ruby had whispered in her ear, 'Where are they, Mammy?'

'No one is better than you Ruby Flynn, remember that.'

As she held the melted snow to her mother's lips, she turned to look at her brother. He lay next to their daddy on the mattress. Something was wrong with Daddy. He didn't speak or move at all and was very cold.

The dog, Max, lay next to where the fire should have been burning and he looked at Ruby with wide doleful eyes. *We are in trouble*, they said to Ruby, *what can I do?*

Where was Max now? Ruby's heart beat faster as she thought of him and her eyes began to fill with tears.

She wanted to ask the man, would someone take Max when they went for her mammy and daddy? Max needed food. Max would die too. But the words were trapped inside her. The vision of soft eyes came into her mind. The long hair around his mouth, which she used to laugh at and call his beard. The smell of his damp coat when they both came back wet to the house and she lay with him on the floor in front of the fire, stroking his belly with one hand, holding a book with another, listening to her mother busy at the table preparing their supper, feeling warm and content.

The image, the smells, the memory all fluttered about inside her head. She opened and closed her mouth and tried to form the word *Max*, but nothing happened, no sound came, she could not speak.

Ruby looked at the adults talking, oblivious to her silence. The man's wife, Susan, had told her she would live here and would attend the school.

'You will be sad for a while, but you will get better, sweetheart,' she had said.

Sometimes, her mammy had called her sweetheart. When she was having her soft moments. When Ruby sat on her knee and rested her head against her soft pillowy breasts. When her mammy stroked her hair and sang softly into her ear. She tried to remember the song. It was elusive, just there, hovering, waiting to be recalled, but she couldn't remember. She could only hear the soothing tones of Susan.

'It is a great opportunity, just fantastic. Make the most of it. Learn every day. Study really hard. That school is the best in Ireland and even in Liverpool. You will leave with something most girls in Ireland don't have, the ability to make your own way in the world. With an education like that, you will be able to do anything, become a nurse, a doctor even, they have more lady doctors now than ever before, since the war. Just you make the most of it, Ruby, turn something bad into something good.'

Susan looked into Ruby's face as she spoke, hoping to find some sign that her words had sunk in, made sense. All she saw was fear, staring back at her.

'It's all too much for her to take in,' said Con, gently. 'Don't upset yourself, it's because you are so close to your time.' Susan nodded and Ruby saw tears welling in her eyes.

She was confused by Susan's words. Why should she make the most of it? She didn't want to live here. When the snow melted, she would escape and return to her cottage. Who were these people deciding the rest of her life for her?

Susan, in her softly spoken way had also said, 'The nuns will look after you and make you very welcome.'

If she had got that so profoundly wrong, what of everything else she had said? Ruby now felt more afraid than ever. The looks the reverend mother shot Ruby, when she thought Con wasn't looking were far from welcoming.

Con continued to speak. 'She is about twelve years old, the housekeeper reckons, despite being so small. The only words she has spoken since we found her are her name, Ruby Flynn. They are known not to have family locally. Flynn was an orphan, himself, by all accounts. I will make enquiries, but without knowing which parish the mother was originally from, I don't hold out much hope… though I do know where she may have once worked.'

Con had finished his tea. His cup tapped the silver teaspoon and it rattled and rang against the saucer as he placed the cup down. She heard the noise of shuffling, the lightest of footsteps, moving along the corridor outside the door and turned her head slightly, to listen harder.

She could hear bells softly pealing, doors opening and closing and muffled voices. The convent, which had been silent until now, was slowly awakening. Her fingers were wound around the thin arm of the chair in which Con sat and they clenched tighter, as though she were reluctant to leave his side. A bolt of anxiety shot through her as he rose to sign the papers the reverend mother had laid out on her blotter. Along with Sister Francis, they huddled over the desk, talking. The heat from the fire burnt the side of her leg and her skin became mottled with ugly red weals. The chilblains on her feet stung, as the freshly warmed blood in her veins forced a way through the constricted and frozen vessels in her almost frostbitten toes.

Sister Francis looked directly at her and smiled again. 'I'll fetch Charlotte. She can look after her for a few days, until she settles down,' she said.

The reverend mother interjected sharply. 'She doesn't require looking after, Sister Francis. You encourage the girls to be weak. She just needs someone to show her the ropes.'

The adults continued talking as they walked out of the office. It was as if they had forgotten about Ruby entirely.

Sister Francis turned back. 'You wait there, Ruby,' she said, leaving the door half open. They were gone and she was alone.

Ruby's head banged with panic. Con had rescued her. She had thought that he and his wife had liked her. Susan had clothed her and fed her soup from a spoon. They had tried to remove the matted knots from her hair. They must feel the same way as she did. She must surely belong to them now, until they could find her mammy's family. Con had spoken to her kindly, like her daddy. She thought he might want to take her back home with him. To his wife and the kitchen with the crib waiting in the corner and the soup pan on the range. To the bookcase against the wall with more books than she thought anyone could ever read and the big lamp and the soft towels. The patterned red rug in front of the crackling fire swam in front of her eyes. She wanted Con to take her back, to the smell of bread, tobacco and safety. Fear rose like bile in her throat and she began to breathe very fast indeed as she controlled the waves of terror, but she could not stop the shaking which began in her knees and now afflicted her hands.

Is he going to leave me? Will he walk away? She felt a cold blast of air race through the room and catch at her legs, as the front door opened once again. She heard muffled voices and words she knew were about her.

'Best not to visit.' 'Regards to your wife.' 'Don't fuss to write.'

Her heart slipped. She tilted her head to one side to strain and hear more.

Will he really leave me here?

Receding, fading footsteps crunched in the snow. A car door clicked shut. An engine fired up.

Will he?

She heard the sound of tyres on compacted snow as the car slowly and carefully moved away and down the driveway.

Does he not want to take me back to his home?

She flinched as the front doors banged shut and she heard the sound of the nun's footsteps moving back towards her; missing was the heavy solid tread of Con's boots.

No, he does not.

The pain of his parting was like a new, fresh loss and yet she had known him for less than a day. She moved not a muscle as she stared at the window, the tears stinging her eyes threatening to erupt. The brass clock on the mantel chimed the hour and in response, the turf shifted in the grate and sent a shower of sparks to land on her feet. She took a deep breath and swallowed a gasp, holding down the panic, the hurt, and the pain, down and down, again. Someone called out the name Charlotte, and a second later the door opened wider.

'Come here, girl.' It was the reverend mother. 'Come here.'

She turned her head, but the reverend mother was no longer looking at Ruby. Her attention was on Sister Francis and a young girl who stood under a dim halo of light. She had a pretty face and long dark hair tied with blue ribbon bows in two plaits which touched her shoulders.

The corridor was dimly lit and the tall shadows of the nuns towered and flickered on the rendered walls. Black effigies, whispering, conferring, long fingers pointing, plotting her fate. The nuns stooping to speak to the young girl who had stood between them were not of Ruby's world. The events of the past weeks had set her apart. No other person could ever know or comprehend the depth of her pain and she could never fit into this world with these people. This place with its antiseptic smell, polished wood and light falling from the brocade fringed lamp.

Ruby fixed her gaze on the vase Con had admired. It glowed in the light from the fire, as if calling her towards the table, and its gold rim burned and flickered, mesmerizing her. The tiny patterns of figurines reflected from the perfect glaze danced mockingly in the flames. Like Ruby, the vase was on fire. She thought she heard her brother's voice whispering in her ear, *We can do it, so we can Ruby, we can.*

'Come here, girl.' A further summons from the door. Not kindly or caring, but abrupt and impatient.

Ruby stroked the vase and ran her fingers over the luminous, powdery glaze, then with one flick of her hand and with all the force of the pain burning inside her, sent it flying from the table and onto the floor, where it smashed at her feet into a thousand pieces. She heard the fading screams of the reverend mother as she disappeared, deep inside her own broken heart.

Later that evening, Con met Thomas in the Doohoma Inn.

'Why do you think they took themselves up there, Con?' asked Thomas as he waited for his Guinness to be pulled.

'God alone knows,' Con replied. 'Seems to me that they had an idea to go out and cut the turf for heat and couldn't get back down again.'

The rescue of the Flynn children had been the talk of the day in the village. The landlord placed Con's pewter mug on the bar and joined the conversation.

'Flynn lost his curragh when the storm began weeks ago, but sure, the man was sick for weeks before that. There won't have been any food in that house for a while, although I have sent up bread meself, and others sent 'tatoes and cabbage. 'Twas the weather that put a stop to it, but we was waiting for them to come down, so we were. I told the mammy meself, sit the storm out down here, I said. Mind, I had no idea then how long it would last and neither did she, but I'm thinking she may have guessed it would be bad and wanted them to stay in their own home with the animals. Did you find the dog? God, the kids loved that dog. Big grey thing, Max I think his name is. He followed them kids everywhere.'

'I didn't,' Con said. 'We saw no dog, did we, Thomas?'

Thomas shook his head as he took the first sip of his pint.

'The mammy, she was a funny one,' said the landlord. 'Too proud they were to ask for help from anyone. People say that she went down a peg or two when she married Flynn. Some say she had something to do with a grand house. Maybe she was from one of the tenant farms on one of the estates. But there's no doubting the nature between her and Flynn now. They was madly in love. Neither God nor man could have kept them apart and none tried, so they say.'

Con finished his Guinness and placed his pot on the bar.

'Come on, Thomas,' he said. 'We have a job to finish.'

'Eh, what job? Have we not done enough for one day, surely to God?'

Con had felt uneasy since returning from the convent.

'Come on, Thomas,' he said again, impatiently. 'We have to go.'

And once again, Con stepped out into the blizzard. The child might be in the convent, but he could do this. She would probably never know, but if it was the last thing he did, he would find her dog.

Back at the convent, Ruby escaped unpunished for breaking the vase. What had saved her was the fact that she turned a ghastly shade of pale and fainted dead away.

'If she stepped outdoors the wind would break her bones in two, she's lighter than a feather,' said Sister Francis, as she carried Ruby along the corridor to the dorm with Charlotte bobbing along in her wake. She said it loudly and ran fast, knowing that while Ruby was at the convent, she would have to watch over her, to save her from the wrath of the reverend mother, which would be fierce indeed after today.

Chapter three

1953

She was awake. Ruby was always the first to wake. Often in the middle of the night. It wasn't the bells of the chapel ringing or even the cock crowing, it was her own urgent thoughts, forcing her eyelids open, escaping the nightmare which had, night after night, haunted her sleep.

In the early days, she awoke screaming. Her punishment for disturbing the slumbering dorm had been severe and now, in the vacillating moments between sleep and wakefulness, she had learnt to control her distress. To lie with her arms rigid, her breathing slow and deep and wait, until her beating heart stilled to a steady rhythm.

'God in heaven, are you awake again? What's up with ye, Ruby?' The dorm bed next to her own would always creak as Charlotte, or Lottie as she was known by everyone, leaned over. Lottie had slept in the bed next to Ruby since that first day at the convent and she had been the first person to hear Ruby speak after a whole year of silence. This from a child who had once talked so much, her father joked that she would drive the fish across the water, all the way to America, just for a bit of peace and quiet.

'Try and get her to speak to you,' kind Sister Francis had said to Lottie. 'Go on, ask her about her family, God rest their souls, anything that will make her talk. Sister Joseph is very sure that when a child stops speaking at her age, she may forget altogether and remain dumb for life.'

Dutifully, Lottie had done as instructed, but received not so much as a whimper in response. After a few weeks of lying awake and staring through the skylight in the dorm, Ruby had studied and worked out the pattern of the constellations in the night sky. They became as familiar to her as the rose trellis paper on the dormitory wall.

Lottie would often wake when she knew Ruby had trouble sleeping. She never expected a reply to her words of comfort. She had learnt to compensate and to speak for Ruby.

'What's the problem? Do ye need the toilet?'

Lottie's face blocked out the skylight as she leaned over Ruby's bed.

Ruby's unwavering green eyes looked back at her.

'Sure, you have bold eyes,' whispered Lottie. 'Suck yer thumb like this, it helps you fall asleep.'

Ruby gave no response, silent, as always.

Each night as she extinguished the lamps, Sister Joseph would say, 'Hands off your penny, girls. Let me see all hands on top of the blankets now, and that doesn't mean suck yer thumb, lie straight.' Then she would walk up and down the rows of beds, tucking the blankets in tightly at the sides and whispering to each girl, 'Don't touch yourself now, 'tis a sin.'

Gently, Lottie picked up Ruby's hand and clumsily pushed her thumb into her mouth. 'Go on now, suck, go on. Look, they all do it.'

To demonstrate what she meant, Lottie began sucking furiously on her own thumb.

'See, that's what you have to do for a bit of peace, ye suck the thumb. You can't sleep ever, Ruby, because ye lie like the boards.'

Lottie was right. Every girl, whether she was aged five or fifteen, noisily sucked her thumb and from that night onwards, Ruby took her first comfort and did the same.

On what was to be their last morning at the convent, Maria, who slept in the bed on the other side of the dorm from Ruby and Lottie, woke to hear them chatting.

'Will you two shut yer fecking gobs, it's still night-time,' she hissed.

Maria had arrived at the convent just a year ago. A refugee from poverty and an alcoholic father. She was not one of the storm orphans, as they had become known in Belmullet. She had been delivered to the door of the convent by a priest. He had declared her to be at severe risk of temptation and sin. In just the year since her arrival, Maria had provided Ruby and Lottie with more of an education than any of the nuns, and they were both in awe of her.

'We need to be up and sharp today, anyway, Maria.' Lottie yawned, stretching her arms up wide as the light from a weak and watery sun slipped into the dorm through the skylight. 'When I was polishing the reverend mother's study yesterday,

I heard her say on the phone there are three housekeepers visiting today to interview girls, and I know we three are on the list, because I heard the reverend mother say so. One of the housekeepers is from a big castle, but Jesus, don't ask me the name, I just heard the word castle.'

Lottie didn't mention that she had also heard the reverend mother say she would be glad of the chance to rid herself of Ruby.

'She broke our beloved Father Michael's vase, she has the devil in her that one, so she does. I will gladly pay a housekeeper to take her.'

Ruby had already been looked over by at least half a dozen prospective housekeepers, but none had taken her, much to the annoyance of the reverend mother.

''Tis the set of your jaw and the boldness in your face,' Sister Francis had whispered to Ruby. 'I don't want you to go, Ruby, but you can't stay here for the rest of your life. Being in service will be one way to step into the big world. Who knows what opportunities will be waiting out there for you?'

Ruby looked coldly at Sister Francis when she said this. Somewhere deep inside, Ruby knew that the set of her jaw and the defiance in her face was all that set her apart from the other orphans in the convent. The girls did everything together, woke, slept, ate, prayed, learned and cleaned. And then learned some more. A routine in harmony with the ringing of the bells. Although the best scholar in the convent and a pride to Sister Francis, Ruby was not quite so good at keeping her own temper in check and she was as stubborn as a mule.

'You were too lenient on her when she couldn't speak,'

Reverend Mother often said to Sister Francis. 'You spared the rod and have spoilt the child.'

In her first year, Ruby often overheard such conversations. There was a general assumption that if she couldn't speak, she couldn't hear either. This had enabled her to live inside her own head with her memories of the days before the storm, recalling not just fragments of time in the past, but sounds, smells and feelings. She could remember, word for word, conversations with her mother, smell the smoke from the crackling fire and feel the wind rush in through the door as her da and her brother returned from a day's fishing. She could hear the soft crackling from the gently yielding straw mattress as she lay down in front of the dying embers of the peat fire and she could still recall the silver shimmer of the sea on a sunny morning and how her eyes hurt from the glare.

Her memories always took her to the final week.

The greyness of the eerie haze inside the cottage that came from the thick snow, which covered both windows. Scraping the black cast iron pan to scratch out the last frozen spoon of the broth her mother had made before she became so ill. She had lain down on her own straw mattress 'for just a minute, Ruby,' and never got up again.

The conversations she had with Eamonn, her brother, but most of all, their fateful last words, came back vividly to her.

'Shall we up onto the turf and cut some to bring back down?' Eamonn had whispered as she huddled next to him for warmth on the mattress between their parents.

'Can we go without Daddy?' she asked. They were never allowed near the cliff edge alone.

'We have to, Daddy won't answer me. He is so cold we have to get the fire going, Ruby.' Her brother began to cough again. The phlegm bubbled in his chest and his eyes burnt bright with a fever.

'Don't worry, I will look after you all right,' Eamonn said, 'but come with me, we can do it, so we can Ruby, we can.'

She could tell he was scared. Scared both of what was outside the cottage and in. He didn't want to step outside alone, without her. There was another reason he wanted to venture outdoors. It was to look for the priest. Eamonn had been sure that when the priest had come to pray over his daddy, he would bring something with him, or send someone straight back. He had done neither, but maybe a neighbour from the village had left something on the road, as they did when his mother bought flour and they took the cart down to collect it. But the road was white and he could see by the undisturbed snow that no one had been there, so now there was nothing for it but to cut the turf. It was the only thing he knew to do, so he wrapped Ruby in their mammy's outdoor shawl, lifted her onto the turf cart and lay the sacking across her knee. But the cold slowed him down and slipped into his bones and the lack of food made him feel dizzy. It took an hour to climb the cliff to the turf bed and to remove two frozen lumps of turf from the neat mounds his daddy had already cut. With what remained of his strength he crawled under the cart for shelter and to rest while he recovered, as his lungs filled and faltered.

Ruby had not intended to break her silence on the morning when she spoke for the first time, but the words, which had been beating on the inside of her brain, unravelled and tumbled out, and as they did, Ruby felt life glide through her veins.

It was Deirdra McGinty who brought about her ferocious explosion of anger. Deirdra was a paying student, the child of a land agent. Like many other pupils, she resented the arrival of the non-paying storm orphans and especially Lottie, viewing her kindness as a weakness.

On the way from prayers to the refectory, Ruby noticed Lottie crying.

Ruby had no need of her voice to ask what was wrong.

'The picture of my mammy and daddy's wedding has disappeared from under my pillow and I know who has taken it but no one will believe me. My mammy and daddy, they were married in Dublin and 'tis a lovely picture. I brought it here, hidden in my liberty bodice on the day I arrived. Sister Maggie says I shouldn't have had it anyway and she won't do nothing to help. I know it was Deirdra McGinty. I saw her rooting around our beds yesterday afternoon. Why would she want the picture of my mammy and daddy? 'Tis the only thing I have left.'

Lottie burst into a fresh bout of raw tears.

'Lottie, stop your squawking.' Sister Maggie's voice rang out from the front of the line. 'You sound worse than a laying hen. What's done is done. Quiet girl.'

Ruby noticed Deirdra McGinty giggling behind her hand to another girl, two ahead in the line. Deirdra never missed an opportunity to let the storm orphans know that her family paid for her to attend the convent and that she was not 'a charity case' like they were.

Ruby had no idea what overcame her. Leaving Lottie's side, she let out one loud scream and hurled herself at Deirdra McGinty, who was knocked flat from the attack.

'Where's the picture?' she screamed.

As she stopped screeching, Ruby wrapped Deirdra's ponytail round her fingers and banged her head up and down on the stone floor.

The shuffling procession of hungry girls stopped in its tracks and stood, open mouthed in amazement.

Ruby had spoken. Ruby had screamed and shouted. Ruby's voice, which no one had heard before today, was so loud it filled the convent and bounced back at them from wall to wall.

The silent girl had not only spoken, she was blaspheming and beating one of the fee-paying pupils to a pulp on the corridor floor, right in front of their eyes.

Sister Maggie shouted for help.

'Get off her, you are killing her, leave her alone,' she shrieked, pulling at Ruby's shoulders.

But Ruby could only hear the rage in her head, which sounded as loud as waves, beating against the Doohoma shore.

It took two of them, Sister Maggie and the reverend mother, to pull Ruby off Deirdra.

'Put me down, put me down,' Ruby screamed as she tried to free herself from the iron grip of the nuns.

Sister Maggie and the reverend mother had each taken an arm and a leg and Ruby found herself helpless, her body arched upwards, with her skirts covering her face as she tried to wriggle free from their vice-like grip while they marched down the corridor with her.

'Open that door,' the reverend mother shouted to one of the girls, as they passed the sick bay. As soon as the door opened, Ruby was swung in and dumped unceremoniously on the bed. She heard the key turn in the lock behind her and she knew she would be there for some time.

'I'm not going to escape,' Ruby shouted through the keyhole, trying out her new-found voice, but no one replied.

The sick bay was cold and bare. It contained nothing but a cast iron bedstead, a sink, a chamber pot, which the maid had left on the floor, and a large crucifix on the wall opposite the bed. The windows were shielded by wooden shutters, which had been pulled and fastened shut.

She could tell the time by the bells calling the girls to prayer and with each hour, her spirits sank further. She cried for the mammy who she knew was not there. She imagined she could smell the peat smoke in her mother's hair and feel the warmth of her breath against her cheek, touching her with the most tender of kisses until she finally fell into a deep sleep.

The following morning, the door opened without the usual jangle of keys. In the shaft of light that fell into the room, Ruby could see the outline of Sister Francis, her saviour. As she felt the hot tears of self-pity prickle her eyes. Sister Francis perched on the side of the bed, took Ruby's hands and held them to her lips.

'Ruby, what are we to do with you?' she said.

Ruby softened at the kindly touch. She saw tears of sympathy returned in the eyes of Sister Francis as she scooped her up from the bed and, holding her close, whispered, 'I have prayed for you child and barely slept while you have been in here. My heart was so heavy. Sister Joseph has been on the door and for the love of God I could not get near you, but it is over now, your punishment is done.'

'I'm sorry, Sister Francis.' The words broke through Ruby's tears.

Sister Francis was filled with joy as her heartfelt prayers were answered. Ruby had spoken. 'I know you are, but Ruby, you must talk to me and let all that anger out. You mustn't bottle it up like that and take it out on others. We've all felt like you did, at times, but if you want to get on in this life you need to learn to handle things a better way than that and talking, now that is always a good idea.'

She held Ruby away from her as she looked at her tear-stained face. 'Promise me that in future you will come and find me when you are filled with the anger. I cannot be your mammy, Ruby, and nor would you want me to be, but I can help you and listen to your problems, just like your mammy would have.'

'She was so wicked to Lottie and upset her and I don't know what happened. I just felt mad and couldn't think or hear anyone, there was just this noise in my head,' Ruby sobbed.

'I know, I know. Life wasn't always wonderful for me and I used to get angry too. I found my solace, here, serving God, but somehow, I don't believe that will be your road to peace.'

Ruby noticed something flit across Sister Francis's face that she couldn't identify. Was it sadness, regret?

'Promise me that you will always come to find me now,' Sister Francis said again, with an urgency in her voice.

'I will,' said Ruby, before whispering in pitiful voice, 'I wanted my mammy.' As her tears began to flow Ruby spoke to Sister Francis for the first time of the life she had lost. Sister Francis stroked her hair, her own heart pained for all the young girl in her arms had endured and she wondered why God, her God, had done this.

'Did you hear where the housekeepers are from?' Ruby asked Lottie.

'What does it fecking matter, Ruby?' said Maria. ''Tis all the same. We are being sold into slavery. I will run away the first chance I can get. I want to go to a house in Dublin and then I can escape with me wages and take a boat to my cousin, she's a nurse in Liverpool.'

'I don't think you can leave, can ye?' said Lottie innocently. 'Do we get wages?'

'Of course you can't leave. Lottie, you are so feckin' dense sometimes. That's how the convent makes its money. From us who don't have family to pay the school fees, it sells us into service and jobs. 'Tis a roaring trade they have going in kitchen and laundry maids. The others, they go off to the university in Dublin, but not the likes of us. If you don't get a wage, never fear, find something to steal and sell. I will and if ye do the same, just make sure ye are careful. Go for something small, silver maybe, eh? Take an ornament or two and then run fer yer life before the Garda leg it after ye.'

Maria laughed. But Ruby and Lottie knew that Maria was from a different world to theirs and on her horizon stood a prison gate.

Ruby had prayed daily that Con and his wife might return to collect her. It was a thought she kept to herself, a hope that burnt deep in her heart. She had spent only a fleeting time with Con and Susan, but she felt that her life in the convent was wrong. Surely, if God had a plan for her, if he did exist, he had meant for her to be with them?

'Do you think the nice man and his wife may come for me?' she asked Sister Francis one day.

Sister Francis looked up from the sock she was darning.

'What man, Ruby?' she replied in surprise.

'The man who brought me here.' Ruby was not now as confident and wished she had kept her thoughts to herself.

'Con O'Malley, the town clerk? Sure, we haven't heard a thing from him since the storm. I don't think we will be hearing from him again. Why, did he say he would?'

Ruby pushed her needle hard into the snowdrop she was embroidering on her tray cloth. It was as though the needle had pierced her heart, so sharp was the pain.

She thought that she must have been mad indeed to have set so much store by Con O'Malley and yet she still remembered the warmth of his coat, the soothing sounds made by his wife and the kindness in their eyes.

'Ruby, get a move on,' a postulant shouted into the dorm. If there was shouting to be done Ruby, the unforgiven vase breaker, was always the first name to fall from the lips of authority.

'Now, girls, after breakfast there are six of you to wait in the corridor outside the mother's room. Are you listening?'

The girls were as close as blood sisters, their bond forged by a unique shared experience and tragic loss. They were all keen to leave the convent, but not to say goodbye to each other.

Waiting on the wooden bench outside the reverend mother's room, they whispered, 'Will they beat us?' 'Will they feed us?' 'Will we ever see each other again?'

They had been scrubbed until their skin was stinging. Their hair was brushed and gleaming. Their cleaning aprons had been changed for fresh.

'Will we stay here, near to Belmullet?' Ruby asked Lottie, nervously.

'I don't know, I just want us to stay together,' Lottie whispered, taking hold of Ruby's hand. She felt responsible for her, even though Ruby now ruled the roost. Lottie knew that she needed to be protected, if only from herself.

The door opened and Sister Francis called Ruby into the office first.

'Look at the cut of you, Ruby,' she hissed, as she guided her across the plush carpet towards the desk where the reverend mother sat. 'Set your face nicely.'

Ruby's eyes narrowed and she glared up at her mentor. Unperturbed, Sister Francis smiled. Ruby reluctantly smiled back.

As Ruby approached the desk, she saw a man and a woman, sitting on one side of the reverend mother.

'Ruby, this is Mr and Mrs McKinnon, they are Scottish.'

Ruby had never before met anyone who wasn't from Ireland.

'They work at Ballyford Castle and are looking for a well-educated girl to join the servants who live and work there.'

Reverend Mother continued. 'Ruby has been with us since she was twelve years old and is now almost eighteen. Along with all of the charity girls at the convent, she has been fully trained in housekeeping and laundry duties. She is also well above the capabilities required to pass the leaving certificate and has even begun training in secretarial and bookkeeping work. We continually develop and stretch our girls so they will be useful employees in the very best places when they leave here. We have a reputation to uphold, Mr McKinnon, and you will not be disappointed in Ruby here, I can vouch for that myself.' Begrudgingly she added, 'She is also a very hard worker.'

The man and woman both looked Ruby up and down. The intensity of their scrutiny made her feel very uncomfortable.

'Where do you come from, girl?' asked the man. His accent sounded strange to Ruby, but much softer than she had thought it would be. She expected a man with such a rugged and wide-set face to speak in a fierce, booming voice. Instead, his was as gentle and as soft as summer rain and she found herself wanting to return the smile he gave her when he finished speaking.

Sister Francis had given the girls very clear instructions that morning. 'Don't speak if you are spoken to, girls. The reverend mother answers all the questions for you. The best way to be placed is not to speak at all.'

'I'm from Doohoma, I am.' Ruby did exactly what she had been told not to do. She lifted her head high and looked the man straight in the eye. Her voice was as strong as his had been gentle.

The reverend mother glared at Ruby.

'Doohoma, eh? Your family fished, did they?'

Now, Ruby did do as she had been told. She hadn't expected to be asked a question about her family. She felt caught off guard and fell silent.

A look of smug satisfaction came over the reverend mother's face. 'Indeed, Mr McKinnon, but since Ruby has been with us she has trained assiduously for the day when she can be usefully employed. It would be a surprise to me if her family were from the fishing community. When Ruby arrived here, she could read very well indeed and her education was already at an advanced level. Not only can she read, she writes beautifully, without error, and can compose a perfect essay. She is learned as well as able and, when she bothers, she can speak prettily too. Sadly, we have little information about her past, being a storm orphan.'

'Come here, girl.' It was the turn of the woman to speak. Her voice was also kindly as she beckoned at Ruby to move forward. She wore a small black hat pinned to her once black hair, now shot through with grey. A tiny veil peeped out from the back of the hat. Her face was pale, long and narrow and her eyes so dark brown, they looked almost black.

Ruby turned to the reverend mother for approval and then crossed the room to stand in front of Mrs McKinnon.

'Hello, hen,' Mrs McKinnon said, then she reached out and took hold of Ruby's chin, lifting her face up to the light streaming in from the window.

'See those eyes?' She turned back and spoke to her husband. Ruby's green eyes flashed back at them both.

'I do and I would say she would fit in very nicely.' Mr McKinnon grinned back at his wife.

Ruby realized that they were speaking in some form of code. As though they shared a secret and she was part of it.

As if she had read Ruby's thoughts, Mrs McKinnon spoke

again. 'We are looking for someone who can read and write well. We will take her.'

The reverend mother almost fainted with relief.

Leaving the convent was traumatic. The girls had been woken, fed, ordered into clean clothes, sold and were out of the door. It was all as quick as that. At the root of Ruby's anxiety was her concern for Lottie. Sweet, kind Lottie, who had always looked after her, even if their roles had sometimes been reversed. They were all each other had in the world.

'There is no use complaining, Ruby, we're only girls, we have no rights.'

Ruby saw red when Lottie said such things. 'Come on, Lottie. Is there no fight in you? Do you think I mean to be a prisoner all of my life? Not on your nelly. Wherever we are sent, we must plan to run away and whoever does it first, must promise to find the other.'

'We will, we'll never lose touch and when we are married, we'll live next door to each other,' said Lottie, excited.

'Aye, and our husbands will be fishermen,' said Ruby, 'and when they fish, we'll make the food and keep the house clean and we'll do it quick so that we can walk on the cliffs and talk to each other all day long while we wait for them to come back.'

Lottie laughed. 'We could even get married on the same day.'

Now it was Ruby's turn to laugh. 'We will, but first we have to escape from all this and I promise you we will, Lottie. It won't last forever, Sister Francis told me. It won't last forever.'

Lottie was placed in a hotel in Belmullet to work as a housekeeper. Poor Maria was taken to work as a laundry maid at a boarding house in Crossmolina and looked far from happy.

'I can't steal fucking sheets, can I?' she said to Lottie, as they dressed to leave. 'I'm just one up from the fecking poorhouse. How am I to make my way out of this backward country? I want to be in Liverpool and then earn the money for a passage to America, not here. Here it's just shite and sheets. The bitches have done for me, so they have.'

'We will find you, Maria,' said Ruby, 'don't give out. We will find you. Just keep your head down.'

Ruby meant it and Maria knew she would one day see Ruby again. The two girls embraced. 'May God be good to you, Ruby,' she whispered as she hugged her tight.

Ruby's goodbye was characteristically eventful. The reverend mother watched on while Ruby and Lottie said their farewells to Sister Francis, who whispered, 'Be nice,' in Ruby's ear.

But even Sister Francis was shocked by what the reverend mother said next.

'Well, Ruby, I cannot say I'm not glad to see the back of you.'

The girls were lined up by the door, ready to depart, bags packed and at their feet.

Ruby felt her stomach lurch and her skin began to prickle. The familiar feelings of hurt and rejection crept in, taking her by surprise. She had expected more; quite what, she was not sure, but not this harshness. She breathed in deeply. Her temper very rarely got the better of her nowadays.

'Do you think the reverend mother might be sad to see me go?' Ruby had asked Lottie. Part of her secretly hoped that maybe she would. That she would say a few nice words and allow Ruby to leave on the same terms as everyone else.

'I think she will,' said Lottie. 'She's grown used to you and although you didn't get along so well in the beginning, I think she will be nice today. This is your last hour. But even if she isn't, don't lose your rag and give her the benefit of your temper, be good.' Lottie had crossed her fingers behind her back and secretly willed the reverend mother to be nice to Ruby, on this her last day.

Lottie's words rang in Ruby's ears as the reverend mother began to speak.

'I shall now have to write to Con O'Malley, the town clerk from Doohoma and give him your new address and the name of your employer.'

Ruby's eyes flashed with anger.

'The town clerk in Doohoma? The man who brought me here? Why would you be writing to him? Why would you *want* to write to him?'

She didn't miss a beat or skip a breath while she stared at the reverend mother, willing her to reply.

'He writes once a month, enquiring after your progress. I don't have to tell you that my replies have not always been the most favourable. Before I had given up on you entirely, the foolish man suggested that you should live with him and his wife. Once their baby was born and things had settled down, they came to visit me with the little boy and said they would like to take you back to their home. I told him that was not a good idea at all and that no child would be safe around someone with a temper as violent as yours. I told him, if he wished, he could see the bruises on Deirdra McGinty. I said the poor child was half dead with the beating you gave her. His wife thanked me, for saving her from making what could have been a terrible mistake.'

Ruby felt rage rising up like vomit in her throat.

Lottie reached out to grab her hand behind her back and squeezed it tight. 'Don't give out,' she whispered. Ruby bit her lip, hard.

As Ruby and Lottie hugged each other goodbye Ruby finally let it out in an ill-tempered tone, 'The only reason I didn't run at the old witch and rip the eyes out of her head was because I have to get out of here now. But I know, if I ever see her again, there will be nothing to stop me.'

'Go now,' said Sister Francis pushing her out of the door and down the drive. Sister Francis was shocked by what she had heard and her own tranquillity deserted her as she too began to cry.

Ruby threw her arms around the nun's neck and kissed her cheek.

'You were good to me, always,' she whispered before she turned her back on them all and ran down the drive to the waiting cart, carrying with her the small embroidered bag, given to her by Sister Francis, with two changes of underclothes and a dress for church on Sundays.

Then she stopped, picked up a clod of wet earth from Reverend Mother's precious flower border and hurled it at her screaming, 'I will come back and get you one day, so help me God, I will.' With that, she stepped up onto the cart with her heart pounding and no backward glance.

She knew that Sister Francis and Lottie would be waving until the cart was out of sight but she couldn't bear to see the tears of the only two people in the world she loved.

Mr and Mrs McKinnon had sent Jack, the man of all trades, with the horse and cart to collect Ruby. Jack was as tall as his cart was long. A man of few social graces, he was never without his scruffy black hat and had trouble using a blade to shave. His ragged-bottomed trousers were tied up with old rope for a belt. Yet despite his general shabbiness Jack was a happy man. What he lacked in refinement he compensated for with good humour and his willowy tallness belied his gentle nature.

Today, the cart was loaded with deliveries for the castle and Ruby had so far spent the journey perched precariously on a sack of flour with a huge oilskin to keep her dry from the rain, which had begun to fall with conviction just as they set off from the convent. But they had only been gone for half an hour and weren't far along the road before the sun came out, shining through the leaves and dappling the road in shimmers of gold.

'The day will be shining warm by the time we reach the castle,' Jack said, breaking the silence. 'Amy Keenan, she makes the sun shine wherever she is and that's the truth.' By the nut-brown colour of his face, Ruby guessed that he spent a lot of time outdoors with his horse and cart. Although Jack was not directly employed at Ballyford he did much of the fetching and carrying and was regarded as one of the staff, having been at the castle since he was just a lad.

Jack told Ruby that Mrs McKinnon, the housekeeper, was from Edinburgh originally and that she was just a dote.

'The McKinnons, now some say they have been at the castle forever, as long as the FitzDeanes. My father, he said that's not true and that his grandfather remembered the first McKinnon who came after the famine and never left. They were bad days they were. The McKinnons, they come from a family of land agents in Scotland and there has been a McKinnon at Ballyford ever since that time.'

Ruby knew about the famine, they had been taught the gory details at the convent and about how it was all the fault of the English.

Jack never stopped chattering and Ruby's head was soon so filled with the names of everyone who lived in the castle, what they did, which family they were from, that she thought her head would burst.

'Have you ever been to a castle before?'

Ruby laughed out loud. 'No, why would I? My mother used to tell me stories of castles though and about witches and dragons rescuing a beautiful princess.'

Jack nodded his head thoughtfully. 'Where was yer mammy from then? Who were her people?'

Ruby fell quiet. It wasn't the first time today she had realized that she knew very little about her mother's background. She still carried her mother's words in her heart. *You have family Ruby, find them.* But she didn't know where to begin.

'You fair lost your temper back there,' said Jack looking

down at her with a frown. 'I'm guessing there must have been good reason for ye to risk being punished for what ye shouted to the reverend mother now?'

Ruby looked sheepish. She fixed her stare on the horse's rump and remained silent.

'Ye don't have to tell me if ye don't want, but ye may feel better to get it off yer chest before ye start at the castle. Can't have things brewing on yer first day and I won't say nuthin, I promise ye that.'

'I feel stupid now,' Ruby replied. 'You really won't tell them at the castle, will you?'

Jack smiled. 'Me? Well, here's a strange thing about Jack, he forgets most things that aren't important and that was not important to anyone, anywhere. 'Tis a new day and a new start for you, Ruby Flynn, just don't go trying those antics on Amy or Mrs McKinnon, if you want to stay alive.'

Ruby smiled up at him, sheepishly. She already liked Jack.

She threaded her fingers around a leather strap attached to the side of the cart and shifted up on the sack, closer to him, in order to see better. She let the oilskin slip from her shoulders and breathed in the earthy smell of the bog. She felt exhilarated and alive. The rain-soaked fields were the deepest green and the clouds were parting to reveal blue sky above, as the sun became even stronger. She relaxed and let her anger fall away, soothed by the rhythm of the horse's trot.

Despite her fear of travelling to a new home and a new life, her heart could not fail to be lifted by the sound of the birds, by the green fields rolling away into the distance and by the rough cragginess of the land.

In every village they passed through, people came out of their cottages and waved. Dogs ran after the cartwheels and barked and children shouted questions up at Ruby. Women stood at their doors with babies in their arms and smiled.

A man cycled past the cart with a sack of potatoes precariously balanced over his handlebars and also held his hand up in greeting.

Ruby asked 'Do you know everyone in these parts.'

Jack laughed. 'Well, I was born here over forty years ago. People leave, but no one ever moves to these parts, so I guess 'tis true, I do know everyone.'

Ruby watched the countryside and the cows grazing and thought about her act of defiance, her final goodbye.

'What you thinking about so much?' Jack shouted, as he slowed the horse and lit his pipe.

'I'm really mad with myself for losing me rag with the reverend mother, because if I ever want to visit Sister Francis, she will never let me through the door again.'

Ruby felt the familiar pain of rejection and hurt throb in her chest. 'She is a truly wicked woman, you know,' she said indignantly to Jack.

Jack puffed on his pipe.

'Well, I was never spared the belt by the nuns when I was a child meself, but I would say now that it never did me no harm.'

This was not what Ruby wanted to hear and she gave a slight snort. 'Will we pass Doohoma on the way?' she asked. She had no idea of her bearings or even where the castle was.

Jack held the reins with one hand and grinned.

'Doohoma, not likely. 'Tis a fair way from the castle but both are near on the shore and face the ocean.'

That news instantly made her feel better. To see the ocean again, where her father and brother fished day after day. Ruby's thoughts of Doohoma sustained her for the rest of journey.

How do I find our house? ran through her mind, over and over.

And even though she knew none of the houses they passed, any one of them could have been her own. She strained to look for her parents and her brother behind the half-open doors or through the small windows.

Ruby's nightmares had lessened over the years and they were replaced by dreams of her future. One in particular disturbed her more than most. She would share it with Lottie when she woke and it was always the same.

'I fancy myself married to a handsome man in a big house with lots of children and I see my little girl running across a lawn and my sons climbing up great big trees. I'm definitely rich and there's a big picnic on the lawn, laid out on a blanket under a tree and my husband, he is very good-looking, Lottie, looks a little bit like the clerk who rescued me and we are watching our children and we are laughing, so we are. Just like my mammy and daddy used to. My husband chases the children and I walk away from them to a place on the lawn where you can see the ocean. I turn back to shout for my husband, but he has gone and the children have disappeared and I run back along the lawn, past dead flowers and bare trees and I start to panic, because I can't find them anywhere.'

As Ruby spoke, Lottie would imagine herself pouring tea

into china cups on the blanket under the tree. Sometimes, she saw herself with a baby and her own husband, watching the children.

'Ruby, you have an imagination like no other. Listen to you with all your grand words. 'Tis just a dream. We are poor and have nothing of our own. Though, you are the one with the looks and the hair, 'twould be easy for you to marry, I would be thinking, and a miracle for me.'

The smell and the sound of the ocean hit Ruby as the horse began to slow to a walk. With the scent of brine in her nostrils, she wanted to catch sight of the ocean the second it came into view. When it did so, her heart stopped bleeding and she felt as if she could jump with joy.

'My daddy used to fish in that ocean,' she shouted up to Jack, pointing and jabbing her finger. Then her heart leapt again as a battered old tank of a fishing trawler pulled out across the horizon and she saw that it was a boat that she recognized.

'I know that boat, I know that boat.'

'Aye,' Jack replied, unimpressed. 'It leaves Belmullet every day and always has. You would have seen it from Doohoma Head.'

The sight of something so familiar from Ruby's childhood made her feel light headed and giddy.

'Can you imagine,' she said, grinning. 'I used to wave to it every day,' and she began to wave again furiously, to the rusty hull.

Jack shook the reins and pulled the horse into a trot around to the right. Soon, the lodge house and pillars came into view and a long driveway meandered ahead.

'Here we are then,' shouted Jack, waving to the porter in the garden of the lodge. 'Welcome to Ballyford Castle.'

Ruby stared straight ahead with her mouth slightly open. She had almost stopped breathing.

Jack, with his horse and cart, had driven Ruby straight into her dream.

Chapter four

Ballyford Castle

'Do we have any idea at all when Jack will be here with the flour?'

Amy Keenan was the cook at Ballyford Castle and she was addressing Mrs McKinnon, who was sitting at the end of the kitchen table, drinking her tea.

'I have no idea, Amy, but he wasn't too long after ourselves. I wish he would get a move on, he has the new girl with him and I have a hundred things to be getting on with, which I can't begin until she is settled in.'

Amy Keenan brought her bread dough down on the table with such a thud that it became difficult for Mrs McKinnon to see her through the cloud of flour.

'Mary, in the name of Jesus, why is it taking ye so long to pluck the chickens? Get a move on, girl.'

'Yes, Amy,' shouted Mary. She was a slight girl who hardly spoke, but she responded to the wink from Mrs McKinnon with a wide and near toothless grin.

'Ah, the new girl,' Amy continued. 'I don't suppose she's been brought to help me in the kitchen, has she?'

'No, I'm afraid not, Amy. She's for the nursery.'

'God in heaven, why would that be? There is no child in the nursery. He's dead. They're all dead, God rest their little souls.' Amy blessed herself as she spoke.

Amy had worked in the castle since she was a girl and had acquired a degree of confidence typical in a woman who rules her own domain. Amy's realm was the kitchen and woe betide anyone who helped themselves to so much as a cup of buttermilk or an oat biscuit without first seeking permission.

'Aye, they are all dead,' said Mrs McKinnon. 'God bless them. Lady FitzDeane was asleep in the nursing chair when I popped my head in this morning. Heartbreaking it is. She's lost so much weight. I'm feared she will snap in two if we don't have someone to help her. Someone who could do a bit of everything including writing the odd letter because she is far too melancholy to write any herself.'

Amy looked dumbfounded. 'Does Lord FitzDeane know?'

'How could he Amy? He's back in Liverpool. He's gone into a new business and bought a ship, so Mr McKinnon tells me. He is living in the big house in Sefton Park now too, so I'm told. He has had it decorated from top to bottom. I don't like him staying in Liverpool. There has been a telephone in this castle for almost five years now, he should be able to work from here.'

''Tis all changing if you ask me,' said Amy. 'Things are so different here now altogether. No fishing parties, no shoots, no balls. It's as if the lady has been in mourning forever and him, Lord Charles, they were his babies too but no one frets about him do they? I've seen the difference since the last one died, he's moving further and further away from us and I will tell you something else too: I reckon that if they had a baby girl, it would live. There is a woman in Waterford, lives in the same village as my mammy's cousin, ten dead boys she had until the girl came along and now she's going as fit as you like. They have her milking and cutting the turf too and they say she's as strong as the ten boys would have been.'

'God help her,' Mrs McKinnon replied wryly. 'I cannot imagine how the mother kept going, losing ten boys. We had five years and five losses and a funeral for each one of them here and I can see the effect it has had on the lady.'

'Mary, stop earwigging and pluck!' Amy shouted.

She turned and filled the kettle at the enormous stone sink and as she did, she thought she heard the sound of the cart in the distance. She immediately stood on tiptoe to look out of the window.

'God in heaven, you don't think he has another woman do you, Mrs McKinnon? I mean, in Liverpool? Maybe that's why he is setting up a new house there. He wouldn't take a mistress in Liverpool, would he?'

Amy turned back and put the kettle onto the range. She had meant to whisper her question. It was one that had been playing on her mind for some time. She felt for Lord FitzDeane. It appeared to Amy that all the attention and sympathy focused on Lady FitzDeane and that the man they all knew with affection as Lord Charles, was forgotten about.

'I don't think so, no,' Mrs McKinnon said impatiently. She looked towards the servants' stairs nervously, to see if anyone was hovering.

'Mr McKinnon is off to Liverpool sometime soon with two chests and papers from the study for Lord Charles. We had thought he was returning to Ballyford shortly, but it would appear Mr McKinnon has to take Ballyford to him.'

Amy took a handkerchief out of her apron pocket and wiped the flour from her eyes.

''Tis a sad state of affairs. I think of those fabulous dinner parties I used to cater for and now, I make pies for the staff meals. Five children born into Ballyford and five children dead. Who would have thought we would be saying that when they first married, eh, and what a day to remember that was? It took me three months from beginning to end to make that cake.'

Mrs McKinnon looked towards the window as she heard the sound of hooves on the cobbled path leading through the arch to the kitchen garden from the main drive. She saw Jack's cart turn the corner and slowly make its way down the path as the wheels dipped in and out of the grooves.

'Here's Jack, so, let's put on a brave face shall we? You know the man has a soft spot for you. Mr McKinnon reckons the reason he fixed up the thatch on that cottage of his is because he is working himself up to make a proposal.'

Mrs McKinnon laughed as she waved out of the window to Jack and went to open the back door.

'Merciful God, he would be a foolish man indeed to do that at our age. That's the notion of a young man. What would he be thinking of?' Amy blushed as bright as the beets she had simmering on the huge kitchen range. 'I'm too old for any of that nonsense and that man surely has more sense than wanting to spend what's left of his life with a woman bigger, stronger and cleverer than himself.'

Amy wiped her floury hands on her powdery apron as she and Mrs McKinnon grinned at each other.

'Can I see the new girl,' said little Mary, hovering behind Amy.

'No, you cannot, not until I have. Get back to the chickens.' Mary scuttled off to sit back on her upturned pail.

Mrs McKinnon opened the door and the first sight to greet her was Ruby Flynn, standing on the doorstep with a white face and a bag in her hand.

'Goodness me, child, you look as though you are about to faint, come away inside,' she said.

Mary, ignoring Amy's warning, rushed forward to greet Ruby and, taking her hand, led her into the kitchen.

'Have ye made me another one of those pies, Amy?' said Jack, lifting his cap in greeting.

'Get off, you cheeky bugger,' said Amy.

'You are a hard woman, Amy. Ye steal my heart by charming my stomach and then ye starve me of the pleasure I have come to enjoy. I dream about your pies, Amy.'

Bustling and blushing, Amy placed a hot potato pie in Jack's hand, then, with a tilt of his cap and a wink at Mrs McKinnon, Jack was back out of the door.

Before he left, he whispered, in an altogether more serious tone, 'The girl, she had a funny turn as we came up the drive, I thought she was about to fall clean off the wagon. She had been right as rain all the way here. I reckon maybe 'twas the size or the sight of the castle that did it. Had to stop for a second, I did. Maybe she needs a bit of Amy's food in her belly. Don't think convent food is up to much for those girls, all stick thin they are.'

'Aye, we will feed her, Jack,' said Mrs McKinnon. 'I treat all my girls well, as does Amy. We look after each other.'

Mrs McKinnon turned to Ruby, as she closed the kitchen door. 'Sit down, girl, and let's get a cuppa and a meal inside you. You have lots to learn over the next few weeks. Now, are you feeling all right?'

Ruby nodded. 'I am fine, thank you, Mrs McKinnon. I think it was the cart, the wobbling back and forth, it made me a bit sickly.'

Mrs McKinnon handed Ruby a cup from the staff press as Amy waddled around the table with a teapot and a slice of the hot pie, baked to perfection with its brown and glazed crust.

'Eat up,' she said kindly. I'll butter you a slice of bread to have with it. Ruby, is it?'

Ruby nodded in response. The smell of the hot pie was reviving her and her mouth began to water.

'I'm away to fetch your uniform Ruby,' said Mrs McKinnon. 'Amy will look after you for a few minutes and no doubt, by the time I return, you will be twice the size you are now.'

'I feed all the staff well here. God knows, there's no one else to cook for,' Amy sighed. 'I reckon I'll have a nice bit of fat sticking to those skinny ribs of yours before the month is out. Drink up and eat the pie now. I've a nice stew for supper. That Mrs McKinnon will have ye run off yer feet by the end of the day. She may be fair, but she expects hard work for her consideration.'

'I'm not afraid of hard work,' Ruby replied defensively.

'That's as may be, but it's not just hard work. There's a reason why she hasn't used one of the girls already on the staff for this job, I'd be thinking.'

Amy settled herself down onto the stool next to Ruby, preparing herself to question the new girl and to find out as much information as possible in the short time she had, just as Mrs McKinnon walked back into the kitchen with clean white aprons and a black dress laid across her arm.

'Thank you, Amy,' said Mrs McKinnon with a hint of irritation. 'I can fill Ruby in on the details of the job very well myself.'

'I was only making polite conversation and trying to explain. It's not like things are normal around here, is it, with a grieving mad woman in the nursery and five small coffins lying in the tomb.'

'Amy!' Mrs McKinnon almost took off her head with one word and a sharp look.

And then in a much softer tone altogether, she turned back to Ruby.

'Ruby, we needed someone with a good education and understanding, you see. It is true, you are here to work in the nursery, only there is something which is, er, slightly unusual, and you need to know. There is no child here in the castle to be looked after. The nursery is empty, except for the mistress that is.'

Ruby took a bite of Amy's pie and gave Mrs McKinnon her full attention as she ate. It was all she could do to stop herself from drooling as the buttery pastry melted on her tongue. She had never before in her life tasted anything as good as Amy's pie.

'You see, Lady FitzDeane, she gave birth to five baby boys in five years and each one perished and returned to his maker without spending very long on this earth. She would like the nursery to be kept spick and span and she spends most of the day in there herself. I have to warn you, she very rarely leaves. But there is a little more to it than that. Lady FitzDeane, she hasn't been doing too well herself in many ways. The doctor visits her every week and God knows, he tries his best, but he thinks she would improve if we had someone to help feed her, pay her some attention, read to her, even. She is a little on the thin side and needs help with the everyday tasks, writing her letters, getting her dressed. It's more a lady's maid job, crossed with that of a nurse, which is why we needed someone of your ability.'

Ruby looked slightly perplexed but simply nodded her head as she wiped the crumbs from her chin. She had only ever heard the words 'lady's maid' when Lottie had said them in jest as she brushed Ruby's long hair and she really had no idea what one was, whereas, having looked after Lottie and Maria a number of times when they had been sick, she had some understanding of the role of a nurse. But still, it was hardly something she had given a great deal of thought to.

She ate the last forkful of the pie and washed it down with the tea. She savoured the salty flavour. The steam rising from the gravy made her want to close her eyes and breathe in the aroma and hold it with her. The food at the convent had been repetitive. She had eaten the same thing on the same day every day for six years. She had never before experienced anything on a plate that made her mouth water.

'Right, if you have finished eating,' Mrs McKinnon said, breaking the spell, 'the others will be in for a break in a moment. It will be a good time to meet them all. Then I'll take you to the room where the girls sleep and from there we will proceed to the nursery so you can meet Lady FitzDeane.'

Just at that moment, the day servants began to file into the kitchen.

'Here they are.' Amy winked at Ruby as she shouted at the staff entering the kitchen through the back door, 'Did ye all smell the pie and know it was time, did ye?'

As the noise in the kitchen grew with chatter, Mrs McKinnon could not take her eyes off the new girl's face. There was another, just like it, which she had once known well, a long time ago and her eyes lingered on Ruby's expression as she responded to the welcome from the other servants.

'At least they appreciate my cooking, even if the lady upstairs does not. My warm boxty, ye cannot beat it,' Amy said to Ruby.

The eight members of staff, male and female, joked with each other and jostled for bigger slices of the pie and the boxty bread, as they all took their plates and mugs and sat along the wooden bench table for their mid-morning break. A young girl who was not much older than Ruby sat next to her.

'Are ye from the convent then?' she asked.

'Don't go scaring Ruby away with too many questions now, Betsy,' said Mrs McKinnon as she moved along the table, filling their mugs with buttermilk.

Betsy wore her dark hair tucked neatly under her linen hat. Her eyes were big and round and almost as black as her hair and she was so gently spoken, she immediately reminded Ruby of Lottie.

'I am. How do you know the convent? Were you there?' asked Ruby.

'No, none of us were. We just heard this morning that Mrs McKinnon was off to fetch a girl who could read and write. I would love to read, I would.'

'Why don't you, then? My mammy taught me,' said Ruby.

'Where are you from then, I mean before the convent?'

'I lived in Doohoma.' Ruby didn't hesitate when Betsy asked about her home..

'Doohoma, eh? My granny came from there. Before she married my granddaddy and moved into the cottages on the estate. I thought there was something familiar, as soon as I set me eyes on you. We used to go back when I was little to visit granny's family and we went to mass. Have I seen you at mass?'

Ruby's face lit up. Could it really be that there was someone in the world who knew her? She had to stop herself from reaching out and grabbing hold of Betsy's arm. 'Do you ever see your family now, do you?'

Before Betsy could answer, another young girl came and sat on the other side of Ruby. She was as thin as Betsy was plump and the lack of welcome in her face made Ruby bristle even before she had pulled out her stool.

'So, you are from the fancy convent then, are you?' she asked, by way of an introduction. 'The only airs and graces around here are upstairs in the castle, not down here in the kitchen, isn't that right, Betsy?'

'Shut yer gob, Jane,' said Betsy. 'How about saying hello or something nice for a change?'

Ruby looked around her, waiting for someone to tell them off for talking. No one had noticed, or at least if they had, they weren't the slightest bit bothered. Ruby was surprised, and told Betsy as much. At the convent every mouthful had to be taken in silence.

'Sure, we is busy working all day. When would we get time to talk if not now? It is so noisy in here sometimes, Mr McKinnon has to shout to get everyone to pipe down when he has the news on the radio and no one even noticed when one of the pigs escaped and was squealing under the table. If Danny had his way, it would have slept there, wouldn't it, Danny?'

A young boy who was tucking into his bread grinned sheepishly back at Betsy. 'I never heard a thing, thought it was Jane whining as usual, didn't I, Jane?' said Danny. 'You will get used to Jane's moaning, miss,' he went on as he looked admiringly at Ruby, 'she never stops.'

Betsy grinned good naturedly at Jane, who dismissed Betsy with a sharp look and Ruby saw her try to kick Danny under the table.

Jane noticed that Ruby was watching her open-mouthed and said, 'You are in our room, with me and Betsy. We never shared with no one else before. Just make sure you don't touch my stuff on the press. Isn't that right, Betsy? We don't want no one touching our things. Anyway, I think I might move into the empty room next door.'

'What things, Jane?' Betsy laughed, but Jane stood up and carried her mug and plate to the sink without answering.

'Take no notice,' Betsy whispered to Ruby. 'She doesn't like no one, does Jane. Someone needs to tell her, no one ever broke a mouth saying a kind word. I've pulled your bed close to mine so that we can talk when Jane is asleep and you can tell me all about yerself.'

'Can I come and sleep in your room too?' Jimmy, the groom and stable boy shouted down the bench.

'Mrs McKinnon, did ye hear that? Jimmy is being bold,' shouted Betsy playfully. Mrs McKinnon hadn't heard, she was deep in conversation with Jane at the sink. Ruby was stunned into silence. 'He's a bad lad is Jimmy,' said Betsy, half scowling half laughing with a definite twinkle in her eye..

Mrs McKinnon now called for Ruby to join her.

'Come along, Ruby, I will take you up to the room to change and then we shall visit the nursery.'

As Ruby stood, the rest of the staff were still joking and chiding each other and making good-natured fun of Amy. The fire boy, stood and threw peat onto the enormous fire burning in the grate. It was his job to keep the fire baskets filled with turf each morning before he went out to work in the garden or with Mr McKinnon to tend the pigs.

At the convent, the peat bricks were counted out; in the winter, they were allowed to burn thirty each day and not one more, regardless of how cold it was. It seemed to Ruby that there were more than thirty blocks burning on the fire right now.

When they reached the girls' room, in a top wing of the castle, she saw that there was a fire grate in here too, and a basket of peat next to the hearth. The fire was already laid, ready to be lit. In winter, the dorm at the convent had small thin icicles protruding from a solid base of ice hanging from the broken and leaking skylight; the girls snapped the icicles off, one by one, before they went to bed, and dropped them into the sink. Lottie had once found them in her bed making her sheets wet and freezing. It was a payback present from Deirdra McGinty.

'I will stand outside the door, Ruby, and leave you to get dressed,' said Mrs McKinnon.

Ruby felt a sense of pride as she buttoned up the crisp black dress and put on the apron and starched cap. She took one look at herself in the long mirror in the corner of the room before she left.

'Well, Ruby Flynn, here goes,' she whispered.

'You will do very nicely,' said Mrs McKinnon. 'Very nicely indeed. This is the main landing, and as you can see...' she moved a few steps over to the highly polished minstrels' gallery which looked down over the main hall, '... it runs all the way around the central hallway of the castle, until it reaches the main staircase.'

Ruby had never seen a place as grand in all her life and stood with her mouth wide open.

'You will catch the midges if you don't close your mouth, my girl,' said Mrs McKinnon, smiling. 'It will take you a little while to get your bearings, and you may even find yourself lost, once or twice. If that happens, you will eventually bump into one of the girls who will put you right. Most of the staff have worked here for years; even Jane, who you spoke to in the kitchen, has been with us since she was twelve. Her mother works in the castle laundry and her father is the lodge keeper. Jane sleeps in the next bed to you, but quite often she slips back to the lodge to be with her family. Betsy's family looks after the pigs and they are tenants on one of the farms. Betsy has been in and out of the castle kitchen since she was a child. You'll notice that the staff mostly call Lord and Lady FitzDeane "Lord Charles" and "Lady Isobel". It's not strictly correct, but everyone likes it, especially Lord Charles.'

They had reached the central grand flight of stairs and Mrs McKinnon paused at the top.

'We never use this flight of stairs. The only time you will see a member of staff on these stairs is when cleaning and polishing is taking place. When you are heading back down to the basement, always use the green door.' She turned and pointed back at the door they had passed through, which had closed almost silently behind them.

Ruby could barely keep herself from gawping at the paintings and the furniture surrounding her. All along the minstrels' gallery, the walls were lined with tall white marble statues. Twenty of them, one in quite a startling state of undress.

'Don't look,' Mrs McKinnon snapped sharply. 'I can tell straight away when the girls have as much as laid their eyes on that statue.' She turned her head and closed her eyes as she spoke, to add effect to the severity of her words. 'I send Mr McKinnon along to dust and clean it along with the rest of them.'

Ruby obediently kept her head held high and her eyes low while Mrs McKinnon explained that Lord FitzDeane's ancestor had the statues transported over from Italy when he had spent a year travelling around Europe.

'Despite it being such a holy country, they appear to have little shame over there,' she said.

Ruby thought they were the most beautiful things she had ever seen. The marble shone, reflecting the light from the chandelier. Cheekily, she let her hand drift across the knee of one of the statues as they walked past. It felt cold. Later, when she was recounting it all to Betsy, she nearly said, 'As cold as anything I have ever felt,' but the words stuck in her throat. It wouldn't have been true. Ruby had felt the coldest things. She had felt ice like wire in her blood, slipping through her veins and puncturing her heart. Like a wound that never heals, she felt it there still. Ruby told herself that the cold in her heart would leave on the day she escaped and made her way back to Doohoma. She knew her heart would heal on that day. As nice as Mrs McKinnon was, escape she would.

'It is a shock to the system to see a painting that size if you've never seen one before.' Mrs McKinnon noticed Ruby staring at a large painting of a family taking a picnic. It was six times the height of Mrs McKinnon and Ruby had to tilt her head back to take in the top of the painting.

There were children playing in a field, with the castle in the background and sitting on chairs around a rug were ladies wearing long dresses and men in tall hats. In the forefront of the painting stood a little girl, holding a plate up to the group while looking back at the artist and smiling.

'Ruby,' said Mrs McKinnon. There was no reply. 'Ruby,' she said slightly louder, 'are you all right? You look terribly pale.'

Again there was no response and Mrs McKinnon watched in horror as Ruby fainted dead away.

Mrs McKinnon shouted downstairs for Jane to fetch the smelling salts and for Betsy to bring a glass of water. As she came round, Ruby thought that never in her life had she smelt anything so unbearable as those smelling salts.

'What was it, Ruby?' Mrs McKinnon asked.

'I'm not sure.' Ruby coughed and spluttered into the handkerchief Mrs McKinnon had taken from her apron pocket.

'You looked as if you had seen a ghost. Had you? Was it a woman?'

'I have never seen a ghost before, I haven't got a clue what one looks like,' Ruby replied.

'Ah no, well you wouldn't,' Mrs McKinnon said. 'Ghosts have no use of the poor. I've never heard of one haunting a sod house, or prowling across an earth floor. Ghosts need minstrels' galleries and oak staircases, like this one. They need old houses and castles. Ghosts are a curse to the rich and it's a blessing to the poor that they don't have to tolerate them.'

'Are there really ghosts here at Ballyford?' Ruby looked about her uneasily, as though expecting to see one lounging against a wall watching her, casually examining a fingernail. 'Surely the heat beating out of that fireplace in the main hall would scare away any ghosts. Wouldn't the dog bark?'

'The dog?' Mrs McKinnon raised her eyebrows in exasperation. 'Rufus?' He sleeps so much, he would never notice if a ghost were to lie down next to him. Aye, there are ghosts, I am sorry to report and they are ghosts with a taste for wool carpets and fireplaces and big soft chairs and sofas. It is a fussy ghost with a taste for splendour and it lives at Ballyford. Oh, don't worry you won't see it in your room. There's no carpet or chandelier in there.'

With the help of Betsy and Jane, Mrs McKinnon had lifted Ruby onto a chair to rest, while she caught her breath.

'You do look shockingly pale,' said Betsy. 'Are you sure you feel well?'

Jane, who was still trying to work out how to put the top back on the smelling salts, decided to take a sniff herself, almost fell over backwards and then dropped the bottle on the floor.

'God save us and help us,' said Betsy, as she picked up the bottle and rolled her eyes.

To Mrs McKinnon's relief, the colour flooded back to Ruby's cheeks.

'Have you ever seen the ghost yourself?' Ruby asked. 'Does it have a name?'

'No, not I. It wouldn't show itself to me or to Mr McKinnon. We shan't have any nonsense with such a thing. I have been here since I was first married and I never saw any ghost,' Mrs McKinnon said, 'but there have been people recently who have reported sightings of a woman on the staircase and on the landing. A guest from London almost screamed the place down when she stayed here a couple of years ago. I thought just then that maybe you had seen her too. Are you sure you didn't?'

Ruby wondered if she should tell her what she had really seen, what it was that had taken her breath away and made her head spin. The little girl in the painting had looked just like her own dead mother.

She thought better of it and merely said, 'Maybe it was the marble statues,' trying to be helpful.

Ruby looked up at the picture again and a shiver ran down her spine.

'I think 'twas Lady Isobel,' said Betsy as she put her hand down and helped Ruby to her feet. 'The poor woman looks like a ghost and surely it must have been her they saw wandering along the gallery. Maybe the light was poor. I remember that woman, she was never off the wine. If ye ask me, 'twas the drink, not a ghost.'

But Mrs McKinnon had had enough talk of ghosts and now said briskly, 'Right, if you have fully recovered, Ruby, on we go. Back to work, girls.'

The nursery wing was separate from the castle. Situated down a corridor that led from the main gallery. It stuck out like an appendage. An after thought of a construction erected by ancestors who would rather not have to see or hear their offspring. When they reached the nursery, Ruby thought that if she hadn't already just fainted, she almost certainly would do now at the sight which greeted them.

A chill hit her as they opened the nursery door. It was hardly surprising, given that the sun had gone and it had begun to rain. The fire in the grate was almost out, which didn't help. Lady Isobel was sitting in the nursing chair by the side of the cavernous hearth and staring out through the leaded windows towards the ocean. The rhododendrons, which ran wild along the perimeter of the grounds and lined the drive, obliterated the view of the beach, but on clear days, the ocean could easily be seen. Ballyford sat on the edge of almost two thousand acres and the view from the opposite side of the castle was of immaculately farmed tenants' fields for as far as the eye could see.

Lady Isobel's manner was wholly vacant and unseeing. Although the rain now beat a tattoo against the leaded windows and whistled an eerie tune as it forced its way in between the cracks, she appeared not to notice. She wore an emerald green silk dressing gown, which had fallen open and exposed a white linen nightdress. The first thing Ruby thought was that she had never seen anything or anyone so beautiful. The weight of Lady Isobel's chestnut coloured hair had defied the grip of a green satin ribbon and fallen in spiralling tendrils around her face, where the skin was so transparent the blue veins beneath were plainly visible. Her collarbone jutted out above the neckline of the nightdress and Ruby thought she appeared so fragile and thin that surely she couldn't be touched.

Mrs McKinnon walked over to Lady Isobel's chair and indicated for Ruby to follow her.

'The new nursery maid has arrived, Lady Isobel,' she announced, gently, as though speaking to a young child.

Lady Isobel started slightly, as if she had been woken from a deep sleep.

'Come here, Ruby, come closer,' said Mrs McKinnon. 'Come and say hello. Let Lady Isobel take a good look at you.'

Tentatively, Ruby took half a dozen steps towards the fireside, at which point it was obvious Lady Isobel became frightened. She began to cry and her cry quickly ascended into a thin, shrill, wail.

Ruby felt a familiar reaction to sudden and unexpected noise grip her. The hair on her arms rose, her skin prickled all over and she fought down the urge to flee. *Run, run, run.* The words beat in her brain and she felt her fingernails dig into the flesh of her hands, as she willed herself to stand still.

'Send her away,' Lady Isobel said, grabbing Mrs McKinnon's hands. 'Send her away!'

Ruby thought she might faint again and willed herself to be strong. She had become used to the noise and now felt her breathing steady to a normal pace. Ruby knew sadness. She knew loss. She knew the kind of grief that could only feel better if you screamed and screamed. Her heart contracted in pity for the bird-like form of the beautiful lady sat before her and now Ruby knew, too, that if anyone could help Lady Isobel, Mrs McKinnon was right, she could.

At last the screams subsided to a quiet sobbing and Mrs McKinnon held out her hand.

'Come here,' she whispered, 'don't be scared.'

Ruby looked into Mrs McKinnon's eyes. She wasn't scared now, not anymore. She allowed the housekeeper to lead her over to the chair. Mrs McKinnon held both Lady Isobel's hands in her own, as much, Ruby realized, to prevent them from lashing out as to comfort the lady.

'This is Ruby, she is here to help, just like you asked,' Mrs McKinnon said softly. 'Remember? We discussed it with the doctor. You need someone to be with you all the time, just for now, until we have you right again.'

Ruby thought she had better do something, to show this was the truth, and that she would be of some use and so she bent down to the fire and began to set light to the turf which Betsy had brought in while Mrs McKinnon was calming Lady Isobel. She picked up the bellows and fanned the almost dead embers and within moments, the flames were leaping up the chimney and warming the room.

Mrs McKinnon smiled and nodded approvingly. 'See what Ruby has done,' she said. 'She will keep the room as warm as toast for you and make sure the fire won't ever go out, won't you, Ruby? I won't have to worry about you sitting in the cold anymore.'

'I will,' Ruby replied. 'I have kept a fire going many times at the convent. We all had duties as well as lessons, and we were taught to clean to a high standard.' She was addressing her remarks to Lady Isobel as much as to Mrs McKinnon, to reassure her of her worth.

Ruby had actually never understood why they were taught lessons to such a high level. Maria had told them it was punish them, carrying an education they could never possibly use. But now, for the first time, as she looked around the room and saw the bookcase, Ruby felt that maybe she could put her learning to some use. She was surprised at her own reaction. She saw the challenge before her and felt excited to embrace it. She willed Lady Isobel to accept her. She truly wanted to help.

That night in the dark of the bedroom, after Jane had fallen asleep, Betsy and Ruby turned in their beds to face each other.

'Well, ye have heard her pitiful crying now,' whispered Betsy. 'Jesus. She may be thinner than a trickle of water but she can give out something mighty when she wants.'

71

'I remember a girl at the convent who sounded just the same,' Ruby whispered back. 'She had been brought in from one of the farms. Found alone, trying to survive by herself, Sister Francis said. A priest brought her in and she was covered in lice. Maria said that she was the child of a brother and sister and that her own mother had been the child of a brother and sister and that was the reason why she was as mad as she was. Screamed the place down she did.'

'Well, the crying, it can scare you if 'tis bad enough,' said Betsy. 'You should have heard her after each of the boys died, my God, 'twas awful. Jimmy says that when her and Lord FitzDeane have gone themselves, her screams will haunt the castle, so they will.'

'How long have ye known Jimmy for then?' asked Ruby. 'You never stop talking about him. It seems to me that Jimmy is the only person who works at this castle.'

Betsy squealed indignantly, but her voice trembled slightly as she admitted that she did indeed nurture a secret passion for Jimmy. As Ruby felt her eyes close, Betsy talked on, describing how her first kiss with him had almost made her faint herself.

'I don't think anyone will ever want to kiss me,' whispered Ruby.

'Sure they will now, why not, you're gorgeous so ye are. I know someone meself already dying to catch yer eye, so he is,' said Betsy.

Ruby wanted to know who it was, she would have loved to have known his name, but before she could respond, her heavy eyes won the battle and sleep claimed her.

*

It took only a few days before Ruby made a breakthrough with Lady Isobel and then a further week before they were getting along well. The first challenge had been to coax her out of her nightdress in the mornings and to consider dressing into day clothes.

For a few days, they were at war and she threw the clothes back at Ruby, until one morning the buckle from Lady Isobel's belt caught Ruby in the eye. Furious now, Ruby hissed back at her, 'Do that once more, and I'll throw them back at you and see how you like it.'

There were just the two of them in the room. Lady Isobel stared at Ruby for a full minute and Ruby thought, *Here we go again, I'm in trouble.*

Nursing her eye, Ruby bent down to pick the belt up from the floor.

Lady Isobel whispered, 'I'm sorry.'

She was so quietly spoken, Ruby almost didn't hear. As Ruby rose from her knees she laid the belt gently across Lady Isobel's lap. Softly done, but the message was clear. This morning was the last fight.

'That's all right,' she said calmly. 'I know you didn't mean it. I know how you feel.'

Their eyes met and bewilderment sat in those of Lady Isobel. A silent question burnt deep within. In Ruby, she had recognized her own pain and loss.

They both knew they had crossed a bridge together and that there would be no more tantrums.

Out on the landing, Ruby found a worried Betsy hovering

behind the door, about to burst in to find out what was happening. She was enraged when she saw the bleeding scratch on Ruby's eye. While she had been looking after Lord Charles's rooms on the first floor, she had noticed the huge effort Ruby had been making with Lady Isobel.

'Don't let her bully you like that,' she said, dabbing the scratch with cold water and a napkin from the closet.

'Don't worry, I won't. I don't think it will happen again. She doesn't mean to, you know, Betsy. I bet it's not in her nature to have a temper. She's just very sad.'

Betsy stopped dabbing and looked at Ruby.

'Is that so? Well, now you mention it, there was no temper before the babies were born, that's true, or so Amy says.'

Ruby took the napkin from Betsy and held it to her own eye. 'Do you know,' she said, as she walked to the window and looked out over the lawn, 'sometimes I have this funny feeling that I just cannot understand. I feel as if I've been here before and that I know the castle, but of course I don't. Sometimes I feel that I was always going to find myself here at Ballyford.'

'I felt like that,' said Betsy. 'But then, I was born in the cottages, over yonder.' Betsy pointed to the row of white cottages on the horizon, in front of the river that meandered through the estate. Ruby guessed there were a dozen or so dwellings. 'I've always felt like I belonged here at Ballyford.'

'It's funny though, you know,' said Ruby, 'the rooms feel as familiar to me as they did at the convent. Mind you, that doesn't mean I'm staying. It's Doohoma for me, just as soon as I can get away.'

Ruby had already confided her plan of escape to Betsy. 'You would never be so bold, would ye?' Betsy said, aghast. 'I would and I am, Betsy.'

Lady Isobel and Ruby spent the following few days in amicable silence, until the next breakthrough. Having picked up a book, without being asked to or even seeking permission, Ruby began to read out loud while Lady Isobel went through her usual routine of staring blankly at a magazine in her lap.

'You have a nice reading voice,' she said softly. 'They taught you well at the convent. *Wuthering Heights* was always my favourite as a girl.'

'It was mine,' said Ruby, full of enthusiasm. 'My mother used to read it to me all the time. I think it was hers, too. Fancy that would ye. We all have the same book as our favourite.'

Lady Isobel smiled, gently. Neither woman registered that it was the first time she had smiled in a very long time.

'Mrs McKinnon told me you lost your mother in the storm.' Lady Isobel sounded nervous, as though she felt she shouldn't ask the question, but at the same time, kindly and curious.

Ruby didn't know how to respond. The boundaries of position and class sat before them. Placing the book face down in her lap, she turned her head and stared at the fire.

Lady Isobel continued. 'I lost my babies. We have something in common you and I, Ruby. We both know what it is like to lose those closest to us. The only people we truly love.'

The tears which sprang to Ruby's eyes were met by those in Lady Isobel's. No more words were spoken. Both women gazed into the fire lost in their own thoughts, each unsure of what to say next, both realizing no further words were required. Knowing was enough. Unknown to anyone but Ruby and Lady Isobel, a bond of closeness and a deep understanding had developed.

From that moment on, Lady Isobel began to show small but perceptible signs of improvement. Mrs McKinnon was beyond delighted with her improvement and made sure that everyone in the castle knew who was responsible. The temper tantrums and fits of crying became a thing of the past.

'You have a great nature with the lady, Ruby,' she said, at staff supper one day. 'If you are all wondering why I am in such good spirits, it's because this young lady has taken a weight off my shoulders and worked wonders with Lady Isobel.'

Jane looked less than pleased.

'Well, she still spends all day every day sat in the nursery. Doesn't seem like much of an improvement to me.' Jane was so quick to condemn Mrs McKinnon's praise. She spoke with her mouth full and crumbs of boxty flew across the table.

Mrs McKinnon scowled at Jane, who was becoming increasingly jealous of the attention Ruby received from Betsy and Mrs McKinnon. Even Mary's face shone with delight when Ruby came into the kitchen.

'Don't speak with your mouth full, Jane, and look at the plank in your own eye first, young lady before you criticize the splinter in the eye of another. The linen room isn't looking its best. I will be making an inspection soon, so get it sorted, please.'

Ruby interjected and brought the conversation back to Lady Isobel. She was saving Jane from further criticism, although

Jane was too consumed by her own penchant for complaining about what others had more than she, to notice.

'I'm about to try and persuade Lady Isobel to move across to the morning room tomorrow,' Ruby said. 'Jane is right, she spends most of the day in there. I swear she spends so much time in that chair, she would be buried under a mountain of cobwebs if no one cleaned the room.'

'We managed afore ye came.' The angry retort flew back from Jane, whose job it had been to look after Lady Isobel's room before Ruby arrived.

'Well, I have managed to dress her each day, Jane.' Ruby would not be put off. 'She lets me choose her clothes and she dresses nicely now.'

Jane snorted with derision..

'Oh shut up, Jane, you started this,' said the normally mild-mannered Betsy, as she stood to gather up her plates and reached for the breadboard on the table. 'Come on Ruby, time for us to get back to work.'

'Don't let Jane get to you,' said Betsy, as they ran up the back stairs.

'Oh, I don't. I will be away from here soon enough, and Lottie and me, we will make our own way. I have my father's cottage. He built it with his own hands and my mother helped. It's mine now. I don't need Ballyford or anyone. I can and I will do it all for myself.'

'Well, sure, until you want a husband,' Betsy said quizzically, 'and what about Lady Isobel? You and she get along great guns.'

'A husband? Well, Lottie would like one and maybe, one day I would too. I don't need a husband though. All I need is what's mine and that's my father's cottage. Then Ruby Flynn can look after herself. I have loads of ideas to make money. You can virtually live off the tatties and fish. I can sew and knit well and Lottie could teach at the school. What in God's name do we need husbands for anyway? And Lady Isobel, she can manage without me. There are plenty of staff who can do my job.'

Betsy began to giggle. 'No husband, are ye mad or what? Do ye not want to lie down with a man?'

'Away with you,' said Ruby. 'Anyway, if you don't stop, I will have a word with that Jimmy about you. I'll tell him yer after lying down with him and soon.'

Betsy squealed and blushed as both girls walked back along the corridor.

'You see those statues…?' said Ruby.

'God, don't look,' said Betsy. 'Mrs McKinnon will know, so she will, she can tell.'

'No, she can't. I look every time I pass, especially at that one, of the boy in all his glory,' grinned Ruby. 'And it's not true, she doesn't know. She can't tell. Go on, take a look yerself, then you'll know what Jimmy has in store for you.'

Betsy clasped both hands over her mouth to stifle her shrieks and then dared herself to take a look.

Linking arms and holding each other upright, the girls walked back along the corridor, weak with laughter.

Lady Isobel stood behind the nursery door about to leave the room and hearing the girls, smiled. She could feel the gloom which had oppressed her for so long beginning to lose its grip, and she knew it was because of Ruby Flynn.

Chapter five

Liverpool

The taxi deposited Mr McKinnon, and the two large cases he had transported across the Irish Sea from Ballyford, at the bottom of the steps of No. 1 Prince Albert Road, in Sefton Park, Liverpool.

'You need a hand with those big cases, mate? Those steps look a bit steep,' the taxi driver said.

'No, no, I will be fine, thank you,' Mr McKinnon replied, with not much conviction. It was his first visit to Lord FitzDeane's new town house in Liverpool. McKinnon preferred to remain at Ballyford.

Until recently Lord FitzDeane had reserved a room at the Grand Hotel for his twice monthly visits on business. His father had always retained a suite, with a room adjoining for his manservant. The new town house created an aura of permanence.

The cab driver was insistent, however. 'Get outta here, old man, I saw yer struggling down at the Pier Head, 'ere gis the bags.'

'There you go, many thanks, now,' said Mr McKinnon,

holding out a shilling. 'Get yerself a pint when you knock off.'

'Go'way mate, I don't want yer money!' The cabbie lifted his cap and with a grin he jumped into the driver's seat and pulled away.

With a smile, Mr McKinnon watched him go and thought that Liverpool was the only city in the world, perhaps apart from Dublin, where the cabbies would do something for nothing.

From the salon on the first floor of the house, Lord Fitz-Deane surveyed the scene below, with his forehead pressed against the cool pane of glass. His fair, almost blond hair hung in curls and flopped across his eyes. He was delighted to see McKinnon arrive at long last and was keen for news from home. He knew that his spells away from Ballyford were longer than they need be. At times he felt lonely. He loved the Irish countryside and when he was in Liverpool, his thoughts often wandered to the river of fish that ran through the estate, to the cows that grazed on his fields, and to the famous pigs. But visits home always resulted in pain. His heart was in Ballyford, it always would be, but for now the agony of all he had lost was too raw.

'Ah, McKinnon, good man, come in and sit by the fire.'

Charles took the cases from McKinnon. He was genuinely pleased to see the man who had been more of a father than a servant.

'You should have left the cases downstairs, I would have carried them up here myself.'

'I wasn't going to let them out of my sight, Lord FitzDeane, and besides, that housekeeper you have looks like she could open them with her teeth in a second.'

Charles flicked the lamp on and walked across to the drinks cabinet to pour McKinnon a drink.

'Fancy a whisky?'

'I do, but is it Irish or Scotch?'

'Well, as it's you, it's Scotch of course.'

McKinnon noted to himself that it was nice to see Charles smile again. It had been a long time. A smile born of relief crossed his own face.

'I will confess, McKinnon, that woman is a dreadful housekeeper. I was served a mutton pie last night so undercooked that I swear to God, it winked at me. Her name is Mrs Bat. I'm sure she spends her nights hanging upside down on a coat stand somewhere.'

Charles handed McKinnon his whisky and the two men sat down, either side of the fire. McKinnon loved moments like this with his boss, the man he had known since he was in the nursery. Due to the fact that the old Lord FitzDeane was never at Ballyford, McKinnon had raised him himself and having no children of his own, he felt as close to Lord Charles as he would have to any son of his own.

Charles leaned forward and threw a log on the fire.

'I've been busy. You know, I'm buying a new ship. She will be a fine spectacle, very new and modern. She carries three times the number of passengers on one crossing than any of the ships of the Blue Star Line. What do you reckon to that, McKinnon?'

McKinnon looked into his glass thoughtfully. His instincts

were fiercely paternal but needed to be phrased in the words of a servant.

'Well, sir, are you sure you're not biting off more than you can chew? I mean, it is a lot of work for one man. You have a lot on your plate already with the estate and the airplanes now, well, there's a lot of talk of the prices coming down and them being used for mass travel. They say that in the future, we will be able to visit any country in the world we want to, on an airplane.'

'Ah, well, strictly speaking, I'm not doing it alone, McKinnon.' Charles was prepared for McKinnon's concern. The reason he enjoyed his company so much was because he imagined it was how it would feel to have a close relationship with a father. 'Rory Doyle is coming into the business with me. He has great enthusiasm and he also knows Liverpool and its people from having lived here for years. Besides, an airplane can't carry the number of people a ship can or even as far. I can't see them ever taking over from travel on the seas.'

'Rory's father was just the same in Ireland,' said McKinnon, 'and his before him. Great men for the craic, a bit too much so, some may say. I thought Rory had his own salvage company down on the docks?'

'He does that. He's one hell of a man, is Rory. You have to admire him and his drive to get on. You'd never guess to see him now that he was born in the Ballyford cottages.'

Charles did not see that McKinnon had raised his eyebrows, sceptically. McKinnon and his wife were possibly the only two people who knew exactly how and why Rory Doyle had managed to buy a salvage company.

Charles pressed on. 'Rory has a fondness for the sea and he's a good business manager now too. The ship will carry six hundred passengers to New York from Liverpool and back. Four days there, one-day turnaround, four days back and we start all over again. Rory knows all there is to know about shipping, and I've been watching and learning from him. I've even spent time working on the ticket sales. But the new business will keep me anchored in Liverpool more often than I would like, I'm afraid,' Charles lied. There were times when he both liked and needed to be in Liverpool and like most men of his class, his input into the business was more financial than practical.

'What, with that housekeeper looking after you?'

Charles leaned back in his chair. 'Do you think Mrs McKinnon could find me a replacement?'

'Now, sir, you know you'll have to come home to Ballyford and ask her yourself. Do you want me to be a dead man?'

Charles laughed. He knew and loved Mrs McKinnon's foibles better than anyone.

'A new girl has begun at the castle,' McKinnon went on, draining the last drops of his whisky. He looked carefully at Lord FitzDeane. 'We fetched her from the convent near Belmullet. She's to work in the nursery for Lady FitzDeane, to give her a helping hand with her personal things. It was Lady FitzDeane's request. Well, it was more of an order from the doctor really.'

Charles swilled his own whisky around the sides of his glass and took a last gulp.

'There's no need for new staff in the nursery. It can be emptied, the dust sheets laid in place and shut up. There will be no more babies born at Ballyford, McKinnon.' Charles spoke stiffly, his voice full of regret.

McKinnon took a deep breath and wished his wife were with him; she would explain this so much better than he ever could. There was so much more to tell Lord Charles about Ruby Flynn, but McKinnon now decided it could wait until he returned home to Ireland.

'I don't think we can lay the dust sheets on the nursery just yet,' he said at last. 'Lady FitzDeane does spend a great deal of time in there.'

Charles jumped up from his chair and with his hand on the mantel, gazed into the fire, remembering the first boy who had been named Charles after himself, his father and grandfather. This baby had lived the longest. Almost six whole glorious months. Months of smiles and laughter. In those early days, Charles playfully fought Isobel to be the first one in the nursery each morning. The love he felt for his baby boy poured from him, the boy loved him back and he knew it. Charles looked deep into his son's eyes and thought that he had never loved anyone or anything as much.

Sometimes, at night, when he couldn't sleep for excitement, he would creep into the nursery while the nurse was sleeping. He would quietly sit on the low velvet-covered nursing chair at the side of the crib and stroke his son's dark, downy hair. He whispered to him gently, promising him Ballyford, the earth and more.

'I will look after you and work hard every day of my life so that you have the very best. I will fight your battles and teach you everything you need to know to make you the most deserving heir God could ask for to take over Ballyford Castle. You will be the best man ever to have been born on this estate, in all of Ireland even.'

He would kiss his son on the small, soft indentation on his as yet un-knitted scalp and let his lips linger there whilst he inhaled the deep warm smell. Flesh of his flesh. He had loved all his sons. But although he would never admit it to anyone, he had loved none as much as his firstborn boy. He knew he would never again feel such an outpouring of innocent, unconstrained love for a child. And that knowledge tore at his heart.

Charles walked over to the drinks cabinet again. 'Refills are in order,' he said.

McKinnon knew better than to argue.

Sitting back down with the whisky, Charles took a breath and said, 'I want my wife to be happy and well, McKinnon.'

'We all do, sir, we hope this girl will help us get there,' said McKinnon. 'We will ask her to coax Lady FitzDeane back into the morning room, slowly ease her away from the nursery. But you must return home, even if only for a short visit. You can discuss with Mrs McKinnon and the doctor about what should be done. It will also only take one word from you to make sure Mrs McKinnon finds someone better than Mrs Bat for this house.'

'You win,' said Charles, raising his glass to his lips and swallowing his whisky in one gulp. 'Next month. I shall return for a few weeks. I have to visit a solicitor here in Liverpool, first, to lodge a number of documents with him to do with the structuring of the company and my partnership with Rory, but then I shall return and do my best to wrap Mrs McKinnon around my little finger.'

'If she ever heard you saying that,' McKinnon laughed, 'she would whack you across your backside with a wooden spoon, lord of the castle or not.' Then in a more serious tone he added, 'It will warm the heart of everyone to hear that news, especially Amy. Lady FitzDeane eats like a bird and Amy has no one to appreciate her fine cooking. Why don't you ask a few of your friends over too, like you used to? You could have a day's fishing on the river, the salmon will be running in July, and you could have a dinner party afterwards. Just like in the old days.'

Charles looked up sharply and McKinnon wondered if he had overstepped the mark.

'How is Amy? Is she still making the best rabbit stew in the whole of the west?'

'She certainly is. You know Amy, the best cook in all of Ireland.'

There was silence for a moment, then Charles said, 'I think that's a good idea. Maybe I should think of doing something social at Ballyford, to blow the cobwebs away and draw a line under the saddest years of our lives.'

McKinnon nodded his head enthusiastically.

'I think that's what should happen. The doctor says Lady Isobel needs something out of the ordinary to break the circle of mourning she has trapped herself in.'

What about resurrecting the Ballyford Ball? Would that be a good idea?' said Charles, with hint of doubt in his voice.

This was music to McKinnon's ears. 'Excellent idea. All

the staff loved the balls and still miss them. They often speak about the last ball, even after all this time.'

Charles said, 'Right, give me a few weeks and we'll get things organized. Rory will take delivery of the new ship; he can manage for a short while. He has good workers in place and a new office right down on the Pier Head, next door to the Blue Star Line headquarters. Tickets are already selling well but I won't be happy unless I can see for myself that everything is in good order. That means I'll have to be strict about my return date, McKinnon. Come down with me in the morning before you leave and I'll introduce you to the staff. You can also catch up with Rory.'

Without knocking, Mrs Bat entered the room and noisily pushed a trolley across to the table.

'Join me, share my pain.' Lord Charles winked at McKinnon once she had finished crashing about with the plates and had left the room.

They settled down to the almost inedible food and talked over their plan to restore one of the great traditions of the estate, the Ballyford Ball. The estate would buzz, the staff would be happy. Lady Isobel's health would improve with the prospect of guest rooms full to the brim and friends enjoying the hospitality of Ballyford once again. 'Let's raise our glasses in a toast,' said Lord Charles. 'To the Ballyford ball and the pleasure it will bring to welcome our friends back to Ballyford once again.'

Never, in the history of time, could two men have been so disastrously wrong.

Chapter six

Ballyford Castle

It was gone midnight by the time McKinnon arrived home to Ballyford. He had made it onto the morning ship from Liverpool back to Dublin. A journey he spent clinging to the rails of the ship, depositing his breakfast over the side. He picked up the car, which he had left parked at the port and drove back as fast as the roads would allow. The journey from Dublin to Mayo always seemed to go faster than from Mayo to Dublin.

As he turned into the long driveway he wound the window down to hear better the rushing sound of the river as it rippled over the stones on its way to the ocean. He noticed that upstairs the nursery light still burned. An owl hooted and he spotted the black silhouette of Lady Isobel standing at the window gazing out into the night and he wondered, *What is she doing? She should be with Lord FitzDeane, supporting him like a proper wife. It should be she running this castle, not my wife, it is too much for her alone.*

The irony that he and Lord Charles had just hatched a plot that would double his wife's workload was lost on him.

Through the kitchen window he could see Mrs McKinnon dozing on a chair by the fire. His heart gave a familiar leap as it always did when he returned after they had been parted. He thought what a lucky man he was. She looked to him as beautiful as she had on the day he had married her.

As he quietly lifted the latch of the wooden kitchen door he dipped his fingers in the holy water and blessed himself, thanking God for his good mercy and his safe return, and asked him not to disturb Amy, who slept in the room next to the kitchen door.

Mrs McKinnon awoke before the door was even half open.

'Oh. You're back,' she murmured, piercing her knitting needles through the ball of wool which lay on her lap, before popping them into a bag at the side of her chair.

'I am that,' he replied. 'Tell you what, Mrs McKinnon, I could never live in that place. What with the noise and the traffic, it's all go it is.'

Mrs McKinnon smiled at her husband. 'Would you like some tea now? I've kept you a ham sandwich, it's under a damp cloth in the big fridge.'

As her husband opened the fridge door, she put the warmed kettle onto the range and yawned. 'Well, it's been a busy day here, too. Did you speak to Lord Charles about his returning home more often?'

'I did and he's coming back in a few weeks.'

That was exactly the news Mrs McKinnon had wanted to hear and she almost clapped her hands in delight.

'Well, thank goodness, you worked a miracle there. How did you manage that?'

McKinnon peeled the damp cloth back from his plate of sandwiches and held them up to his nose.

'You can't beat that smell can you? I reckon the best pigs in Ireland are bred here at Ballyford. And I'll tell you something else, Mrs McKinnon, the potatoes in Liverpool, they are dreadful specimens, awful, white and watery things. I would say they're not even good enough to feed the Ballyford pigs.'

'Is that all you have to tell me? You spend some time with Lord Charles in Liverpool and you come back in here talking about potatoes?' Mrs McKinnon turned a look of amused astonishment on her husband.

'No, not at all, give me a minute will you, woman. He took me to the office in Liverpool this morning for an early breakfast before my crossing and God knows, I wish I hadn't eaten it. He's bought his new ship, the *Marianna*. He wants to have her sailing on the Atlantic, from Liverpool to New York and back every day of the week he says. I met the man who works as his gaffer down at the Pier Head as well, a Mr Kimble, he seemed like a decent chap. They have an office now, a big one full of staff, right down on the Mersey in a huge white building, selling tickets over the counter, mad busy it was in there. People were lined up from when we arrived, early in the morning. They are selling the first tickets half price and there was an unholy scrum, I can tell you. Lord Charles isn't actually running the company, that is the job of Rory Doyle, would you ever believe it?'

'Rory Doyle, well I never.' Mrs McKinnon shook her head in disapproval. 'Lord Charles could never see any wrong in that boy. I don't suppose he knows that Rory was over here last week, visiting his mother? As usual, it was supposed to be a secret and no one was to know. The problem with his mother is she tells Miss McAndrew next door everything and she tells me. Likes to keep in my good books, does Miss McAndrew. She was telling me today there has been a McAndrew in that cottage for over two hundred years. I'm amazed it's stood for so long. Oh and another thing, I know he met up with Amy. He always does. Keeps her dangling on a string and both of them well into their forties. She would never say a word to me, of course. She knows what I would have to say about it all.'

'Maybe he's altered?' said McKinnon hopefully, between bites. 'Maybe Lord Charles is aware of a side to his nature that we never knew. After all, Amy's not a bad person and she sees something in him, if what you say is right.'

Mrs McKinnon sat down at the table and watched her husband eat.

'Well, I'll tell you what's worrying me now. I need Lord Charles here. Who is going to look after Lady Isobel if he is to be working in Liverpool all of the time? He can't be expecting you to do everything on the estate. You aren't the lord of the castle, you haven't the authority, he needs to be seen at your side, he should be here. Did you tell him about Ruby?'

Mr McKinnon had not told Lord Charles the full story, as instructed by Mrs McKinnon. He knew that could all come later.

Evading the question, he asked, 'How is Ruby shaping up? Has she found her way around all right?'

'Well, you know, we have seen such an improvement. I never would have thought it possible and it's undoubtedly all down to Ruby. Oh, I know Lady Isobel isn't as she was when she first came to Ballyford, but I can see a fairy footstep of improvement every day.' Changing the subject, she added, 'I have gossip, mind, listen. The main reason I'm worried about Rory Doyle working with Lord Charles is that apparently he has gambling debts and isn't doing as well as his mother has been cracking on. Miss McAndrew, she heard that from his mother herself, the horse's mouth so to speak. He was after her for money, would you believe it and her nearly ninety. He is convinced she has a pot of gold somewhere.'

'Well, I'm sorry to disappoint you, Mrs McKinnon, because I know you can't abide the man, any more than I can myself, but not only is he doing very well at helping Lord FitzDeane, his own salvage company is going great guns. He is a changed man, not the rascal he was when he lived here at Ballyford. I saw him today with my very own eyes. If he is a man with troubles and in debt, there was no sign of it today. I would say Miss McAndrew has got that one wrong.'

Mrs McKinnon was sore that her gossip had fallen on stony ground.

'Well, if he is doing as well as you say and if there was ever proof needed that blood money could do well for a man, there you have it. I wouldn't be so quick to believe it myself. Miss McAndrew, she doesn't get anything wrong.' Mrs McKinnon rose from the table with a flounce. 'God in heaven, that man was always trouble. Did you not see fit to warn Lord Charles?' Mrs McKinnon had only ever felt hatred for one person in her life and it was him. She and Mr McKinnon shared secrets that they could share with no one and at the centre was Rory Doyle.

At times she felt she would explode with her knowledge. She avoided Rory Doyle's mother like the plague, relying on her neighbour Miss McAndrew for information, lest she should one day be unable to control her tongue.

'Warn him? What would you have me say? Do you think he would believe me if I did? I would be opening a can of worms, that's for sure. Is that what you want, now that Ruby has arrived? I'm afraid that until we have something concrete to say, with irrefutable evidence to back it up, we have to ignore any gossip. I know you have it in your head that he only ever pretended to like Lord Charles, that he really hated him and everyone at the castle. Well, even you have to admit, it sounds a bit far-fetched. Anyway, never mind Rory Doyle, you know the light is still on up in the nursery, don't you? I saw it as I drove into the yard.'

'God in heaven, no.' Mrs McKinnon shook her head. 'She went to bed hours since. I took her up a Horlicks and switched off her main light myself. She must have got back up. I'm glad Lord Charles is coming home. The long nights seem to be difficult for her to bear alone. At least down here we all have each other. I'd like Ruby to stay with her at night, but it's too much to ask.'

Mrs McKinnon lifted up the near-empty teapot and walked over to the range to refresh the leaves with boiling water. 'Did he say what he wanted to do while he was home?' She placed the full pot back on the table and sat down.

'Well, I think he wants to have a chat with you about the Liverpool house, and we also talked about resurrecting the Ballyford Ball.'

Mrs McKinnon gave her husband one long hard look. A look he knew well.

'The Ballyford Ball? Do you remember how much work that was and how much younger we were than we are now? Ruby has only just persuaded Lady Isobel to wear a day dress, never mind fancying her up for a ball. How in God's name do you think we will manage that?'

McKinnon looked glum. 'Well, if anyone can work a miracle around here, you can. When he arrives home, you talk to him about it. He was only considering it.' He wanted to reverse out of the conversation as quickly as possible now that the notion of resurrecting the Ballyford Ball hadn't been received quite as well as he'd hoped and now said, 'Let's turn in.'

As they climbed the stairs to bed Mrs McKinnon said sharply, 'By the way, how did you get back so quickly? I hope you didn't drive more than twenty-five miles an hour.'

McKinnon laughed guiltily. 'I thought you liked a man with a bit of the devil-may-care about him?'

As they got into bed he snuggled up behind his wife and placed his hand on her bottom.

'I'll tell you what,' he whispered into her hairnet, 'you know how to make an old man feel young again in that flannelette nightie.'

'Get away with you.' Mrs McKinnon slapped his hand away. 'You may feel sixteen, but you're really sixty.'

With a sigh Mr McKinnon rolled over. Only he knew that it was really a sigh of relief. His mind might be willing but his body, in recent years, had certainly become weak. Now, as he lay on his back with his arms folded across his chest, listening to his wife's gentle breathing, he thought, *Yes, this will suffice, me pretending still to be the raging, sex mad bull of old and she stubbornly refusing. Far better than failing to rise to the occasion and suffering the shame of failure.*

Chapter seven

'Jack is driving Jane and me to Belmullet on the cart tomorrow morning,' said Ruby to Betsy. They were scraping porridge bowls into the scullery sink following breakfast and helping Mary to clear up.

'It's not fair,' said Mary sullenly. 'I never get to go nowhere. No one ever sends me to the shops. I'd love to go to Galway one day, I would. Or Belmullet; I would love that.'

Ruby instantly felt guilty. 'Oh Mary, shall I bring you something nice back? Would you like some sweets? Mrs McKinnon has given me a shilling to buy some treats.'

Ruby reached out and pulled Mary to her, tucking her under her arm and kissing the top of her head. Mary was such a simple soul that she felt protective towards her.

'If you went to Galway, Mary,' said Betsy, 'we'd be terrified of losing you. God, can you imagine how heartbroken the lads would be, 'cause they all love our Mary.'

Mary giggled and pulled out from Ruby's embrace, her face bright red. 'Would ye stop!' she yelled, as Jimmy walked into the scullery with his bowl.

'What's that?' said Jimmy. 'Our Mary's not going anywhere,

there would be too many hearts broken around here and mine, sure now, it would be broken the worst of all.'

Mary ran from the scullery, shrieking with delight. Her day of peeling potatoes and scrubbing the scullery floor had just become that much more bearable.

'I wonder why Jane and not me?' Betsy said to Ruby and Jimmy, feeling hurt. 'Mrs McKinnon promised me I could go next time I had a day off.'

'I think Jane overheard Mrs Mack telling me I could have the day off and she gave out big time. I think she just caught Mrs McKinnon when she was busy and wore the poor woman down. You are too easy-going, Betsy. Jane kicks off so much she has them all half scared of her.'

Ruby felt guilty imparting this information, but she was already quite clear in her mind: Betsy was her friend, not Jane. Betsy had helped her settle quickly into castle life and that had in turn helped her work with and improve things a little for Lady Isobel.

Jane walked in through the scullery door to join them at the sink and shouted at Mary to follow her.

'What's going on in here?' she demanded to know. 'Amy sent Mary in for the vegetables and she ran back out without them.'

Mary, who had followed behind Jane struggled to lift the wicker basket full of vegetables. 'Jane, will ye take the other handle?' she asked, sheepishly.

'No,' replied Jane, walking over to Ruby and Betsy. 'Ye aren't complaining about me going out are ye, Betsy? Don't ye dare. Ye and Amy are always slipping off to visit your mammy's sister's lad at the pub in Belmullet and ye never take me.'

'I wonder why that might be,' replied Betsy, tartly. 'You must come with us next time,' she added pointedly, looking at Ruby and ignoring Jane as she bent down and took the handle of the wicker basket, which was banging painfully against Mary's knees.

As it was, the rain the next day was far too heavy and the road too muddy for the cart to take the extra weight of the girls alongside the provisions.

'Just wait until there has been a few windy days on the trot to dry out the mud,' Mrs McKinnon said to the disappointed Ruby and Jane.

But the rain persisted every day and felt like it would never stop again and so eventually Jack took them in his precious new van. Mr McKinnon had said that if the rain kept up he would take the girls in the car himself, but the car couldn't fit everything in that Amy needed, especially the sacks of flour and the special new mix for the pig feed which Mr McKinnon was becoming impatient for.

'Don't get mud on the seat or put your feet on the dashboard,' Jack said, as soon as they were sitting on the front bench.

'Can we breathe, Jack?' Ruby asked, cheekily.

'Away with you, madam,' he replied. 'It has taken my whole life to save enough to buy this van and I shan't live long enough to buy another, so we must look after it now.'

'Where do you earn your money to save?' asked Ruby, puzzled.

'Well, the estate needs me most days, but I have work from

the village too and I do a lot of fetching and carrying from Dublin for the shopkeepers in Belmullet and the villages. Not everyone pays me in money, mind. I had my roof thatched and it didn't cost me. We all do things to get by and help each other.'

As Ruby examined the van, she wondered if Jack would help when she finally put her escape plan into action. For now she was just happy to have a day off. She had never before had a day off from anything. Despite Sunday being a day of rest, it was prayers, church and jobs as always for the non-fee-paying girls in the convent. She had decided that today she would use the freedom to track down Lottie, even if it meant stepping in and out of every hotel bar in Belmullet.

'God, I cannot believe I am going to find Lottie,' Ruby said to Jane when they were well along the road. 'Can you? There can't be that many hotels in Belmullet. I just have to ask around and find out which one she's working in.'

'Why would I care either way?' replied Jane, with indifference. 'She's nothing to me.' It took a lot more than an acerbic Jane to put Ruby off her track.

'Imagine, she could be only yards away from me and not even know I was there. I couldn't sleep last night thinking of the things I had to remember to tell her next time I see her, not knowing at the time that it would be today.'

Ruby had decided to entirely ignore Jane's rudeness but she did wish that it was Betsy sitting next to her in the van. Despite her best efforts, Jane's moods threatened to spoil the happiness of her day.

As the van turned onto the Belmullet Road, Ruby read the list Amy had given her. Amongst other things she wanted six ounces of two-ply baby pink wool, which had apparently arrived from England last week. Amy planned to knit a matinee coat for her niece in Chicago.

'There will have been a run on it,' said Jane gloomily as she led the way to the shop. 'They will all be after it when the news gets out that it's in. They haven't had pink in for months. I thought that maybe Amy would have slipped away and bought it for herself but she's in a right tizz because Lord FitzDeane is coming home sometime soon and she wants to make his favourite things to eat.'

'Will I get to meet him?' Ruby asked.

'Well sure, why would ye not, stupid. He's not invisible. We all work for him, don't we?'

Ruby was still determined not to take offence.

'Amy does love her cooking. She will be glad of the chance to make some nice things and with a bit of luck, maybe we will see some of the leftovers,' Ruby said cheerfully.

'It isn't just Amy in a tizz,' Jane continued. 'The gardeners haven't stopped cutting and pruning and Mrs McKinnon hasn't stopped ordering us all about. Don't ye have ears, Ruby? Have you not noticed how busy everyone is? If there wasn't a list of things Amy and Mrs McKinnon needed, I think they might have cancelled our day out. The only person who isn't bothered about Lord Charles coming home is Lady Isobel.'

As Jane spent barely a moment in Lady Isobel's company, Ruby wondered how she had noticed this, but her loyalty towards Lady Isobel forbade her to reply. She sometimes confided in Betsy, who she knew she could trust, but never in Jane.

When at last Ruby and Lottie met, their squeals of joy could be heard outside the hotel and right down the main street in Belmullet.

'What kind of commotion is that?' said the barman Tony, , Amy's cousin as he came up into the bar from the cellar. Tony knew Ballyford well, which was news to Lottie.

'My giddy aunt, Lottie, would you look at the cut of you, you look grand,' said Ruby admiringly.

'Not at all, 'tis you who looks grand. Ye look just like Rita Hayworth, doesn't she, Tony? If I hadn't known it was you coming through that door, Ruby, I'd have thought she had checked into the hotel herself.'

'Go on Lottie, take an hour in the town,' said Tony, as he slammed a wooden crate onto the bar. 'You and Rita Hayworth have some catching up to do and then ye can come back here and tell me all the news of our Amy, Ruby.'

Lottie had her apron off and her coat on almost before the words had left his mouth.

Later, in the café above the shop where Ruby had bought the wool, they looked out into the street and saw Jane and Jack, searching for Ruby.

'Shall I tap on the window for her?' asked Lottie.

'God, no, she has a mouth on her so sour she would turn the milk. Let's have a few minutes and I'll say I never saw them. Lottie, we have to escape soon, you still want to, don't you?'

Lottie looked sheepish. 'Well, I do quite like it here, you know. Tony, he's a nice man to work for and I'm making friends in Belmullet. At night, all the young ones, they hang about on the street and outside the pubs and the hotel and the craic is great. We are out there until it's dark. And in the pub there's a ceilidh at the weekend, with everyone dancing and the fiddlers playing and it's just fantastic, so it is.' Lottie's face lit up, as Ruby's fell.

'Well, there will be that in Doohoma as well, but you could be a teacher, Lottie, you are so clever. You surely don't want to stay here, do you?'

Lottie thought Ruby looked as if she was about to cry, so she said, 'God, no, of course not, but let's just wait a little while. Give me a few weeks, maybe a few months. I'm only getting five shillings a week, with my board and keep. How much are you getting?'

Ruby was ashamed to say she hadn't asked and didn't know. Lottie knew Ruby well enough to have guessed this was the case. 'Well, get the cut of you with your big running away ideas and you don't even know how much money you have!'

'But we will be away from here before Christmas comes, won't we?'

'Of course we will,' said Lottie, hugging Ruby, knowing deep down that she didn't have Ruby's burning desire to be free. Lottie was safe and she was having fun. Her existence was a million times better than it had ever been at the convent. Life, for the first time, was being good to Lottie and she was scared to move, to alter the direction of the wind that was blowing such fortune in her direction.

When it came time to say goodbye, Jack almost had to peel Ruby and Lottie apart. 'Come on, little lady,' he said. 'You can come back soon, can't she, Tony?'

'Aye, she can that. We need another, if she wants to leave Ballyford and come and work for us. I doubt she could match Lottie though, she has been a great bonus to the hotel. Chats away to all the guests she does as bold as you like and they all love her.'

'Eh, enough of that, this lady belongs at Ballyford, don't you, miss?' said Jack.

As Ruby climbed into the van with Jane, Jack's words spun around in her brain. *This lady belongs at Ballyford.* It was true, she did feel as though she belonged there and with each day the feeling got stronger. She needed to escape sooner rather than later if the pull of Ballyford was to be resisted.

The servants were getting ready to go about their work when Mr McKinnon made his announcement. Ruby was in the process of untying a knot in the back of Betsy's hair and the kitchen was filled with the noise of clattering oat bowls being loaded into the sink for washing.

'Tomorrow, Lord Charles finally arrives at Ballyford.'

'Thank the Holy Father, at last,' said Amy.

'It's because of your constant chatter and complaints that he's returning so soon, Amy,' said Mr McKinnon, with a grin. 'That and because you're his favourite.'

Everyone giggled, but none more than Amy who turned crimson.

Mr McKinnon spoke over the laughter. 'Apparently, he dreams of your chicken and leek pie with the savoury cream sauce when he's in Liverpool and he only gets to eat it when he is at Ballyford. He is yet to meet anyone in Liverpool who even understands what he is talking about and the woman who cooks for him, well, if she wasn't enough to drive a man to drink, I'm sure I don't know what would be.'

'Well, 'tis nice to be appreciated an' all but I need to get to work,' said Amy, with a flourish. 'Lady Isobel eats less food than I throw out for the birds; I need to stock up. Get those bowls washed, Jane. Everyone else, out of here. I have work to do. And someone tell Jimmy I need more onions and to bring me two big birds.'

She threw the skinned rabbit back onto the platter and slid it under the cover. The evening stew abandoned, it was now to be chicken and leek pie.

Ruby had not joined in with the laughter and hung back from the other staff, who were gathered around Mr McKinnon in order to hear better. Her plan to escape was all worked out in her mind. Jack had told them that he was waiting for six bicycles to be shipped from Liverpool into Dublin and that he was away to collect them in the van. If Ruby could get hold of one of those bicycles, then she would have her own means of transport and could be gone.

But now she felt reluctant, and she didn't know why. Though she felt so very sorry for Lady Isobel, now that Lord FitzDeane was coming back she supposed Lady Isobel would not need her as much. This was her opportunity to escape. So why did she feel filled with dread? As though things were not going to work out the way she had planned?

Chapter eight

Liverpool

'Shoeshine, sir?'

Charles FitzDeane looked down at the boy standing on the corner of Exchange Flags. He knew the lad. He stood in the same place every day and often cleaned his shoes. It gave him some amusement that the boy he tipped by day failed to recognize him at night.

Charles had walked through bomb rubble on his way to get a cab to drive him into Liverpool from Sefton Park. His shoes were dirty and in need of a polish, but where he was heading clean shoes would be out of place. He walked through bombed-out wasteland every day in Liverpool. Nothing had altered, since VE Day. Liverpool had been torn and ravaged and the energy of the city's residents had been focused on existing. On healing. On the making good of who and what was left. The rubble had remained, waiting for someone to notice. A miserable and unintended memorial, fashioned from towers of fire-blackened bricks, to the people who had lost their lives.

Tonight, Charles definitely did not want his shoes to be shone and his eyes avoided the boy's expectant gaze. If he had

105

been dressed in the clothes he had worn earlier that day, on his way to his solicitor's office, the boy would have known him straight away and realized that he had already brushed his shoes once that morning.

Charles flicked a shilling his way as he passed and the boy leapt up to catch it.

'Thanks mister,' he shouted, with a look of amazement on his face. 'Ta for the bob. Don't you want yer shoes cleaned then?'

Charles held up his hand in recognition of the thanks and smiled at the boy's enthusiasm as he walked away and disappeared into the fog.

Charles had fallen for Liverpool the moment he set foot on the dockside. The people and the vibrancy of the city, war-damaged but pushing slowly towards recovery, captivated his imagination. He could smell prosperity on the Mersey air, a means to increase the fortune he had been left for the benefit of his yet-to-be-born sons. He had even loved the humorous cheekiness of people like the shoeshine boys, always in the same place on Exchange Flags.

Tonight, the fog was everywhere. It rolled down the Mersey River like a bolt of unfurling grey chiffon and tumbled over the edge of the riverbank. It hung around on the decks of boats and crawled across the docks and up the streets into the city. It cowered in doorways and squatted on street lamps, dulling the yellow sulphur light to an eerie blur. It filled the air and the lungs of babies and children and it stalked the easy prey of the old into their badly heated homes.

'It's a right pea-souper tonight, sir,' the boy shouted, even though Charles was lost to the fog.

Earlier that evening, Mrs Bat had almost delayed Charles by retiring much later than usual.

'I will bring you your tea tray at six, then,' she said, in her usual surly manner, as she deposited his dinner on the table with a thud so hard that the dinner plate leapt up from the tray and rattled as it landed, sending his watery gravy slopping over the edge.

'And I will put your breakfast with it, although what any God-fearing person can eat before mass, I have no idea.' She fussed and fiddled about the room, as though sensing his impatience and deliberately delaying her departure.

As soon as she had left, he bolted down his supper and made his way to his secret room on the top floor, the room to which only he and no one else held a key. There he changed his clothes for those he was now wearing. He sat on a wooden chest and waited until the housekeeper closed the scullery door and descended the rear steps. Once he had heard the latch fall on the wooden gate, he followed her out into the unlit back entry.

If Charles had simply needed company tonight, he could have taken himself to London and spent a few nights at his club. He would have met friends for dinner and found any number of young ladies willing to supply what he was looking for. It always amazed him how much easier it was to persuade the daughter of a duke to bend to his will than it was the daughter of a docker. The dockers' daughters were riddled with guilt and the fear of shame. They went to church, believed the priest and trembled at the thought of confession.

'I can't,' the last one had whispered. 'Me mam says that if I darken our doorstep, me da will kill me.' Charles knew she was referring to becoming pregnant.

Charles had considered taking a mistress and keeping her in London, but he realized that wasn't for him. Charles adored the dockers' daughters, these Liverpool girls most of all. He thought that they were more like Americans than any others he had ever met. Not so strange, given that Liverpool faced out across the Atlantic towards America, turning its back on England. He loved their irreverence, their soft skin and a willing lust for life to match his own, but mostly he loved the fact that they allowed him to release his pain.

He knew of no other way to cure the hurt, except by burying himself in the scent of an unknown woman. It worked. For a short time afterwards, he could concentrate, think and be free from the pain that haunted him and which without fail or warning, always returned. Not one of his Liverpool conquests knew his true identity and that was how it would remain. He genuinely loved the girls he met, for the time he was with them. He envied their simple, uncomplicated lives and the feeling of power and pleasure it gave him to hand them money, then watch their faces light up. Their lives were so unlike his own. They couldn't ever know who he truly was. The lord of a castle. A man who detested his own life. His life was a lie and he knew it, but at least his Liverpool girls prevented him from falling into a pit of loneliness and despair.

But his thoughts tonight were full of one particular Liverpool lady, Stella. That he had remembered her name after their first night was a feat in itself. Usually he forgot a girl's name before her French knickers returned to full mast. Stella made him laugh. To be fair, all Liverpool girls made him laugh. Brought about by a lack of a social filter, or an awareness that there are things one just shouldn't say or do.

Stella had set her eye on Charles from the moment he walked into the bar. He knew instantly that bedding her would be dangerous. There was something about her that set alarm bells ringing and told him to be careful, but at the same time he wanted to know her more.

She was a virgin, and the discovery had come as a surprise to him. He remembered every second of the first time he had taken her. At the thought of her sweetness, of her desperate eagerness to please and accommodate him, his stomach clenched. He had hardly fumbled with her blouse before she reached up and undid it for him. His impression had been of one who was skilled, until he felt her violently tremble in his arms.

'Is there something wrong,' he had whispered thickly into her hair.

'No not wrong, it's just that it's me first time and I want to get it right. Will it hurt?'

Charles was thrown: he wrapped his arms around her to stop the shaking, while he gathered his thoughts for a moment and wondered what to do.

She decided for him by placing her mouth over his and his hand inside the blouse she had opened. When he tried to pull away to speak, to make sure that this was what she really wanted, she put her hands around the back of his neck, pulling him to her, kissing him harder as he heard her first gentle moans.

He wished they were somewhere else. He didn't want this girl to remember her first time in a back entry, but it was too late. She had won, he was lost and as he entered her, as gently as he could, she shuddered and contracted, drawing him in. He held his breath and steadied himself; savouring the moment, relishing the dizziness in his head and the oblivion it brought. He bent his head and kissed the curve of her breast, inhaling the scent of her, holding on. He took her nipple into his mouth. Instantly, he felt her respond once more as she rose against him. Stella was hungry for life. He could hold himself back no longer and succumbed to the pleasure of release she gave him.

It was not his usual style, but he waited with her and they shared a cigarette before he left.

Not one of the Liverpool girls he had met before had been as willing, as hungry or as exuberant as Stella. She amused him, pulled him into her world of optimism with her talkativeness and her funny accent. He knew where he could find her, if he wanted. He knew. And it nagged at him. As he walked through the back alleys he wondered what Stella, the Liverpool girl about town, would make of the Ballyford pigs.

'I never knew that pig farming was such an attractive proposition to so many beautiful young women,' a friend from university had said to Charles, with a hint of sarcasm, during the days when life was good.

Charles had laughed out loud as his friend continued. 'No, indeed, it is a fact that every beautiful woman is fascinated by the price of wheat and bacon, adores fishing and has always wanted to visit rural Ireland. I wonder what it is that attracts them to the incredibly wealthy and landed Lord FitzDeane.'

That comment had hurt.

As Charles turned onto Tithebarn Street he thought about Rory, a man who knew all about pigs. He remembered how Rory had taken Charles under his wing at Ballyford during the long periods of loneliness when his parents were away. It was Rory who had always landed Charles in trouble with Mrs McKinnon when they were boys.

'You spend too much time down at the cottages my boy, you need to keep away from that Rory. All the Doyles are a bad lot,' she had often chided him when he was younger.

She was right. But he had hung around with the servants and Rory Doyle because he was a lonely boy in need of friends. His parents spent most of their time in London and he had been raised at Ballyford by Mr and Mrs McKinnon. As far as he could remember, he had never once sat on his mother's knee and the only affection he could ever recall had come from the Ballyford servants. Sheets washed, floors scrubbed, brow kissed.

All in the line of duty, and Rory Doyle, well he was a hero in Charles's eyes. Tall, older and with deep, dark Irish eyes, which flared with daring, it was Rory Doyle who taught Charles to ride and sat with him on the side of the river at Ballyford and told him tales of the people who lived in the cottages. But suddenly, without warning and when Charles still a boy, Rory had disappeared from Ballyford overnight and hadn't returned until the morning of the wake for Charles's father, years later.

Now they were both men. Rory, in his late forties, made Charles feel, at thirty-three, as if he was still a young man.

Charles regarded Rory almost as family. He knew him, liked him and more than that, he trusted him, too.

He wondered, not for the first time, why Rory had left Ballyford so suddenly. But none of that mattered now. They were working as a team, united by the *Marianna* and the new shipping business.

They had met that lunchtime in the new office and their recently appointed assistant had made them fancy sandwiches and a pot of tea. Rory's desk faced out over the Mersey and for a few moments they had sat and watched the *Royal Iris* as she loaded her passengers and the dredger, making its steady way across to Birkenhead. Rory was keen.

'Sure, I can do it,' he said enthusiastically, when Charles asked him could he manage the company whilst he went home to Ballyford. 'My lad is virtually running the salvage business, and why wouldn't I want to help my Lord Charles?' Rory winked to dispel any notion that he was being facetious.

It worked. It always did. Charles had no idea how much Rory loathed the FitzDeanes. If he had any notion that Rory had spent his life winning his trust and favour, while all the time despising him, he would have been shocked to his core. Rory Doyle was a charmer who used people with ease and without conscience.

'Are you still a rouge on the tables, Rory?' Charles asked, sheepishly. Like everyone else, he had heard the tales of Rory's gambling.

'Well, let's put it this way, shall we...' Rory crushed his cigarette into the ashtray with exaggerated force and picked up and examined an egg sandwich. He began to pull the threads of mustard cress away from the sides. 'When I gamble, 'tis only with me own money, not anyone else's, so I'm thinking that would be legal now and classed as me own enjoyment.' His smile belied the bristling edge to his voice.

Charles laughed out loud. 'That's fine. It's none of my business what you do with your own money, Rory. I'm not prying. Just showing concern, that's all. I had a reason for asking: would you like to become a full partner in the business?' Charles asked this question out of the blue. He could see he had irritated Rory with his question about gambling and wanted to make it up to him. Without his being aware, it had been the cycle of their friendship since their boyhood days.

'I need someone who can give the business their all. Work seven days a week, if necessary, to make the *Marianna* a success. If there is one thing you know, it's shipping.'

Rory thought for a moment. Even he hadn't expected this. He knew he had to pick his words carefully and took a bite of his sandwich to buy himself some time.

'I will give it my all, lord Charles,' he said, sombrely and without enthusiasm. 'You know I will do that anyway, you don't have to make me a partner, you know.'

'No, I want to, you deserve it. I can't expect you to put the work in and not take the rewards. I want to pay you as an equal in the business,' said Charles with full enthusiasm and an almost pleading voice.

It worked. Rory smiled.

Charles was in the middle of developing his plans to expand the Ballyford holdings and in that year, Rory had taught Charles most of what he knew about shipping. It was reassuring for Charles to have someone older lending a helping hand. Rory was rough around the edges, but skilled and competent. What let him down was that his eye was always on the bigger prize. The one he could attain with lady luck and no effort from himself. Greed was his vice and on occasion it had nearly taken him down. But Charles had found himself leaving more and more of the day-to-day running of the business to Rory. It had been the same when they were kids. Although Charles had been the heir to the castle, it was Rory who lorded it around the estate.

Tomorrow morning, Charles would set off for Ballyford on the first boat and leave Rory in charge of tying up the remaining loose ends of the deal.

'Thank God for Rory,' Charles said out loud, as he hurried along into the foggy night. If it weren't for him, a trip back to Ballyford at this crucial stage of the process would have been out of the question. Charles had sworn that, when he married, he would never leave Ballyford and now here he was deepening his business interests in England and Ballyford was the place he dreaded visiting more than anywhere else in the world.

Tonight, however, he knew exactly what he had to do. He had abandoned his suit and bowler hat, the uniform for men of business in Liverpool and wore shabby trousers and a worker's donkey jacket. His brown brogues were down on the heel and he had placed a workman's cap on his head.

The clothes had been the most difficult part of his deceit. Unable to give this task to any servant, he had visited a pawnshop himself and pretended he was buying the clothes as an act of charity for a lady from the church.

He was shocked at the bluntness of the woman behind the counter.

'Are you sure those trousers aren't for you?' she asked him, with narrow eyes. 'It's just that yer awful particular like about whether they fits yer or not. How d'ya know he's the same size as you? You just told me you never met 'im.'

Charles handed the money over and fled out of the door. Liverpool women were as sharp as a Stanley knife and twice as clever.

The lights of the pub he was heading for twinkled in the smog ahead, urging him along. The fog was disorientating and he hoped he would have no trouble finding a cab back to Sefton Park when he was done. Looking up and down the street first, he slipped into the pub. Charles knew it wouldn't take him long. He would be back home by ten, in bed by half past and up at six, ready to face the formidable Mrs Bat.

His eyes alighted upon her immediately. She was standing with three other girls by the jukebox and was swaying to the music. She wore a mid-calf length red dress with a square neck, which fell in soft pleats. Her dark and tightly crimped hair sat stiffly on her shoulders. It was not a style any of the women in Charles's circle would adopt. The style alone defined her class; that and her lips, which were painted a bright cherry red and complemented the dress. That was enough for Charles. A man from his background could never be seen with a woman who wore crimped hair and red lips. The women in his social circle had never set foot inside a pub and would not be seen outdoors without a hat, kid gloves and a matching handbag.

At least Stella wasn't one of the religious ones. The 'not on the first night' girls. How would he have told her kindly that there would be no second night? And yet here he was, breaking his own rules.

He bought himself a pint of Guinness and sent over a gin and orange. Five minutes later she was by his side at the bar.

'Well, I knew you'd be back.' Stella grinned.

Despite himself, he grinned back, as he remembered to slip into a more working class accent. 'How's that then? You psychic or what?'

She laughed as she swilled down her drink, her eyes twinkled and she blushed. 'You were me first, I wanted yer to come back.'

Charles looked around the bar and whispered in her ear, and she giggled again.

Half an hour later he slipped her twenty pounds while she straightened her skirt. She almost fainted with the shock.

'I can't take that,' she said. 'I'm norra whore, I just fancied yer, you've got nice eyes.' She grinned up at him and wobbled precariously, placing one of her hands on his arm while she tried to replace the high-heeled sandals, which had slipped off her feet at the height of her passion. Charles was taken aback. The twenty-pound note was equal to a month's wage for a girl of her age and position.

'Come back to my place and meet me mam and our kids. I don't want yer money.' As she spoke she slipped the twenty-pound note into her handbag, which she had retrieved, having earlier discarded it unceremoniously on the floor. Her contrary nature fascinated Charles.

'No, I know that, girl, but go on, I won it on the gee-gees – go an' 'ave a laugh with yer mates. I'll find yer soon.'

And that's where he left her, standing by the bins looking bewildered as he slipped away into the enveloping fog once more.

Back home he lay in his bed and wondered yet again why he did it. He knew in his heart that it was to prevent himself seeking solace in the arms of his wife and risking another pregnancy when he returned to Ballyford. He would be tempted, he always was. This made it easier, this and the knowledge that when he returned to Liverpool, his little Stella or any one of many beautiful Liverpool ladies would be available. He and Isobel had given up the pretence of loving one another a long time ago, but she was his wife, he was a young man and in his marriage was where his needs should be met. But he could not go there. Never, ever again.

While Charles slept, Rory sat on the late train to Euston. It had been far easier than he had imagined to persuade Charles to use Nicholas Nathan, the maritime lawyer he had met whilst running his salvage company, who had often made visits to Liverpool to meet him and haggle over the value of salvage. Mr Nathan also liked gambling and Rory had introduced him to the card schools in the back rooms of Bold Street. They had become good friends over their pints of mild and whisky chasers in smoky bars and had dreamt up a plan to make both men rich. Nicholas Nathan often travelled to Piraeus in Greece on behalf of a shipping line which was expanding into cruising the Mediterranean, and he had made some interesting if dubious contacts from the shipping world.

Rory had lost huge sums on the poker tables and on horses at Aintree. He was concerned that Charles had somehow got wind of this. Rory kept his gambling under cover. He owed too many people not to. Charles's comments had put the wind up him. The offer of a partnership, with a substantial financial payment, had arrived at a crucial moment and then the ideas had just simply run away with him. Charles had unwittingly helped Rory to seal his own fate. It had been easy to transfer the failing salvage company to his wife and his son and a brilliant plan of Nathan's. It held the debtors off for a little while longer. What had not been so easy, was persuading Amy to leave his note in the castle.

'I want to know what's in it first,' Amy had said. They had met in secret in her mother's cottage on the estate. Poor Amy, she was so easy for him to manage. He had once told her he would take everything from Ballyford and precious Lord Charles and Amy had laughed at him. Soon she would laugh no more.

The business and his wife, that would do. Rory smiled to himself. For now.

'Tea, biscuits, cake?'

A guard pushed a wooden trolley towards him with an urn balanced precariously on top. Rory instinctively shifted in his seat away from the aisle and took some coins out of his trouser pocket.

'Tea please,' he said as he smiled up at the guard.

Rory felt good and wished he had something stronger. He had worked hard to get Charles to invite him into the business.

It had taken years. It had been exhausting winning his trust. He knew Charles carried guilt with him every day. The sins of his father haunted him and no one knew that better than Rory himself. Rory had been his father's accomplice. An accomplice who had never been paid in full. The best-kept secret. Guilt. A powerful emotion. As he sipped his tea and gazed out of the window, watching the lights of industry twinkle in the night sky, he mused over how willingly Charles had agreed to his plan.

'I don't think you should use your own solicitor in Liverpool for this deal,' Rory had said as they stood on the Southampton dockside, looking up at the towering sides and the blue and white striped funnel of the *Marianna*. 'Maritime law is quite specialized. The Blue Star Line used a man from London, a maritime lawyer by the name of Nicholas Nathan, because he was the best.'

Charles knew that what he felt right now, looking up at the ship, was a diluted version of what he had felt on becoming a father. But this is safer, he thought to himself. 'Really?' he replied. 'Why was he the best?'

'Well, because he has the brain, I suppose. Look, she's a big ship and worth a lot of money for a start. Let's use a serious brief in London and then we can bring on board a local solicitor in Liverpool to tie up the ends.'

'My father used a solicitor in Dublin,' said Charles. 'I haven't had much need for one over these last few years and anyway, I have never thought much of my father's solicitor, reminds me too much of him for my liking.'

'Well, there aren't many other options in truth, Charles.

At least Nathan will know all the pitfalls, as an experienced maritime solicitor. Always important to put the right person in charge of the job.'

Charles glanced back up at the towering funnels. He wanted to object, but felt churlish because he didn't really know why. Rory knew shipping better than he ever would. If he felt this was the right man to use, he had to trust him and let him know that Charles respected his opinion. After all, he had known Rory for all of his life. He suppressed his instinctive wariness at the prospect of using a solicitor he didn't know. Maybe owning a ship is like having a child, he thought to himself. The inherent degree of possessiveness. The mistrust of anyone other than oneself taking control.

'Yes, you are quite right, Rory,' he said, with more confidence than he felt.

'Good, I shall visit him immediately,' said Rory, seizing the moment. 'We don't want any delays, time is money and we need to use someone we can be sure knows the job and can push along.'

'When we get back to Lime Street, let's head over to Sefton Park for me to collect the contract,' said Rory, sensing Charles's hesitance and pushing the point to his favour. 'If I can't see the lawyer today, I'll visit him tomorrow. I can leave it all to him.' Rory slapped Charles on the back and the two men walked back to the waiting car chatting.

Charles could not shift the feeling of uneasiness resting in the pit of his stomach. 'I think McKinnon is right, Rory,' he said as they drove away from Southampton docks and he looked out through the car windows at his new purchase, diminishing in size as it retreated from sight. 'I think I do need a spell at Ballyford.'

'Ah, well, I was there meself to see mammy, 'tis just the same,' said Rory.

Rory was delighted. Charles being out of the way for a few weeks was perfect. Everything was going to plan. Charles was completely unaware that he had just taken the worst decision of his life.

Rory spent the night in Euston station and met Nicholas Nathan for breakfast in the station café at first light. Rory chose the bacon and egg on toast and Nicholas the smoked kippers. They both lit up a cigarette while they were waiting to be served.

'I still can't get used to being able to order kippers and eggs in a café so easily,' said Nicholas. 'God, the war lasted a bloody long time.'

Over breakfast Rory explained what he wanted to achieve. 'It can be done,' said Nicholas almost an hour later. 'It is a very bold and daring plan, but between us, I think we can achieve it. I'll need sixty per cent, mind.'

Rory's toes curled. Sixty per cent? That was far more than he had expected. However, 40 per cent of this deal was better than 40 per cent of nothing, in the grand scheme of things. He was in no position to complain. If he pulled this off, his debts would be cleared. His own son would be secure and the thugs who had waited at the corner of the road when he left for work only the previous morning, would stop demanding that he pay back his debts. The patience of the men he owed the money to and had gambled away in the smoky back rooms of the card schools was running short. He knew that it was only a matter of time before they let his wife, Margaret, know the perilous position he was in. Losing the house would kill Margaret, but not until she, or more accurately her brothers had killed him first.

'You don't like the FitzDeanes, do you?' Nicholas said.

'I never liked any man who broke a promise. I left my home to do his dirty work. My mammy cries every time I see her and her head has hung in shame ever since. She has barely set foot outside her cottage since that night. The man was an evil bastard who ran me out of me own home. I will make him pay, and from his cold tomb he will know it. No one gets away with cheating Rory Doyle. He gave me only half the money I was promised for doing what I did and then the bastard made me wait for years before he went and died. Charles could never know what happened. I would be cutting of me nose to spite my face if I told him. There's nothing to be gained by going down that road. This is my chance, my retribution you might say. I hate the fecking FitzDeanes. What did they ever do to earn their money? When did any of them ever slave for an honest days pay?

'Sins of the father, they never truly go away, do they?' said Nathan.

'Some sins are worse than others,' said Rory, stubbing out his cigarette. 'The myth is they was good landlords during the famine, but that's just a load of shite. They put one poor girl into the Galway poor house.'

Nathan detected bitterness in Rory's voice. It made him uncomfortable. He met people like Rory every day of the week in the courts of justice. Those born with sense of entitlement. The irony of the thought was lost to him as he made to leave. 'Remind me never to cross you,' said Nathan.

'You already have,' Rory grimaced, 'with your sixty per cent.'

Rory and Nicholas left the café separately. Nicholas to his office, for a dishonest day's work. Rory to the washroom for a quick shave and then back to platform four, for the train back to Liverpool.

An uncomfortable and unfamiliar sense of guilt swamped him as he stood and waited for the train. A vision of himself and the young Charles, fishing together on the banks of the river at Ballyford ran through his mind. But then he thought of his mother in her cottage, who once lived happily at Ballyford, chatting to Miss McAndrew at the front door each day. Now, she cried every time he saw her. Knowing and hearing the whispers and the stories that had followed her son around for years. She hated it. All he had wanted to do was make a better life for her. The Doyles and McAndrews had lived next door to each other at Ballyford for hundreds of years. His biggest mistake was not realising this was what made his mammy happy.

He thought of Amy, who he had picked up and dropped over the years, always knowing he needed someone working for him inside the castle. Amy had been more than useful. He had nurtured a fondness for her, knowing that she had spent her entire adult life in love with him. But from the day the old lord did him over, there had been no room for love in his life and he dropped Amy, along with everyone and everything else. The only thing that had driven him throughout these years was the need to get back what was rightfully his. He had used Amy once again, only last week and he vowed to himself that it would be the last time.

He had smoked almost an entire packet of cigarettes during breakfast and now stubbed yet another out on the platform floor. Kicking it out onto the tracks with the toe of his shoe, he looked down the line at the approaching train and whispered, 'It's almost over, almost.'

Chapter nine

Ballyford Castle

Mrs McKinnon had made everyone in the castle work longer hours since the night Mr McKinnon had returned from Liverpool with the news that a visit from Lord Charles was imminent. In the preceding days, the rugs were rolled up and the dust sheets removed from the furniture in Lord Charles's study. Each piece of stone was damp-dusted and every surface and floorboard polished until it gleamed. In the library, every book was taken down and dusted individually.

'It's a good job I wasn't asked to do that job,' said Ruby to Betsy, popping her head round the door of the library one morning. 'I would never be finished until I had read the lot of them.'

'I wish I could read,' said Betsy from her position halfway up a ladder, 'but then, I suppose Mrs McKinnon would have asked someone else to do this job. What's this book called, Ruby? It has a beautiful cover.'

Ruby placed the clean towels she was carrying to Lady Isobel's bathroom on a chair and reached up to take the book out of Betsy's hand. She studied the spine and the cover and then, opening the fly page, felt her heart quicken. The stamp on the inside of the cover read: *Ballyford Castle library, 1935.*

'Well,' demanded Betsy, breaking the silence. 'What does it say then?'

'The book is called *The Strange Death of Liberal England*, and I've never heard of it, but the stamp on the inside looks familiar to me. Do they all have it?'

'Jesus, how would I know?' said Betsy. 'Here, take a look yourself.'

Ruby stood at the bottom of the ladder. She took a book off the shelf, blew the dust away and opened it. There it was again, the Ballyford ink stamp.

'God in heaven, what's up with yer?' asked Betsy. 'Have ye seen a ghost again, or what?'

Ruby smiled weakly. 'No, I never have seen a ghost, Betsy, it just feels like I have. Can I take this one?' Ruby had continued browsing and found a book she knew both she and Lady Isobel would enjoy.

'Don't ask me,' said Betsy. 'I only clean the bloody things. Is it for ye?'

'No,' said Ruby, 'I want to take it to read to the lady. It's called *Rebecca*. I think she might like it. I better be getting these clean towels to Lady Isobel, or Mrs McKinnon will be sending me up a ladder to join you.'

As Ruby neared the nursery, she turned her thoughts to how she and the mistress were rubbing along. They occasionally chatted and Ruby had noticed how soft she had become towards Rufus, the dog. She might stare wistfully out onto the lawn while she stroked Rufus, but she was calmer, more serene.

Lady Isobel made an unusual request of Ruby.

'Could you please do something for me and pop into Belmullet? I am expecting a letter to arrive any day now, but I don't really want anyone to bring it to me except you. If I send you in the trap with Danny, could you collect the post for me?'

Ruby was delighted to be asked. Her mind raced ahead and wondered what her chance was of popping in to see Lottie – she wasn't sure if Danny would wait around.

Mrs McKinnon was less than thrilled at the sudden change of plan and inconvenience at a time when everyone was so busy.

'Lordy, there is so much to do. Why can't Jack collect the post as he usually does?' She immediately altered her tone. 'If she's keen to get to the post, that's a great sign of improvement. Maybe there's a magazine she especially wants to read. If that's what the lady wants, that's what she shall have. Go now to the post office and be straight back for twelve. No dawdling.'

They left with the horse and trap at a pace.

'Jesus, could the lady not have sent you another time?' asked Danny. 'Did she have to choose today? We've so much to do before Lord Charles arrives.'

'Danny, could we stop outside the hotel and call in and see Lottie on the way back?'

Danny knew all about Lottie, they all did. She and Ruby wrote to each other frequently and Ruby often read Lottie's letters out loud over supper. They were always full of tales of life in Belmullet and it was now the case that the entire staff were excited when a letter arrived from Lottie, even the McKinnons.

*

That night in bed, Ruby described the day and the trip to Belmullet to Betsy.

'It would have been grand altogether, if Danny hadn't got himself lost and made us late back. I wouldn't have minded, but there wasn't anyone he didn't know. How could he have got lost? I reckon he slipped away to see his granny, but he won't say so. And that made Mrs McKinnon give out to us so bad when we arrived back. I was close to dropping him in it, I was, for making us that late. He had no notion of the time.'

'Did you see Lottie again?' asked Betsy.

'I did. Would you believe, she is learning to knit. She says they make special jumpers out on the Islands and that we can learn to make them too and sell them for money to live on when we escape to Doohoma. The man who works behind the bar, his people were from Doohoma and he told me my house is still stood there. Oh aye, as solid as a rock he told me.'

Betsy always listened patiently to these plans. 'Ye will never leave here, Ruby,' she laughed, gently, not wanting to burst Ruby's happy mood bubble.

'I will that, Betsy. I'm desperate to get back to my home. The stable boys have told me they know where Doohoma is. Jimmy tells me he knows my house, too. Everyone knows where my house is, except me.' Ruby punched her pillow in frustration. 'Jimmy said there are houses still standing empty since the famine, waiting for the relatives to claim them. I won't be long. It is no castle, but I will claim what is mine.'

'I had to look after the lady while ye were gone,' said Betsy, changing the subject as she pulled herself up the bed. 'God, I'd rather be up the bloody ladder. I don't want to give out about her, but Mrs McKinnon told me the mistress was a very spoilt young lady who always had her own way. Mrs McKinnon also said that being an only child has made her a very demanding and difficult mistress to work for. Sure, even her own da had despaired of her and he never visited her, once she was married and living at the castle.'

'Can you imagine that?' said Ruby. 'All that money and you don't speak to each other. How can anyone who lives like they do have any problems at all?'

'Well, Mrs McKinnon thinks the world of her, so she does,' said Betsy. 'She likes you too.'

'God, I almost wish she didn't,' said Ruby. 'Jane has been teasing me, nasty girl that she is. She keeps saying I am Mrs McKinnon's pet.'

'At least you get to work on the first floor with me, Ruby. Jane only does the laundry. Imagine that. 'Twould drive ye crazy, so it would.'

Ruby turned on her side and held her pillow to her chest. 'Do you know, Betsy,' she said, 'I think Mrs McKinnon knows more about me than she cracks on. I have no idea how. I sometimes think she even knows my secret plan. It's the way she looks at me. I feel as though sometimes she is digging around in my head, trying to work out my thoughts and so, this morning I told her that I feel as though I have been at this castle all my life. She looked taken aback, but I told her I had a notion that I have always known these rooms. I could have been born here, I said, it feels so much like home to me.'

'Go on then, what did she say?' said Betsy, who had rolled over to face Ruby. The dying flames from the night peat were dancing their last on the stone walls and the room was filled with a warm orange glow.

'Well now, Mrs McKinnon looked as though she was the one who had seen the ghost. She put both of her hands on my shoulders and almost shook me near to death, she did. "Why do you say that?" she as good as shouted at me. God, I was speechless so I was and then the next moment she gave me a hug and said she was sorry. That woman is all over the place at the moment. She has too much work on with this big castle.'

'Well, maybe you were here once, in a different life,' said Betsy as, exhausted, they both drifted off to sleep.

Chapter ten

'What are you doing in here?' Ruby opened the study door to see Betsy standing beside Lord Charles's desk, staring at the telephone. She had searched the castle to find Betsy to tell her that the coffee was ready in the kitchen and Mrs Mack wanted to check that they all had clean aprons and caps on.

'Shh,' hissed Betsy, 'I have to listen. When the telephone rings, I have to run down to the kitchen and tell Mrs Mack that Lord Charles is on his way up. They have a phone at the lodge house and Jane's daddy will ring here and then I tell everyone else. I'm worried I won't hear it though. She has already checked my apron, twice.'

'Jane and the girls are telling me he is gorgeous, is that so?' Ruby had sat herself on the desk and was swinging her legs. 'Are you staring at that phone in case you don't hear it ring – do you listen with your eyes?' she laughed.

'No I do not, you eejit, now away with you, Ruby Flynn, I've just polished that desk and his study is one of the first places he will come. I want him to know I look after it well for him.'

'God, everyone really wants to be in Lord Charles's good books, don't they?' Ruby had no idea why, but she felt slightly put out by what a tizzy everyone was in today as they anticipated the arrival of Lord Charles, and yet no one had mentioned Lady Isobel.

'And, to answer your question...' Betsy tore her gaze away from the telephone and grinned at Ruby. 'He is more gorgeous than you can imagine.' As she spoke, the telephone rang. 'Oh God in heaven, look what you have made me do!' screeched Betsy almost jumping out of her own skin with shock. 'I didn't see it ring, I nearly missed it.'

'What? What have I made you do?' laughed Ruby. 'Just pick the thing up and speak into it.'

Betsy picked up the receiver and put it to her ear as she had been shown. Then without saying a word she replaced it nervously on the handset.

'He's coming up the drive. Quick!' she screamed as both girls fled from the room. Ruby's cap flew off and she turned back to fetch it.

'You go on, I'll catch you up,' she shouted to Betsy.

It occurred to Ruby that no one had bothered to let Lady Isobel know Lord Charles had arrived and she took it upon herself to pop into the nursery before she joined the others on the steps.

'How many tons of wheat do we expect to harvest from Maughan this summer?' Charles pointed out of the car window to one of the castle farms on the side of the hill.

'We will know in the morning, m'lord, when we drive over,' said Mr McKinnon. 'I know you don't agree with me, but I think we should turn that arable land back over to the tenants.

We are spreading ourselves too thin. Our pork is the best in all of Ireland and in high demand. I want to show you some plans I have to double our herd over the next five years. There are feeds being produced in England that help to boost the growth of the pigs. I have used it on two of the sows and you can see the difference already. I reckon that if we put our minds to it, Ballyford could become one of the biggest meat producers in Ireland and even beat the English at their own game.'

Charles looked at McKinnon and frowned. How could he tell him that his heart was now in shipping and no longer in the estate? His life had altered in a way he could never have imagined and he with it. Ballyford had been cruel to him and he could barely face it. It had taken every ounce of resolution to step on the boat earlier that morning.

'I had thought I might fly across today, McKinnon,' said Charles, knowing that any second now he would catch sight of the river. In the past, it had never failed to tug at his heart and he wondered if it would do the same again today. Or would it disappoint him, like everything else associated with Ballyford?

'But I still love the boats, you know,' he said. 'Air travel will never take over from boats. Too expensive for the common man and that is where the money is. It is all in the volume. Rory and I, we are going to make the tickets for the passage to New York on our ship so inexpensive, we will be the liner of choice. There are sometimes queues of up to fifty people at a time down on the Pier Head, waiting to buy tickets to America.'

McKinnon felt intense disappointment. His heart sank as he thought of how Lord Charles used to speak about

Ballyford. McKinnon didn't trust Rory Doyle any more than Mrs McKinnon did.

Charles saw McKinnon's face had fallen.

'Ballyford just isn't something I can give my time to, McKinnon,' he said, trying to let him down gently. 'I need to concentrate all my efforts on the shipping company. Rory Doyle and I have big plans. I want us to be the biggest shipping magnates in Europe, outside of Greece. We have worked together long enough, McKinnon, we know each other's ways. You just give me a report once a month as to how you are getting along. You have license to manage the farm as you see fit. You know the estate like the back of your hand. Just don't cover the land completely with pigs.'

McKinnon kept his eyes straight ahead and his gloved hands firmly on the steering wheel. He knew he would have to be bold. Ballyford had to be more than a folly to the FitzDeane family. Charles was as good a landlord as any of the existing tenants could hope for and they liked, even wanted, to see him around. His ancestors would never be forgotten for their benevolence during the famine.

It was obvious to everyone, servants and tenants alike, that the young lord was drifting away. They had been filled with such hope after his father's death. His father had been the least popular of all the FitzDeanes. When Charles had brought his bride to Ballyford, there had been huge excitement, but hope had sunk into the ground along with the FitzDeane babies.

McKinnon remembered the early days. He recalled the words of Lord FitzDeane as they had ridden out together to the O'Neils' farm the week before the wedding. Charles had filled McKinnon's heart with his words as they had ridden back home.

O'Neil had been too ill to bring in his own harvest. Farm workers from across the estate had provided assistance, some working through the night by the light of lanterns, as anyone with an hour to spare rode across the country, before the rain that they could smell heavy in the air arrived and destroyed O'Neil's year of toil and along with it, his income and rent for the following year.

Charles had heard that O'Neil was dying and wanted to see if there was anything he could do to help. O'Neil was barely out of his forties and he had young children. Charles had known him all his life and felt a keen sense of responsibility, in a way his father never had.

The sun was setting over the hills and dipping down into the ocean. His father had been dead for less than a year and his head was bursting with ideas.

'I don't need to live in England, McKinnon. It is here I want to live and raise my family. I want my children to love Ballyford as much as I do, but unlike my father I want to be with my children. I want to hunt and fish with my sons and for us to be close, like father and sons should be, before they have to be sent away to school. I want to fill Ballyford with children and for it to be a happy place. You and I, McKinnon, will work with the pigs and the farms. We will travel to England and study some of the new methods farmers are using over there. We can invest in the new machinery. Now the war is over, it is all happening in London.'

McKinnon beamed from ear to ear. 'They say there is new

machinery being built which will change how we farm, but not here in Ireland, surely?'

'That is right McKinnon. The English will recover from the war and lead the way, then we will jump on their coat-tails and Ballyford will benefit. They are building tractors and combines like you cannot imagine. One day, every farm will use motorized equipment instead of manual labour. It will be more efficient and if we can be ahead of the game here at Ballyford, we shall continue to prosper. No one will ever remember the famine again, there will be food for all.'

The tenants chose to never mention Charles's father, but instead still spoke of the kindness of one of Charles's forebears and of how he waived the rent during the famine. They remembered the sacks of wheat flour, secretly delivered to Ballyford and then distributed amongst the farms. And every so often, they spoke of the famished girl, the witch, who he had rescued from starvation and when they mentioned her, they spoke in whispers. They never spoke of the curse out loud but they knew it still haunted Ballyford.

McKinnon changed gear as the outline of the castle came into sight. He turned a steep corner, in through the gates and motored past the flaming fuchsia bushes that lined the driveway. In the summer months they would drip blood-red blooms, and today they dropped a low curtsy in the ocean breeze to Charles, the lord of the castle, as he drove by.

Rhododendrons fanned out away across the lawn in a burst of crimson. Behind them, as they neared the castle, the ocean changed from a glimmering quiver of sunlit silver to the brooding still, flat grey of Irish slate.

McKinnon plucked up the courage to speak in the few minutes he knew he had left.

'Well, I'm as excited as you about the plans for the shipping company. Tis all security for the future of Ballyford. The war did show us all that no one knows what is going to happen next and they sound like very grand plans. It seems to me, though, that people might decide not to cross the Atlantic, but that they will always need rashers to eat. I think you could become the largest pig producer in all of Ireland, if you were so inclined. We can't export enough to England. They love Irish bacon over there and the Danish, they are beginning to push their way in, now that the war is over and they are back on their feet. I wouldn't underestimate the Danish.'

Charles nodded. 'There are so many Irish in England, the Danish will never make an impact with their pigs. Not over ours. I think half of Ireland is in Liverpool and they won't eat anything, other than rashers from home. Everyone I meet seems to have a connection to a family from Mayo.'

'Look, Lord Charles, I am happy to keep things ticking over, but you are the lord of Ballyford.' McKinnon sensed that he had touched a raw nerve. 'It needs your direction, not mine. See, already I have the wrong idea about our pigs and the Danish threatening our exports. We need you here at Ballyford.'

'Well, let's drive out tomorrow first thing and see these giant pigs, shall we? Do you have anyone in mind to help us manage this expansion to our giant swine herd?'

'You could do worse than Amy's brother, I reckon,' said McKinnon.

Charles smiled. That was the Irish way. Family first. Every

worker on his estate was related to someone else. Most of the staff were born and died on the estate.

'I might have known.' He grinned at McKinnon who did not look remotely sheepish.

As the main entrance to the castle came into view, they saw that everyone who worked at the estate was standing on the steps, waiting. Some servants and gardeners were running down the last yard of lawn to take their place in the line-up. Mrs McKinnon was boxing Danny across the ears for being late and shouting at the others to fall into place quickly.

The phone call to the castle from the gate lodge had worked well. Betsy had run down the gallery and the main stairs to let Mrs McKinnon know that the car had turned in through the gates and in turn, she had harried the remaining servants outside onto the steps. As the car drew up, an errant peacock squawked and ran across the front of the car, sending Mrs McKinnon into a fluster. She took a handkerchief from her apron pocket to scare the bird back onto the lawn.

Charles watched the bird as it sauntered away, fanning out its iridescent blue and green tail feathers in a pompous display of outrage. Far from admiring the beautiful bird, as he once had, he wondered now if he should take his gun and shoot it. His stomach was in a knot at the prospect of seeing his wife. His good mood had evaporated as soon as the staff on the steps had come into view. He turned back to face the house, took a deep breath and mentally prepared himself. He glanced up at the windows on the first floor. They looked back at him, black and hollow.

Somewhere behind them lay his obligation. He knew his wife

would not be waiting on the steps, or smiling at the window. More likely she was waiting patiently in her room, perched in front of her mirror, as she prepared words of poison, ready to strike and wound.

Your fault. Your family. Your curse.

And it was then, as he steeled himself to leave the comfort of the car and search for his wife, that his eyes fell upon her. She was standing on the top step, at the back of the crowd of servants. Her back was tall and straight. A smile of what could have been amusement hovered on her lips and she squinted in the sunlight towards the car. The wind had caught at her red hair and pulled out a large strand. She put her hand up to tame her tresses. Irritated, she battled the gusts of wind and secured her cap once more. Then she stood on tiptoe to look over Amy's head.

The sun was shining directly on the car window and Charles shielded his eyes. He knew he had those few seconds when he could see her, but she could not see him.

'You found her then,' he whispered to McKinnon, his voice hoarse and almost angry. 'Why didn't you tell me?'

'I thought it best to wait, Lord Charles, so that you could see for yourself that I had made no mistake.'

'God in heaven,' Charles whispered, placing his hands flat on his knees. He took a deep breath. 'You have made no mistake, McKinnon. She must never know, you realize that, don't you? We can repair what my father did wrong, but the past is too dangerous to rake over. We don't even know how much is truth or just cottage gossip. No one must know but you, me and Mrs McKinnon.'

'Me and Mrs McKinnon, we both know that, Lord Charles. We never will tell anyone. She works as a member of the staff. Lady FitzDeane needing a nursery maid was convenient at the time.'

Charles looked at McKinnon. He had no words, but he did not need any. Both men were locked in a mutual understanding.

Charles broke the silence. 'Right, well, let's go and get the greetings over and done with. There's Mrs McKinnon, not looking a day older.'

It took all Charles's strength of will to keep his eyes focused on Mrs McKinnon and to avoid looking directly at Ruby. Knowing he had done the right thing to repair the damage caused by his cruel father was already a tonic. He felt his heart settle. It was as though one of many dark clouds had moved and was slowly drifting away, out of his life.

He was unable to help himself. His eyes met hers and his pulse quickened. She roused something deep within, which he shut down instantly. History would not repeat itself, not during his time at Ballyford. She smiled at him, the slightest of smiles. Not a smile of welcome, more one of curiosity, a faint amusement even. He felt his frozen heart begin to thaw and he knew that despite himself, the darkest, coldest secret was now his private warmth.

That night, when they were in bed, Ruby could not settle and as was her way, chatted to Betsy. Jane had long gone to sleep in another room, irritated by their closeness and constant talking.

'Betsy, I have a secret.'

Betsy didn't like secrets. 'What?' she whispered, wanting to know, but at the same time fearing the answer.

'Well, you know when Lord Charles arrived, how he kept his head bent low as he spoke to each of the maids on the steps and then Mrs McKinnon said to him, "And here is Ruby, the new maid for the mistress"...'

'Yes, I know, I was there, I heard her.' Betsy was now leaning up on her elbow, peering at Ruby.

'Well, when he turned his face to look at me and I looked back at him, it was there again, that feeling of knowing something. As though we had met before. I couldn't breathe, Betsy. My knees were weak and do you know, for a moment, I couldn't feel the wind at all. I had a warm feeling all through me and his look, it made my heart beat faster. I swear to God, Betsy, I swear to all that's holy, I do believe it happened to him too. I felt I had known him and he, well, he knew me. He did, Betsy, I know he did.'

Chapter eleven

Ruby was bemused by the excitement that rippled throughout the household after the arrival of Lord Charles.

'Holy Mother, it has sent everyone into a complete frenzy,' she said to Amy, as she set Lady Isobel's tray for tea, at the wooden bench in the kitchen.

Amy was busy, bustling and puffing around the stove. Mary, excited to see Ruby, her favourite, was already by her side, wanting Ruby to sit down on the stool.

'Let me play with your hair,' Mary pleaded. 'Go on, Ruby, let me.'

Ruby looked at Mary's hair. All the staff wore their hair in the same style, chopped short by Amy who had no time for vanity. As a new arrival, Ruby had thus far escaped the lure of Amy, her scissors, and the promise of convenient styling.

'Go on then, just for a minute, Mary,' said Ruby. 'I have masses to do this morning.'

'Everyone is in a state, except the mistress, that is.' Amy frowned. 'Mary, don't brush Ruby's hair in here.'

Mary pulled a face at Amy behind her back.

'That's half of the problem. If she was more willing to see Lord Charles, things could get back to how they were around here. She needs to know what she's missing. Men like Lord Charles are few and far between. I don't think she understands. The way she is in her mourning, it affects us all, so it does and Lord Charles the most, I would say. She drives him away and she will drive him into the arms of another woman, if she's not careful. It would help if she moved out of that nursery and back into the morning room, Ruby. Can you not coax her, like, make her move away from the sadness? Oh, 'twould make such a difference.' Amy placed a steaming tin dish on the bench and wiped the sweat from her brow with a cloth. 'My aunty says 'tis the hands of the dead children, they are pressing down on her and holding her in the chair, so she cannot move, even if she wanted to. They will not let her go. 'Tis not her fault, 'tis the babbies, so it is.'

'Oh, no, oh no, that's not true, no they are not now,' said Mary seriously, as she put the pins back in Ruby's hair. 'Sure, Mammy tells me they are all in heaven, sat with Jesus and having a whale of a time with all the other dead babies and Mammy says anyone who says that they are still here will go to hell, so they will and that will be you, Amy, if you talk any more like that.'

'Oh, shut up, Mary and get on with your work,' said Amy, exasperated.

Ruby felt slightly alarmed. 'I'm sure Mary is right, Amy. Does your aunty really think they are in the nursery?' Ruby was intrigued. She knew that Amy's aunt was a legend with her prophesies, because Amy had told her so.

'Oh, aye, she's always right. Now don't say nothing to the McKinnons, but my aunt, she has been in a right state just lately about the lady.'

Mary leant her chin on the table, her bright, watery eyes focused intently on Amy

'She used to be a maid here, for the old Lady FitzDeane, and when I told her you were coming to look after her she gave out, so she did, crying with the relief. "Oh, thank the Holy Father," she said. "Make sure she watches over her, I have had the most awful dreams and prophesies about the lady." I told her only last night, no better watcher could the lady have than Ruby.'

Ruby smiled. She knew herself that it was true. There was hardly a daylight hour that she had not spent with Lady Isobel since she arrived, and even Ruby could see the improvement. Especially since she had begun reading to Lady Isobel every day.

'She says she's been having dreams about Ballyford too, waking to her own screams and a cold sweat. They all go to my aunty to have their fortunes read, even your pious mammy, Mary. She's the first there so she is, on her way to confession.' Amy thrust her chin forward towards Mary's face. Mary gasped. Her mammy was the first into mass every morning and the last out after Angelus every night.

'Well, tell your aunty not to worry,' said Ruby. 'Lady Isobel never wanted to eat when I first arrived. It has taken some persuasion, but she eats a meal now and doesn't pick any longer. It's been exhausting trying to persuade her, but she really does look better. I don't think there's anything to worry about anymore, as long as we don't have too many mornings like yesterday.'

The previous morning had been a difficult one. Ruby began with her usual routine of cajoling Lady Isobel.

'Come on now, I made this in the kitchen myself, this morning. Amy didn't mind, she said to me, "Go on Ruby, you know just how Lady Isobel likes her eggs. I've even chopped them up in the cup for you and put a nice bit of butter in so they slip down easier." You know what a dragon Amy can be when anyone else steps in her kitchen but she didn't complain once. "Nothing is as important as Lady Isobel's breakfast, you lot can all starve," she said.'

Painfully and slowly, Ruby had persevered. She never abandoned her main objective: to ensure that every last spoonful of the chopped eggs in the pretty china cup were eaten. It had all been worthwhile but had taken almost an hour, until the eggs were stone cold. Ruby was aware that there was something untoward upsetting Lady Isobel and it was not the homecoming of Lord Charles. She had noticed her reading the letter Ruby had collected from Belmullet before she carefully slipped it into her pocket.

'I swear to God, if she didn't have you she would have starved to death by now. No one else has your cheek. One word from the lady and everyone folds like scared rabbits, except for you. It has been that way since the day she arrived, with her fancy, hoity manners, but you have a way, you do. I wouldn't cross you, so I wouldn't.'

'Well, I need to be brave, Amy, chopping an egg in your kitchen and helping myself to the salt the way I do. I'm always waiting for the roar when you see me.'

'You cheeky madam.' Amy grinned and Mary chuckled: she hung on every word Ruby spoke.

'Here, grab a cuppa before you run back upstairs. Mary, stop gawping. Make yourself useful and pour Ruby some tea. It must be thirsty work, kneeling by the side of her chair for so long, trying to make her eat.'

Mary poured Ruby a steaming mug of tea and ladled three spoons of sugar into the cup. She stared at Ruby, watching her drink.

'It's not that she doesn't want to eat, you know, Amy. When she pushes her tray away I know it looks that way, but I know her really well now. There is something stopping her. Perhaps it's hard to eat when you are crying inside.'

'Well, 'tis a sad state of affairs for the poor woman.' Amy had dropped her voice to a whisper. 'But she's not the only one to suffer in this way. My mother had fourteen of us and only six lived past twelve years of age. I would say that was a lot harder.'

Ruby didn't know what to think and so she waited for Amy to continue, as she knew she surely would.

'And one of the women in the tenant cottages, pregnant six times and never carried one all the way. All born like pink skinned rabbits they were, drew a breath and died. There's no one to spoon-feed her chopped eggs and that's a fact. If she didn't get out of her bed and carry on, how would they manage? If her husband didn't work they would have no home or food in their bellies. No, the truth is, Ruby, melancholy is for the rich, not the poor and I'm not saying I don't have any sympathy for her predicament, or that I didn't love each one of those little boys. I did. Brought them down here to the kitchen, the nurse did and I held each one in my arms, before they died. Lovely little boys and there was never a father who loved his sons more than Lord FitzDeane, but life goes on and she needs to realize that and snap out of it.'

Ruby felt sad. She couldn't argue with a word Amy had said, but she also felt deeply for Lady Isobel.

Amy continued. 'I've always done my best for her, Ruby. I know you think I'm harsh, but surely 'tis time she thought about what is important, and in that I include Lord Charles.'

Ruby picked up her cup and finished the last of her tea.

'Well, Amy, I can't say any of that to her. I'll just keep doing what I do, which is looking after her as best I can. I can't think of all those other people, because I didn't know them, I can't allow myself to feel grudging towards her, because I don't think it's like that. Something serious is up, she needs me and my job is to look after her. There is something much deeper going on with the lady, I just don't know what it is.'

'Aye, you do that,' said Amy. 'Keeps you in a job too. Come on, pass me that cup and let's not say anything of this to anyone else. Feelings are divided here as to how Lady Isobel should be treated. Mrs McKinnon won't hear a word said against her. And you Mary, keep your mouth shut if you want a roof over your head and food in your belly. There are plenty of girls like you in the cottages looking for kitchen work.'

If anyone had ever bothered to give Mary a second thought, they would have known she was the most loyal of all the Ballyford staff. A loyalty soon to be put to the fiercest test.

Chapter twelve

Upon first sight, Mrs McKinnon forgave Charles for having been away for so long, and Charles now spoke the words he knew were expected of him. 'I shall head straight upstairs to see Lady FitzDeane.'

Mrs McKinnon noticed he looked pale.

'Was it a bad crossing yesterday?' she whispered to Mr McKinnon. 'He looks exhausted.'

'Not at all, the sea was meant to be as smooth as your backside and they did make good time. He needs some of your care and Amy's cooking. You have no idea the shite that woman in Liverpool forces him to eat.'

'Merciful God, keep that language to yourself, will you,' Mrs McKinnon laughed.

Upstairs on the gallery, all was quiet as Charles stood outside the door to the nursery, hesitating, with his hand hovering above the newly polished brass door handle.

'The doctor has visited this morning as usual,' Mrs McKinnon had told him before he made his way to the stairs. 'He says the same thing every time he visits. She needs feeding up, lots of fresh air and to be forced back into living a normal life.'

Charles ran his fingers through his hair nervously. He knew what Mrs McKinnon thought. She had never voiced her feelings to him, but hadn't she been the woman who had raised him? Didn't he know her as well as she knew him? Her disapproval needed no voice. It was there, accusing him, whether she knew it or not, in every line on her face and in the tone of every word she spoke. She would prefer him to remain at Ballyford and to play the role of the dutiful and loving husband. She would never understand that Isobel blamed him, hated him and with her hatred for him, his own feelings for Isobel had perished and died.

Charles took a breath, turned the handle and entered the room. Isobel didn't move as he almost tiptoed across the room towards her. She sat bolt upright on the sofa facing the fire and was as still as the gallery statues. It struck him how thin she appeared, even from behind.

As he neared her, he gently said her name, but there was still no response. He walked around the back of the sofa and sat on the chair next to the fire. Maybe she had spent her anger and there would be no further histrionics. He realized that he was holding his breath, just as he always did these days in the presence of his wife.

'Hello Isobel,' he said. 'Did Mrs McKinnon tell you the news? I'm home for a few weeks. How are you feeling?'

His words felt distant, as though he were addressing a stranger. He didn't know what else to say. After all their years of marriage, there was no subject they could broach which failed to evoke memories of desperate sadness. There was not a single holiday, Christmas, ball, birthday or event he could refer to without its being marked by the progression of a hopeful pregnancy or a funeral procession of despair. He could feel the pain in the room and he knew it would always be like this. *It will never leave us and she will always blame me.*

Isobel turned her head to look at him.

'Hello Charles, it's nice to have you home,' she said.

Charles was stunned. This was not what he had expected. His wife had torn at his skin, beat him with the fire irons, spat and sworn at him, but not since the death of his last son had she greeted him. Maybe this was why McKinnon had been so keen for him to return, to see the improvement for himself.

'Yes, it is nice to be back at Ballyford,' Charles replied. 'Is there anything I can get for you? Mrs McKinnon is bringing some tea just now, she should be here any minute.'

'I don't need anything, Charles. What I need you cannot give me.' Her voice was almost pleading and Charles felt his heart slip. 'I just need to see my babies and they need me.'

Charles remained silent. She had raised his spirits and then dashed them on the rocks of disappointment. How could he say the only thing that was true? That there were no babies.

Isobel turned back to the fire and continued. 'Charles, they miss me, they are only babies, they always needed me. They are so cold in the crypt. You feel that, don't you? You must feel it too?' She whispered her words with an intensity that suggested they had been on her lips for weeks, just waiting for him to return.

Charles wondered if they would ever have a normal conversation again.

Welcome home, Charles. We have missed you. How is business?

Tears threatened to flood his eyes. Her words, her grief, the mention of the crypt, all of it. His sons had been put to the back of his mind when he was in Liverpool, they were part of a life from which he had detached himself. The things he ran from, the memories, were now crowding in, making it difficult for him to breathe.

We have you now. You are trapped, the ghosts of Ballyford whispered.

He imagined the voices of his ancestors calling out to him from the crypt, chiding him for not visiting his sons. He had sworn he would never, ever visit again until he himself was laid to rest. Since the day he had laid the small coffin of his last dead son on the cold, Kerry slate slab, he had sworn that was his last. Now, he wanted to run out of the nursery door, down the stairs and all the way to Dublin, to catch the next boat back to Liverpool where there was no one who knew. To a life of pretence, free from the pain. Where he didn't have to be Lord Charles of Ballyford, father of five dead sons and husband to a wife driven mad with grief.

Was his life to be devoid of normality for as long as he lived? Was he to be trapped within this circle of despair forever? He remembered how Isobel had run at him with a fire poker in her hand because she believed he had had her babies poisoned, just one of the many phases she had passed through. There had been others. She had alternatively blamed the maids,

151

McKinnon, Amy, a witch, his father and grandfather. There had been so many phases of anger and blame, remorse and despair, that Charles had lost count.

There had been a time when he and Isobel were happy. When they spoke of their future. When they both cried with joy at the birth of their firstborn.

He had wanted to fill Ballyford with children and she loved his ideas of breaking with convention. Not for him the stuffiness of her English peers. Isobel needed no persuading to be a real mother. Many of their friends thought she had lost her mind. Well, thought Charles, if she hadn't then, she certainly has now.

He had no answer at hand to respond to the madness contained within her words. As they sat there in silence, Mrs McKinnon walked in with the tea tray, followed by Ruby, who moved straight to the fire and threw half a dozen blocks of peat onto the dying flames. The normality of the familiar sound of Mrs McKinnon pouring tea through the silver strainer into the china cups was a welcome relief. Charles needed both the tea and a diversion.

'You have a letter, Isobel,' he commented, to break the heavy silence. 'Is it from anyone I know?'

Isobel picked up the letter that lay on her lap and instead of handing it to him, as he thought she would, she slowly folded the envelope and slipped it into the pocket of her skirt.

'No, Charles, not from anyone you know.'

Charles thought this was odd, but he was distracted by Ruby who had stretched across and picked up the fire tongs to push the peat blocks further back into place.

Watching Ruby brought the Ballyford secret to the forefront of his mind. He and Ruby were sitting in the very room from which his father had banished her mother, Iona, from Ballyford forever, when he and Iona were children. It felt like only yesterday. It was the shame of Ballyford and Ruby would never know.

His grandfather perfectly understood the nature of his son, Charles's father. He had summoned Charles to his bedside and made him promise that Ballyford would always be responsible for Iona and that Charles would care for her.

'Put right whatever your father will do wrong once I have gone,' his grandfather had whispered. 'Protect her.'

Charles had failed, but at least he had found her daughter.

Only days old, Iona had arrived at Ballyford one cold winter's morning, wrapped in rags, with a note pinned to her shawl. She had been carried into the kitchen to the cook and the note and the child were promptly delivered to Charles's grandfather. The note was chilling. It claimed the child belonged to Ballyford and that in order for an old and dreadful wrong to be put right, she should be taken in and become Ballyford's own. The note struck the fear of God into Charles's grandfather. He had heard the story himself, from his own father and from the moment the lonely man laid eyes on Iona's face, he had taken her into his heart, the castle and his will. He had sent out to the cottages for the local apothecary, Miss McAndrew to come to his study. She knew things about Ballyford that others did not, as had all the McAndrews before her. Whatever they discussed on that morning was never repeated to anyone. He had been unable to help himself from showing the child adoring affection, the only baby girl to arrive at Ballyford for many generations. He also saw caring for her as the way to absolution. A man of many mistresses, he knew he had sinned often in his lifetime and the death of his wife had brought home to him his own mortality. All he had left in his old age were his disagreeable son, his adored grandson, Charles, and the beautiful baby girl, Iona, found in the stables.

Young as he was, Charles knew that his grandfather's death wish was wasted. He had no power to force his father to honour the words of a dying man. What then happened was catastrophic and Charles knew that the people in the cottages whispered of the girl from the famine to this day, and claimed that here was history repeating itself.

But now, having failed in his promise to protect Iona, here was her daughter kneeling before him, stoking a fire. The sight of her lifted his heart and he slowly warmed inside as he watched her at the stone hearth. She must never know and yet he wanted to know her more. He closed his eyes, remembering Iona with her red hair.

'Your tea, Lord Charles.'

Charles started and saw that Mrs McKinnon was placing a shawl around the shoulders of Lady Isobel and leading her out of the room. It was Ruby who held his tea.

'Your tea, Lord Charles.'

Ruby said it again and as he reached up, he noticed her hair escaping in red tendrils from under her cap. He realized he must have drifted off to sleep for just a few seconds.

He knew that hair, and those eyes. Those same green eyes had belonged to her mother. Iona would have still been young.

She had been his only company as a child and his closest friend. She had shared his nursery and Mrs McKinnon had looked after them both with equal care. Although she had been older, he had loved Iona and the loneliness he felt at her loss when she was taken away had never left him. Thoughts of guilt and self-hatred for not being able to save her were never far from the surface. Despite his pleas and screams of despair he had failed to persuade his father to protect her. His mother, who lived her own life in the London house, neither know nor cared. The whispers were that Iona was dead. Kidnapped. Disposed of. He heard them around corners of stairs and in the midst of huddled servants who fell silent as he approached. He knew they were untrue. It was wild cottage gossip. He could feel she was alive and what was more, she was nearby. Of late, thoughts of Iona had haunted him. She was always there, hovering on the edge. Entering his dreams and forming his nightmares. Iona had plagued him. Renewing his search for her yet again, it was no surprise to discover she was dead. He had known. He had felt it. He woke on the night of the storm and he had shivered at the eerie emptiness that filled the castle and he knew, wherever she had been taken, now she was gone.

The sound of the cup rattling on the saucer brought him to his senses and he noticed as he reached for it, that Ruby's own, thin and delicate hand trembled in response.

He dared to speak, although he didn't trust his own voice. 'Are you quite settled at Ballyford?'

'Oh yes, Lord Charles, I really am,' she responded with genuine enthusiasm. 'I do love it here.'

Charles raised his eyebrows and smiled. He had expected a

polite 'yes, thank you'. He had hardly ever managed to extract a word from any of the maids. They were either too shy or Mrs McKinnon trained them never to answer him, he wasn't sure which. If this one had been trained, she was paying no attention.

'And my wife. Have you, er, managed well?'

'Oh, yes, no trouble at all. We get along just fine now, Lady Isobel and me. She loves Rufus, you know. I bring him in here every morning now and she likes to stroke him and tickle his belly. Rufus is becoming very fond of the lady, too.'

'You manage better than I do, then,' he said, leaning forward to stir the tea again.

'I am just her maid,' Ruby replied. 'She expects nothing more than that from me. It is only hard when she becomes excited. It takes Mr and Mrs McKinnon to help, then. I can't manage on my own.'

They both heard the nursery door click then and saw Mrs McKinnon returning with Lady Isobel.

Lady Isobel looked coldly at Charles.

'Lord Charles has some news, don't you?' Mrs McKinnon nodded furiously at Charles.

'Oh, I'm very sure my husband has news, don't you Charles? Is it news from Liverpool?'

Charles looked at Mrs McKinnon with a confused expression. 'Do I? Do I have news?'

'Mr McKinnon tells me you are thinking of resurrecting the Ballyford Ball again soon, aren't you?'

Charles felt his heart sink. It had seemed like a good suggestion at the time.

'I hadn't thought much about the detail, Mrs McKinnon,' he replied. 'I had planned to work with Mr McKinnon on the estate. I'm only here for a few weeks or so before I have to return to Liverpool.'

'Yes, but as you know, the doctor thought it would be an excellent idea. He said Lady Isobel must return to what she knew and was familiar with. He said that would be the best medicine.'

Charles knew at once that this was a trap. Mrs McKinnon was always one step ahead of him. She wanted him to stay for longer and this was her way of making it happen.

'The doctor is a man, Mrs McKinnon, with six living healthy children. The Ballyford Ball hardly sounds like a prescription he would have learned in medical school.'

Charles sounded exasperated even to his own ears. He saw Mrs McKinnon's disappointment and he hated himself.

He looked at Lady Isobel and she met his gaze without animosity. Her look puzzled him, for a fleeting moment he saw a total clarity of thought in her eyes and she had looked amused. As though she too knew what Mrs McKinnon was up to.

'However, it seems to me that I am ill qualified to disagree with the experts. What do you think, Isobel? Shall I invite some of our friends over for a ball? Shall we let our neighbours know that all is well at Ballyford? We could have a day's fishing and you could spend some time with your old friends.'

To everyone's utter amazement Isobel replied, 'Well, maybe the doctor is right. I think it might be good for me to see people again.'

For a moment the only noise in the room was that of the

teapot gently simmering on the silver tea-light stand.

Charles found himself turning to Ruby. 'What do you think? Is it a good idea?'

But this time Ruby did not reply and looked down at her clasped hands in embarrassment.

Charles instantly realized his faux pas in having addressed a servant with such a personal question and turned to Mrs McKinnon.

'Sorry, I have been up since dawn and the journey is always exhausting. Is this a good idea, Mrs McKinnon? Could you, Amy and the rest of the staff cope?'

Mrs McKinnon's back straightened in indignation.

'Was it not me speaking just now? Did I not say that I thought the doctor was right? He charges enough, so he should be.'

Mrs McKinnon bent down and stroked Lady Isobel's hands as though soothing a small child.

'Wouldn't that be something for us all to look forward to? We could go through your ball gowns together, you and I and we could alter one down to fit you, now that you are so much slimmer. I will write out the invitations and Ruby will help, as she has a good hand. It would be no trouble for you Lady Isobel.'

Lady Isobel stared at Mrs McKinnon, this woman who had helped deliver her babies and been at her side throughout every ordeal. The woman she and Charles both trusted and regarded as a mother. To the relief of everyone in the room, she nodded.

'There we go,' said Mrs McKinnon. 'The Ballyford Ball

shall happen once more. It will be just like the old days.'

Charles dared not speak. The old days held nothing but memories of pain and loss. He could not remember the last Ballyford Ball. It was a blur. Unimportant to him, but essential to the staff, the status of Ballyford and their way of life.

'We had better pick a date then as it will take some time to organize.'

Once again he looked at Ruby, who smiled back at him. Her smile said, *Well done you, all will be well.* And then, undeniably, she followed with slight narrowing of the eyes, a puzzled expression, *I think I know you.*

Charles was suddenly aware that the history between them both had a life of its own. He should have made more effort to find Iona earlier. Before his father had been laid to rest in the crypt, they had scoured all of Ireland from shore to shore, but it was as though she hadn't wanted to be found. As though she had not forgiven him. And all the time he had thought how could anything good to come from Ballyford, when the wishes of his dying grandfather had been so callously ignored. The McKinnon's thought they knew where she had been taken, but hopes were dashed when they discovered they were wrong.

Mrs McKinnon led Lady Isobel out of the room. Their hushed voices spoke of gowns and gloves and polished tiaras. Charles looked down at his hands, determined not to look at Ruby as she cleared away the china cups. The silver sugar tongs clattered as she laid them on the tray. Both of them knew that each was waiting for the other to speak.

He fought with his own instincts and neither looked away

from the fire nor moved, as she left the room. He heard the door click, as the tea trolley rolled out onto the wooden floor of the gallery.

Charles let out a deep sigh. He was here, alone in Ballyford and it looked as though it could be for a month, instead of the two weeks he had originally planned. He would write to Rory. He could return to Ireland and visit his mother at Ballyford. They could deal with business at the same time. Charles felt his urge to return to Liverpool draining away. The castle called out to him, there was a reason to stay at the place he had once loved with all his heart. It was pulling at him in the familiar way he knew all too well.

Walking over to the fire, Charles picked up a silver framed photograph of his firstborn son from the stone mantelpiece.

As always, his eyes filled with tears as they rested on the image of his son and he felt his heart contract with familiar pain. It had the same effect every time and he wanted to scream out the only word that ever came to him. *Why?*

He pushed his thumbs into his eyes to stem the tears as his eyes lingered. It was as though he was seeing the picture for the first time and he wondered if his pain would ever lessen.

He turned to leave the nursery and without warning felt a premonition of fear run through his veins. His skin prickled as Ruby stood silently by the door, waiting.

'Did you want me for anything?' she said. 'You seem very sad. Is there something I can do to help?'

'No, thank you. Nothing,' he replied, walking past her. As he did so, his eyes met hers and she held his gaze. She was near enough for him to reach out with his hand and touch her face. He was overcome by an urge to push back the strand of hair that had fallen across her eye. She was trying to blink and blow it away, not wanting to raise her clasped hands. She shook her head and the wayward hair lifted and then fell to the side of her cheek and her eyes held his, unblinking, still. The air between them felt charged, alive and waiting for the past and the future to fuse and connect.

She knows. God, she already knows. How can she? he thought. He felt his own pulse, hammering in his throat and, afraid of what he might do or say, he pushed past her and strode purposefully away towards the safety of his own study.

Chapter thirteen

Ruby and Jane had retreated to the linen room. It was the place where all gossip was exchanged, away from the eyes and ears of Mrs McKinnon and Amy, both of whom were well aware of what went on there.

'We grew up gossiping in our mother's kitchen and on the front step,' said Amy to Mrs McKinnon. 'These girls have been in service since they were children, best we make sure they can have a little gossip or they will never learn.'

This made Mrs McKinnon smile. Scottish, buttoned up, proper, she was astounded by the capacity of Irish women to talk and secretly envied them this rich source of entertainment.

In the linen room, a damaged linen basket had been overturned and the castors removed to provide a makeshift table. A collection of damaged chairs from the castle were scattered around the room, awaiting attention and repair. Some had even been in this state of limbo waiting to be sent to England since before the war.

Ruby and Jane had arranged to meet just after breakfast. Jane had caught Ruby on the stairs.

'Meet me in the linen room after the lady has been served her morning trolley and save me some bloody coffee.'

Ruby had wondered what Jane wanted to discuss, but her thoughts soon turned to Lord Charles. Betsy had been right to describe him as gorgeous. Ruby had never met or seen a man who looked or dressed as he did, other than in the magazines that arrived for Lady Isobel from London. She could even smell him as she bent and served his tea. She had been alarmed at her own reaction. He mouth had dried, her pulse had raced and she felt her scalp tighten. Within minutes, she had become curious, if not fascinated by the man who was, in effect, her employer and the husband of the woman she had come to care for.

Ruby had not seen Lord Charles since yesterday. She had no business being in the study, that room was the responsibility of Mr McKinnon and Betsy, who kept the fire burning. But despite her best intentions, Ruby found herself looking for him at any opportunity. Each time she heard footsteps on the landing, she crept to the door and peeped outside, without really knowing why. She reasoned with herself and fought with her own thoughts and emotions. *I only want to see him, I'm just curious,* she told herself over and over, knowing that she would reveal her thoughts to no one, not even Betsy or Lottie.

Nevertheless, at the allotted time, Ruby made her way to the linen cupboard, pushing the trolley in front of her and Jane came in through the door, struggling with a large plate.

'I got us two hot bracks while I was in the kitchen,' she whispered. 'Amy is in a good mood today and sure, that can't have anything to do with Jack being sat at the kitchen table, can it?'

Both girls laughed.

Ruby always knew by breakfast time what mood Jane was going to be in for the day. It was anyone's guess whether a sour and miserable Jane would turn up for her oats and milk or a bright and cheerful one. The pleasant Jane turned up rarely but when she did, the entire staff breathed a sigh of relief. As Jane now dragged up a chair and Ruby poured the coffee from the silver pot she had used to serve Lady Isobel, she was thankful Jane was in a good mood today.

'Does Amy know we are up here?' Ruby asked.

'Stop, are ye mad?' Jane said. 'I haven't half done yet. She would be in here after us, dragging me out by my ear. Amy has no issue with a good natter, mind, she just likes to know the work is done first. God, ye should hear her giving out if something gets behind. A proper scold she's becoming these days. I reckon she is sweet on Jack, but gives out that she isn't. I would bet all my spare knicker elastic, she and him, they'll be kissing soon.'

Ruby flopped on to a chair next to Jane.

'God, don't let her hear you saying that, or she'll be kissing you with her hand, I've no doubt. I don't know why Amy isn't married, she's very pretty, even though she always smells of cabbage water.'

Jane threw Ruby a confused glance. She thought Amy smelt lovely.

'I reckon she's still sweet on Rory Doyle, although God knows, he left the cottages years back. She lived behind the

Doyles and they were to be married. Then suddenly, for no reason at all, he upped and disappeared in the middle of the night. Away to Liverpool, they say. He has his own wife and family now, but every now and then he sneaks back and when he does, there's no talking to Amy. No one is supposed to know he has snuck back, mind, but his mammy can't help telling everyone. My mammy says Amy has never forgotten or forgiven him. In fact,' Jane leant forward and whispered, 'my mammy saw him sneaking into Amy's mammy's cottage only a few weeks back and Amy snuck in, just after him.'

'Poor Amy, she must still love him, to make herself so available like that. Does she know why he just suddenly left?'

'Someone does, but they won't tell me,' said Jane. ''Tis a big secret. Ballyford has lots of secrets, so my mammy says.'

Ruby decided she felt sorry for Jack. She already didn't like Rory Doyle if he was standing between Jack and happiness.

Jane emptied the last of the buttermilk from the jug into her cup, before pouring the leftovers from Lady Isobel's coffee on top.

'How is the lady today?' she asked. 'Has she scratched yer eyes out yet, like she tried to do to me after the second one died?'

'No, not at all. She seems quite perked up today, maybe the Ballyford Ball is a good idea, after all. Mrs McKinnon wants me to start helping her to write out the invitations this afternoon.'

'God in heaven, no one would ever ask me to do that,' said Jane. 'I can't even write my own name, never mind anyone else's.'

Ruby had stood and begun idly wandering around the linen room, opening drawers in the press and bending down to peep inside, while Jane sat on her chair, swinging her legs. Ruby had to resist the urge to wriggle her nose. Jane often smelt and sometimes, like today, the smell was stronger than at others. Daily wash-downs at the sink and a belief that cleanliness is next to godliness were essentials at the convent. Ruby was amazed by how little contact the staff at Ballyford appeared to have with the bathtub.

Ruby was impressed with the standard of tidiness in the linen room, though. Shelf upon shelf of sheets, pillowcases and towels, all folded to the same size with the creases neatly lined up. The precision of the stacking, the whiteness of the sheets took her breath away.

'Don't touch the press, Ruby,' said Jane with a hint of concern.

But Ruby couldn't help herself and if it hadn't been for her love of order, the pleasure in the brilliantly white sheets, rotated carefully every week, she never would have spotted it. It was the slightest of bulges, some way above her head.

Ruby could only just reach the outer sheet and as she pushed hard on the bulge with her fingertips she felt something firm resist her touch.

'Would ye stop!' Jane almost screamed, jumping to her feet and placing her cup down on the tray. 'No one is allowed to touch the linen, only me and Mrs McKinnon and she'll kill ye she will, favourite or not. Stop!'

But it was too late. Ruby tugged hard and quick and before Jane had finished speaking, the sheet pulled free of the press to fall down at Ruby's feet.

'Oh, Jesus, Holy Mary Mother of God!' In a flash Jane had

scooped the sheet up from the floor and was trying desperately to restore its precise and perfect folded lines.

'Help me, will ye?' she hissed.

Ruby looked up at the gap that had now appeared and spotted what had caused the bulge; she could just make out the outline of a hessian sack.

'Help me instead, will you?' she said to Jane. 'Look, I can see something hidden behind there.'

'Feck, no,' Jane shouted at her. 'What are ye doing, are ye mad? Mr and Mrs McKinnon only allow us in here if we touch nothing. I do the laundry and even I can't do that. They will have me shot for this.'

'Ah, go on,' Ruby pleaded. 'I promise we will leave everything exactly as it was and they will never know.'

'We can't leave it as it was, because it is already different. I need to get this sheet pushed back in, before the others fall down. Now, get out of my way Ruby, ye fecking eejit.'

But before Jane could protest any further, Ruby dragged the upturned basket over to the press and pushing her toes into the wicker, she scrambled on top. Just in the nick of time, Jane quickly grabbed the plate of half-eaten brack before it fell.

The wicker crackled and snapped in objection and Ruby wobbled slightly as she grabbed hold of the shelf on the press. Now she was at eye level with the gap in the sheets and could see the hessian bag clearly.

'I see it,' she hissed down to Jane.

Jane had worked at the castle since she was eight years old. She had been trained by Amy and Mrs McKinnon. She knew the value of her job. She had been told by her own mammy a hundred times that the Holy Father had blessed her and ensured she was warm and fed. But she also knew how useless she was and how close she often came to losing her job. If it hadn't been for Amy, who had saved her neck time and time again, she surely would have done so by now.

Jane felt sure now that she was about to faint and if she hadn't been rooted to the spot she would have run down the stairs, screaming, to Amy. She had been told very clearly by Mr McKinnon, 'One more false step Jane, and you are out. We need workers here, not people who create work.' She had known for sure, he was deadly serious.

Once again, Ruby tugged at the sack and was surprised at the resistance. She wobbled. Jane put her hands out and grabbed at Ruby's feet. She could see in her mind's eye Ruby flat out on the floor with a broken neck.

'Get fecking down now, or I swear by all that is holy, I shall run down the stairs and fetch Mrs McKinnon.'

Jane's threat was cut short by the sound of the hessian sack and its contents landing on top of the basket with a thud. Ruby put one hand on the basket to steady herself and leapt down nimbly, her feet barely making a sound on the wooden floor.

For a second, both girls stood and looked at each other. Jane was wondering what in heaven was happening and how much trouble she would be in and Ruby was asking herself which side of the line Jane would fall on. There had been the same division at the convent. There were those who, like Ruby, pushed at the boundaries of authority, and those like Jane, who would obey the rules with their dying breath.

'Look,' Ruby whispered, 'it's tied up in a knot and I'm going to undo it, have a look and then tie it back up and put it back exactly where I found it, so stop panicking. You want to know what is in there, now, as much as I do. Don't lie.'

Jane said nothing. It was a sin to lie.

Ruby picked and picked away at the knot.

'I have it,' she said, tipping the sack upside down.

Out fell a very old, dark wooden box. With relief Ruby saw that it had a clasp, not a lock.

'Oh, Jesus, put it back.' Jane was almost in tears. She had now turned a ghastly shade of white and was obviously truly afraid. 'I have a bad feeling,' she said from between the fingers she had clasped across her eyes. 'This isn't right, there's something bad about it. Please Ruby, there are stories and I will tell you about them, but now please, just put it back. Me legs are shaking, Ruby, please.'

The *please* was more cried than spoken, and then Ruby heard a sound like trickling water. She looked around, confused, and then it dawned on her. Jane had wet herself.

Ruby knew she had to be quick now. Lifting the brass clasp, she looked inside and then gently, tipped up the box, so that Jane too could see. A knitted shawl, large enough to wrap a baby in and a once white linen baby dress, now grey with age flopped out onto the top of the basket.

'God, would ye look at that,' said Jane, whose colour had slowly returned. 'None of the lady's babies were ever dressed in that. I used to help with the washing, 'twas my first job when I came and I did the baby clothes too, God rest their souls.' Jane blessed herself. 'I washed them all, I did and I never washed those. They are so old, more like what we use in the cottages than in the castle.'

'Whose are they, then?' asked Ruby.

'I don't know, but they're definitely not from here. God, have you seen the cut of the clothes the lady dressed the babies in? That's them in that press there, but ye can't look, I forbid ye.'

Jane bravely pointed to a smaller press, and although Ruby was curious to see and felt almost challenged by the word 'forbid', she concentrated on the job in hand.

She opened the lid of the box wider, but inside it was empty. She picked it up and studied it, to see if there was a name written on the side and it was then that she noticed a carved indentation in the wood. Slipping her fingers in, she found that it was the handle of a small drawer. Ruby pulled, the drawer resisted. It was not going to open easily.

Her earlier audacity was now fading and she realized time was slipping on. *Shall I leave it and come back another day?* she thought, but just at that moment the drawer surrendered to her pressure.

'Oh, here's a letter,' she squealed.

'Well, that's no fecking use, I can't read,' said Jane who was now very intrigued. She moved towards the door, turned the handle and popped her head outside, to check if anyone was looking for them.

'It's all clear,' she whispered as she tiptoed back. 'But please, Ruby, hurry up will ye, for God's sake. I'm near having a fit here.'

Ruby opened the letter and read quickly, muttering to herself as she did so, but Jane could not understand a word she was saying. She was surprised to see how the blood left Ruby's face as she read.

'What does it say?' asked Jane nervously, not sure that she wanted to know.

A feeling of dread had crept into the room and Jane was afraid as she looked to Ruby for an answer.

Ruby gave Jane a hard look, but said, 'I will read it to you, but first bring me a chair, please.'

Jane grabbed two chairs and pulled them over to the press. 'Well, go on then. Jesus we don't have another five minutes, let alone all day.' She was trying hard to be brave, and almost, but not quite succeeding. 'Ruby, will ye stop. Ye are scaring me now, just bloody get on with it.'

Ruby picked up the paper and began.

To Lord FitzDeane

I leave this baby in your stable. She is well wrapped and warm in the hay and I know she will be safe until she is found.

She is the first daughter of Ballyford. Long ago, her ancestors were once of Ballyford too. Her line may be broken and long forgotten, but this child belongs with you. Care for her. Make her as your own, for always. Only she can right the wrong of the past. Should her line be broken, should she be cast out or disowned, Ballyford shall pay a terrible price. The sins of your fathers are not forgotten.

*

'Merciful God, you are a great one for the reading, Ruby. What does it all mean? Is that the curse the storyteller talks of? Ruby?'

'How would I know?' Ruby replied sharply. 'I have never heard the story. It's from someone who can write and not many on the farms can, can they? So, I don't believe it could be anyone from around these parts. I don't know if it's a curse or not. The babies here, they've all died, haven't they?'

'Well, not all, Ruby. Lord Charles is here, isn't he? But it is true, there has been a lot of sadness here. Some of the boys from the estate went to fight in the war, in the same regiment they were and fought in the same battle and none of them came back. Everyone cried for weeks. 'Twas the only time Mrs McKinnon has ever taken to her bed, so they say. Lord Charles's daddy, he died not long after that, so he did, but I get confused between them all. There are tales about the castle, Ruby. Of the child that was found, but I can't talk about that because 'tis bad so it is. No one speaks of it and now I'm wondering, were these her clothes? But Mrs McKinnon, she was here then, although she was probably the age we are now. This box and all, it cannot be her clothes, can it? You should come down to the cottages when the storyteller comes, he knows everything, him and Amy's mammy, she's the fortune teller, and Miss McAndrew, they know everything they do.'

Ruby sat looking at the letter and was surprised at how her hands trembled. Putting the folded sheet on top of the basket, she picked up the baby clothes and pressed them to her face inhaling deeply the lingering smell of something she could not place. She failed to prevent tears springing to her eyes, as a powerful sense of something already seen and known possessed her.

Jane did not like the expression on Ruby's face. She found the tears in her eyes alarming and the atmosphere in the linen room oppressive.

'Quick, would ye be here now,' she said snatching the shawl and dress out of Ruby's hands. She began to fold the baby clothes and replace them carefully in the box. 'Come on, Ruby, would ye, or we will both be thrown out of our jobs and onto our arses.'

Ruby gently slid the letter back into the darkness of the hidden drawer and the box into its place of hiding. She tied up the string, then without haste climbed onto the basket and put the sack back into place. She covered it with the sheet, just as it had been before and pushed the wicker basket back in, covering the damp patch on the floorboards.

Jane picked up the plate and made towards the door with Ruby following.

'Anyway, I never got to tell ye why I wanted us to meet in here,' Jane said. She wanted to dispel the atmosphere as quickly as possible. Ruby was acting very odd and Jane didn't want to discuss the letter any further. 'I heard a man called at the castle and he was asking about ye. Said that Jack had told him he had taken a girl himself from the convent to the castle and her name was Ruby. He was from Doohoma and I heard him tell Lord FitzDeane that he was the man who rescued you from the storm and took you to the convent in the first place. He wanted to see you. Anyway you could have knocked me down, because Lord FitzDeane had a very long chat with him, so he did.'

Ruby stopped in her tracks and looked at Jane.

'Did he now?' she said, walking towards the door. 'And no one thought to tell me? We will see about that then.' She stormed out of the door, it swung back and knocked the plate Jane carrying clean out of her hands.

'Merciful God, Ruby, has the devil himself got into ye today?' Fortunately, the plate had bounced off the rug without breaking. Jane dropped to her knees and picked the crumbs up from the rug one by one, then pushed those remaining into the carpet with her fingers. 'Don't ye be cursing anyone today now,' she said as she rubbed. 'There's been enough curses around here I'm thinking.'

But Ruby did not answer. She was marching straight towards Lord FitzDeane's study.

Chapter fourteen

Amy stood at the range and stirred the soup in the huge, black, cast iron cauldron that hung on the crane. It would be served at midday to the staff, along with the bread she and Mary had made earlier that morning. As Amy stirred she pondered her situation. She knew that life had passed her by, just as it had many women in rural Ireland who earned a living, or rather existed, in domestic servitude.

'It's not that I mind not having had the children,' she confided in Mrs McKinnon, 'but I wish I'd had a bit of the other a few more times than I have.'

'Heavens above, you should thank your lucky stars you got away scot-free, if you have indulged already outside marriage,' Mrs McKinnon replied. 'I hope you went to confession? Think yourself lucky, Amy, there's no joy in the creation of excuses and feigning headaches and bad backs half of your life, I can tell you. The novelty soon wears off.'

'Away with ye.' Amy waved her wooden spoon at Mrs McKinnon. 'I've heard that bed of yours groaning for dear life, there's no excuses you can make that I would believe.'

Mrs McKinnon blushed. There was an element of truth in what Amy said. But no more. *Thank God.* It had taken her forty years to learn to say no with conviction. Even then, it was as though her refusals had driven him crazy. It was as if he had found a new source of erotica in her full-length flannel nightdress and her wire curlers tucked under her terry-towelling turban. He had never stopped bothering her, but she had not relented, no indeed, those days were over. At his age, Mr McKinnon should be very grateful for a good meal, clean sheets and his laundry done. And she told him so almost every day.

Nothing Mrs McKinnon could say would convince Amy that she hadn't missed out and her dissatisfaction had intensified over the past year. Rory Doyle was a secret. It was one she had nursed and kept warm, blinded by his words. She had believed him, believed that at any moment she would turn a corner and life would be there, waiting for her, asking what had kept her so long. Yet when the moment came, he ran from Ballyford, leaving Amy behind, alone and weeping.

Rory Doyle, the man she had fallen head over heels for when she was only a slip of a girl, had used her and left her, but despite that, if he wagged his finger again, she would run to him and she knew it because that was how it always was. It was madness. He was married, loved another, it was a sin, but she would happily burn in hell for one more night with him, just as she had done on so many occasions over the years, before fleeing to confession, just in case she should drop dead without warning. When he wanted something, he knew where to find her and how to get it. Usually it was information about the goings-on at the castle. He was a nosy one all right, was Rory.

The last time he came she had, as usual, done as he asked, but this time she felt uncomfortable and torn with a guilt that no amount of time in the confessional would ease. Rory had gone a step too far. He still made her feel as if she was the most beautiful woman in the world, even though he always disappeared in the middle of the night and only ever returned under the cover of darkness and in secret. It had been so long and yet, when she lay her head on her pillow at night, he still filled her thoughts and the memories. His words and his touch, but mostly his laugh, remained with her. Despite all that, in her heart she knew that it had to end. She could not undertake one of his errands ever again, even though to refuse him would mean that she would be discarded forever.

Amy knew that she had been wrong about her life. She had failed to emerge from the shadow cast by Rory and she had been oblivious to the passing years and the futility of the passion she nursed for him. Her life had never begun. Over time, she had learnt how not to be jealous of others good fortune, but it was hard. She was gone forty, fat and forgotten and it was not meant to have been this way.

She had never wanted to work as a trainee cook in the kitchen, or to be someone's secret lover. She had held onto her dreams to train as a nurse in Dublin. Amy had worked hard at her studies with that hope lodged firmly in her mind and, apart from the McKinnon's, she was the only member of staff who could write.

'You will go up to the castle at Ballyford and provide food for us all,' her mother said, crushing all of her dreams in one sentence.

'I think knowing what it's like to be loved is what makes me more dissatisfied,' Amy confided in Mrs McKinnon. 'There was no other lover like Rory Doyle. It's the knowing what I'm missing which is the hardest and who wants mutton, after you've enjoyed a nice bit of spring lamb.'

'Shh, keep your voice down, Amy, we don't want anyone else hearing you. If I were a different sort of housekeeper, you would be out on your ear, with immoral chatter like that and as for Rory Doyle, think yourself lucky. You had a narrow escape. Neither I nor Mr McKinnon have a minute for the man. Mr McKinnon is lying awake at night worrying about the fact that Lord Charles has left him in charge of his shipping business while he's back in Ballyford and that's more than can be said for Lord Charles who appears to have been completely taken in by him since he was in the nursery. He would never hear a word against Rory when they were kids and Rory was the biggest rascal on the estate. I can tell you this Amy, if either you or Lord Charles knew what Rory Doyle was really capable of, neither of you would go near the man.' Amy remained silent. She knew very well what Rory Doyle was capable of.

The soup began to bubble so Amy slid the cast iron lid across and then, lifting the handle, used both her hands to shift the huge pot over onto a cooler section of the plate. She shot Mrs McKinnon a sharp look.

Amy's hair was scraped up into her frilled and starched white cloth hat, but the sides had long since frizzed out with the steam, a result of her early morning baking and soup-making endeavours.

'Are you ready to roll out that pastry, Mary?' she snapped. 'The trouble with you Mrs McKinnon, was that you were jealous of how, when Lord Charles was just a boy, he took so much notice of Rory and would ignore you. It's time you let that go.'

Silence descended upon the kitchen. Mary looked from one woman to the other as they locked horns. Her mouth dried in fear. She knew this exchange could result in Amy storming out of the kitchen. It was always the same. The mention of Rory Doyle's name always caused animosity between the two women who ran Ballyford.

Mary licked her dry lips and then broke the atmosphere as she made an almighty row, slapping her dough on the table.

'Lord Charles wants to feed his guests pies, not ask them to visit a dentist, Mary,' Amy shouted as she watched Mary slap the pastry down overly hard.

Unperturbed, Mary smiled back.

'And get on with peeling the fruit.'

Everyone had noted how grumpy Amy had become of late and because she ruled the kitchen, her mood was bringing down the rest of the castle staff.

'I have, Amy,' said Mary sullenly. 'I have enough for four apple pies. Is that not enough?'

Mrs McKinnon slipped away into the scullery.

'Aye, that's grand. 'Twill do nicely,' said Amy as she cast a glance at Mrs McKinnon's retreating back and grinned to herself; on this occasion she had won.

Later that morning, as Amy stood at the sink to rinse her hands, she noticed Jack alighting from his cart and making his way towards the back door.

Was it him? Amy thought. Was he really my life, waiting for me to notice? Have I been blind? Have I been spoilt by Rory and been too fussy?

Half an hour later Jack was still sitting at the kitchen table unable to keep the grin from his face. Amy had chosen to be nice to him, something that didn't happen very often. Jack didn't notice Mary raise her eyebrows or roll her eyes when Amy greeted him at the back door.

'Would you like another egg with yer rashers, Jack?' Amy asked, putting a plate of bacon and fried eggs, speckled with blackened fat, in front of him.

Jack could not believe his luck.

'If I didn't know better, I would say ye was trying to have yer wicked way with me,' he said. 'Eggs and rashers, I'm usually lucky to have only the lashing from yer tongue when I bring the goods round.'

Amy plopped herself on the stool opposite Jack. After wiping her hands on a cloth, which she then discarded. She picked up the teapot.

'Will ye have a sup?' The teapot hovered over the mug. Jack could have sworn Amy had winked at him.

'Aye, I will,' he replied, bemused.

She poured them both a cup.

'Well, you don't always get treated badly here now, Jack and 'tis a long time since we had a ball. There's much I need and I can't think of anyone else who can get what I want for the table. I will need more than one delivery from Dublin and I need provisions from Galway. Will ye be able to manage, Jack?'

'Well, ye know, I would do that for nothing,' he said, tucking into the best Ballyford bacon rashers.

Amy spooned the sugar into his mug. 'I know that,' she said, 'and sure, I know I can trust ye with the list an' all. It's just that it's been years since I have catered for a ball in the castle. I'm rusty. I'm not sure if can do it anymore.'

'Get away, never have I heard such a load of rot. Ye run this place, don't ye? Mrs McKinnon thinks she does, that's for sure, but 'tis you, everyone knows that.'

Amy looked more than pleased at his words, even if they were untrue, and for a moment she preened, studying him as he ate, as if seeing him for the first time. *God, I have been blind*, she thought to herself. He had everything she needed in a man. A kind nature, a nice cottage, a cowshed of his own, even though his new van lived in it, covered up each night in rags. And he had no children. A bonus. As she watched him place a forkful in his mouth, a dribble of bacon fat ran down his chin and Jack licked it away. Amy shivered, more with pleasure than horror and allowed herself to contemplate what a future with Jack would be like. She was a prisoner in a castle in the wildest part of rural Ireland. Amy was truly desperate.

'Did ye hear we had the town clerk himself here from Doohoma?' she asked, dragging herself mentally out of his bed and back into the kitchen where she belonged. Jack stopped eating and looked up with interest.

'I didn't, no, but he did ask me plenty of questions when he knew I had brought Ruby up from the convent to the castle.

He had been trying to trace her family and he said if Lord FitzDeane was home, he might call in.'

'Well, call he did,' said Amy, as Jack cleaned his plate with a slice of bread. 'It was a big chinwag they had, too. Fancy the master discussing servants with the clerk. He may have told him about the Ballyford ball. If you ask me, he's bitten off more than he can chew with the lady not being quite right.'

Once Jack had finished, she took his plate over to the enormous stone sink and began to rinse it under the tap.

'Well, 'tis the talk of the village and all around for miles, I'd say they were discussing it in Galway now,' said Jack. 'The news is that Lady Isobel must be well recovered from her loss to be throwing the Ballyford Ball and sure, isn't that a relief, after all this time.'

Mr and Mrs McKinnon walked into the kitchen together. They had been to visit two families of brawling tenants, each one threatening to murder the other in their beds and all over a stolen chicken. The fact was, no one had stolen anything, the chicken had a mind of its own and exercising good judgement, had hopped into the Ballyford stables.

'What's the talk of the town, Jack?' asked Mrs McKinnon. 'God in heaven, am I dying for a cup of tea, or what? That lot would make a saint weep.'

'Did you knock their heads together?' asked Amy.

'If I had thought it would help, I would have,' said Mrs McKinnon, 'but as it was, the only thing that would work with that lot was the threat of eviction and even that took a while to sink in. Not one of them seemed to care that there would be no food for the children if they carried on. You know, I'm still not sure we have done enough good. Maybe we should call out the Garda, Mr McKinnon?'

'Not yet. If anyone dies, we will.' Mr McKinnon ladled himself a large portion of soup from the pan and dragged a chair out for himself. Wearily, he tore up a hunk of fresh bread. He looked at Amy and asked, 'Why is Jack being fed like the lord of the castle? Bit of hanky-panky going on here is there, while we are out refereeing the tenants?'

Amy flushed bright red and Mrs McKinnon, the hostility of the morning forgotten, rushed to her rescue.

'I'd be careful if I were you, Jack,' she said. 'There's a ball coming up. Never believe the promises of a woman who has to cater for eighty people, especially if they are made to a man with his own van and contacts in perishable provisions.'

Jack laughed. 'Aye, I'm not so daft as to think that a woman as beautiful as Amy here would give me a second look.'

Flustered, Amy jumped up and began to smooth her skirts and to pin her errant hair back into her cap.

'Aye, well, you're a man of sense altogether, I would say, so I would,' said Amy, tapping her spoon on the table and looking Jack square in the eye, all notion of romance banished. 'Can you get me anchovy paste and quail eggs from Galway?'

'What did I tell you?' Mrs McKinnon said triumphantly.

Jack picked up his cap. 'I can that, Amy, and there's strawberries to come every day into Galway, from the airport in Dublin. They will be just in time for the ball.'

Jack had delivered a consignment of six pushbikes to the castle, which were now stacked on the back of his van, waiting to be unloaded. It was Mr McKinnon who had sent him off to Dublin the previous day.

'Would you believe it, Jack,' Mr McKinnon had said. 'I was happy with the horse and then Lord Charles got the car and now we are to have pushbikes, too. Mind you, very handy indeed for the staff to get about.'

Jack wouldn't argue, but for him it would always be a trusty Irish cob and his pristine van. Jack was a man of means.

He had been sure there had been a change in Amy when he had arrived at the castle. There was a look about her, a softer, come-hither quality around the edges. As he left the kitchen, he looked back at her.

'I'll be back tomorrow then, as usual.'

'Bye Jack,' shouted Mr and Mrs McKinnon.

Amy resumed her earlier air of dejected misery at the range, as she stirred the soup, deep in thought.

'Mary, lay the table,' she snapped as the staff began to filter into the kitchen, one by one.

Jane was the first in, dashing down the stairs in a fluster.

'What on earth is up with you, miss?' asked Mrs McKinnon.

'Nothing, Mrs McKinnon,' replied Jane meekly.

'Don't wait for grace.' Mrs McKinnon had already moved on. 'The garden lads won't be in for another half hour and it looks like Ruby must have her hands full. She is usually the hungriest and the first down.'

Jane stared intently at her bowl as she began to eat and with each spoonful, felt calmer. She had been in and out of this kitchen since she was a girl and if there was one thing she had learnt in life, it was to try and keep your mouth shut, if you had the choice.

They would all find out soon enough that Ruby was in the study, giving Lord Charles hell, but it wouldn't be Jane who told them.

Chapter fifteen

Although she had marched down the corridor towards his study as though pursued by the devil's own handmaidens, once Ruby reached the large oak door, she stopped dead in her tracks. Despite the thickness of the wood, she could hear a voice speaking on the other side.

'Well, I'm truly glad to hear that and so, the deed is finally done. We are officially a partnership Rory, we must drink to our exciting alliance when you arrive at Ballyford.'

Ruby leaned in to hear better and pressed her ear to the study door.

There was a long period of silence. She could hear only her own breathing and the distant rotating of the blades cutting the grass at the front of the castle. She stepped back and peered over at the minstrels' gallery, wondering if anyone other than Jane had seen or heard her storming along. But the only living soul was Rufus, stretched out in front of the hearth in the hall. Hearing her move, he lifted his lazy head and looked straight at her. He yawned and put his head back down on the stone floor, satisfied that it was only Ruby, who had never taken him running through the woods or thrown him a sausage from the cool store. Knowing that she was very unlikely to do either at this moment, he made himself comfortable once more.

'You lazy hound,' she whispered to him.

Moving back to the office door she heard Charles's voice again.

'I shall meet you myself, Rory,' he was saying. 'I can't wait. Everyone is excited about your arrival, especially Mr and Mrs McKinnon. They told your mother to expect you, when they were at the cottages this morning.'

Ruby knew that was a flat-out lie. She had heard enough of the whispered conversation between Amy and the McKinnons to know that, if it was Mr Rory Doyle from Liverpool he was talking to, the McKinnons couldn't bear him and were living in dread of his being invited as a guest to the ball. Mrs McKinnon had told her he was not to be trusted and if Lord Charles could have found a less well-disposed gentleman to work with, she would be surprised.

After a few moments she heard the click of the handset being replaced and she gently tapped on the door. Ruby was cross with herself. Her temper, usually so dependable, had deserted her. She knocked on the study door once more, slightly louder.

'Come in,' he shouted breezily.

He had his back to her and was sitting at his desk in front of the window, facing out over the front lawn.

As she stepped into the room, she had no idea whether or not it was polite or acceptable to walk into his sanctuary and so she stood, stock-still, a few feet inside the door.

'Ah, Ruby.' He swung around on the green-leather chair. He lounged back with one hand in his pocket, and his legs splayed out in front of him. She felt thrown by the intimate familiarity of his pose.

She could smell him. She hadn't expected that.

Ruby felt diminished. The furniture dwarfed her. But she knew that the following moments were important and she took a deep breath before she spoke. She had to get this right, or she would leave this room a fool. The FitzDeane ancestors looked contemptuously down at her from the walls. She thought she saw the mouth of a wigged and pretentious man curl at the corners. She began to wonder, was she mad? Before she could reply, as if sensing her fear he spoke again.

'Is Lady FitzDeane well?'

Ruby almost sighed in relief. Her hands clasped together tightly in a little ball before her. He had handed her an opening. She wondered, was her hair in place, did she look presentable? Was her apron clean? She had been in such a state of blind anger she hadn't checked and now, as she stood before him, it was the most important thing on her mind.

'Yes, m'lord, she is very well indeed.' Her voice croaked. She was angry with herself. This was not Ruby. Ruby did not cower in front of anyone. As she took another breath she felt her confidence return and she prepared to fire her onslaught.

She licked her lips. She looked him over and pinned him to the chair with her stare. He was her prisoner. She was ready.

'I hear, Lord FitzDeane, that the clerk from Doohoma was here, making enquiries about myself and I demand to know why I wasn't told. I demand, I do.'

Ruby's legs wobbled slightly but she willed herself not to flinch.

Charles FitzDeane was speechless. He couldn't help but be amused by her ferocity and the sparks in her eyes.

'He didn't call at the castle to see you, Ruby, he came to see me and on entirely private business. You must never believe castle gossip.'

'But, but I know it was about me and that makes it my business too.' Ruby was flustered. She had expected him to tell her that he had no time to be dealing with such lowly people as town clerks, that he had dismissed Con without even hearing what he had to say, but instead he made her feel as though he were laughing at her standing in his office interrogating him. She was amusing him. His expression altered in an instant.

'What makes you think it was about you?' His voice was now cooler and shot through with steel.

Ruby felt scared. This was not turning out as she had planned when she had stormed through the corridors in a fit of indignation. She had expected him to apologize, to pick up the phone right away and call the clerk so that he could speak to Ruby at once. But he did none of that and instead sat and held her in his gaze. The tables turned. She felt as though she might disintegrate before him.

'It's Doohoma,' she whispered. 'He's from my home. I wanted to see him, because he's from Doohoma and it was him who saved me.'

Charles rose from his chair and walked across the floor towards the window. He stood with his back to her and she found that so much easier. It was when he was facing her, his eyes piercing into her, that she found it difficult to speak.

'Doohoma was where you lived?' His voice had softened slightly.

She knew it was not really a question, she could tell he already knew the answer and the thought, *How?* fluttered across Ruby's mind. The McKinnons would know, but surely they didn't discuss the staff with Lord FitzDeane?

She didn't reply. Instead, she stared at the red carpet and at the intricate black diamond pattern around the edge.

The atmosphere in the study was tense and she thought, *There's dust on the desk. Betsy, where are you?*

She sometimes deployed this diversionary tactic when she thought about Doohoma. It was as if her mind played tricks on her. She distracted her thoughts away from a potential source of pain by concentrating on things of no substance. A bit of dust here, a raindrop winding its way down a window there. In the convent, she would fix her gaze on the second hand of the large wall clock and count the seconds until her thoughts had moved on.

Charles turned from the window and spoke again. His voice took on a very different tone and one that Ruby did not like.

'Did you live in Doohoma? Did you live in a cottage facing side on to the sea, did your broken boat, with its nets, rest at the bottom of the cliff with the rope fixed to a rock? And did your donkey shelter at the side, under a sod shed?'

Ruby's mouth opened and closed. She felt as though she had been punched in the stomach and as the blood rushed to her face she tried to remember to breathe. Memories crowded in and completed the landscape. A little boy saving the peat, her brother. A woman hanging out the washing, her mother. A dog running and barking around her, Max. But where was she, was she there? Could she see herself? Of course she could, she was there, handing the washing up to her mother and looking out to the ocean for her father, who waved his hand in greeting as his boat came in closer. As he did even now, every time he caught her unaware and sailed into her dreams.

The noise she made as she cried was inaudible. It had brewed inside her for years, gathering strength, pushing away at the edges in her sleep, and now, Charles had dismantled her defences and with just a few words had left her bare and raw and vulnerable. She had nowhere to hide. She was here, standing before Lord FitzDeane and she could not stop her heart from breaking.

'I am so sorry,' he said, moving quickly towards her and gathering her into his arms. He was unprepared for his own reaction as his muscles hardened in response to her yielding feminine softness. 'I should have explained to you. I did discuss you with the town clerk. He thought he had traced your mother to Ballyford. I'm afraid I had to tell him he was quite wrong. He described the house to me, just in case it jogged my memory, but I am sorry to say he was mistaken. He had thought nothing of it, before, but when he heard you had been brought here, he thought it worth mentioning. I also told him that when you next have a day off, I would lend you one of the new bikes, which I have had delivered to the castle from England, to ride to Doohoma yourself and you could visit him then. He was keen to see you. Said he felt a responsibility, having rescued you from the storm.'

Ruby could not believe what she was hearing. She would see her home again and the clerk. There was a link to her past. Someone from Doohoma, who both knew her and cared about what had happened to her. It meant everything. The things she had wished for in the convent, they would be hers, at last.

'Thank you so much, Lord FitzDeane,' she said between sobs.

She knew that she now needed to leave the room. She was in danger of humiliating herself and embarrassing him further. She wouldn't have to steal a bike, he was giving her one for a day and letting her go.

'Oh, God, me and my stupid thoughts,' she said out loud as she wiped her nose. 'Does he know I will be coming?'

'He doesn't, Ruby, but he said you can knock on his door at any time and that you would be most welcome.'

She was now devoid of anger and filled only with elation. She felt ashamed for having lost her temper. Drying her eyes on her apron, she realized he had moved her gently away from the paintings and towards the weak sunlight streaming in through his window. She thought he was wonderful. He had more than redeemed himself. Lord FitzDeane had no idea that he had spoken words that from that moment on would support a lifetime of devotion.

Charles moved to the desk and picked up the Waterford carafe, which was washed and filled with fresh water each day by Betsy. He poured the clear water from Ballyford's own mountain stream into the crystal cut-glass tumbler which sat, always ready, next to it.

'Here, before you dash away, have a glass of water. I swear

that the water from our streams has fabulous restorative properties. If I could, I would bottle it and sell it, except I know everyone would laugh at me, trying to sell something provided for free by the good Lord.'

Ruby smiled at him through watery eyes.

'Thank you,' she gasped gratefully gulping the water. She took the handkerchief from her apron pocket and unself-consciously blew her nose loudly. She checked that her hair was in place under her hat, before she replaced the handkerchief in her pocket.

Charles found that he didn't want her to leave his office and his mind scrabbled for a reason to make her stay.

Ruby looked up and her eyes, still full of tears, met his. The moment seemed to stretch into forever, a hundred messages flashing between them as their eyes spoke. She saw the pulse throbbing in the side of his neck and the colour rise in his cheeks. She knew that it was there again, a deep familiarity between them. She was aware, without a shadow of a doubt that he would not have spoken to her, or looked at her in such a way, if they had been in the presence of other servants. There was a knowledge, an acceptance between them. It was there in the way he now said her name and smiled at her. It was as if he regarded her as an equal and not as a servant. But she had no idea why.

Charles dragged his gaze away as he absentmindedly placed the linen cloth back over the carafe. Ruby was filled with gratitude and something else she could not identify. Something which bound her to this man's life, this castle. His world, past and present.

The phone on his desk rang and the shrill noise ripped apart the ambiance of familiarity which had settled between them. He looked at her apologetically.

'Thank you,' she whispered simply. The smile that followed held a deeper meaning, which neither understood.

And with that, Ruby turned and left.

Charles dealt with his business call quickly and, once he replaced the receiver, put both hands in his pockets, deep in thought. Through the window, he watched Danny and Jimmy and the rest of the garden boys lay down their raking tools, before they ran inside the castle for lunch.

He smiled to himself, feeling warmed by the things he had once loved to distraction about Ballyford, but from which he had derived no pleasure in recent years. The green of the grass, the laughter of the gardeners as they worked together like generations before them and the feeling of being responsible for the wellbeing of others, all this lifted his heart.

But the lies he had told Ruby lay like a weight in his gut and dragged down the smile from his face, as he thought of her tears.

He had ridden out to Doohoma only yesterday, to find where Iona had lived. Charles thought deeply about what he knew of the past. It wasn't much. Iona's arrival in the stable had put the fear of God into everyone. He had to prove to himself that she had really lived, to see what had become of her, and in Ruby he had touched her life. The only other people who knew who Ruby really was were the McKinnons and Charles realized that Mrs McKinnon knew even more than she had ever let on to him.

And now she was here. He was thirty-three years old to Ruby's eighteen and in her presence he felt like a young man once again. She made his heart beat faster and his mind fill with foolish thoughts. Charles knew he would have to fight hard to conquer his natural responses to Ruby. When he handed her the glass of water, he had felt a burning need to hold her tightly in his arms again. A need that had almost got the better of him. But down the corridor sat his wife.

'How can a place so beautiful be so cruel?' he whispered out loud.

He heard his father's voice. 'I shall rid this castle of spirits and sin,' he had shouted to Charles, who had begged and cried as Iona was carried away and handed to a faceless stranger, waiting on the other side of the door.

Tears filled Charles's eyes. He turned to the marble effigy of his hated father. 'But you never knew, did you, Father, you never knew that the darkest sin casts the longest shadows.'

Chapter sixteen

The daylight was fading fast and the fall of the light from the brass lamp on the escritoire was contained by its dark burgundy shade. A soft, amber pool illuminated the writing blotter and guided the hand that held the pen. The rain and wind beat ferociously against the tall leaded windows and drowned out the sound of the careful scratch of the gold nib on card as fine as vellum, the hissing of the peat as it gently burnt in the fireplace and the occasional stomach rumble from hungry Rufus, lying next to Mrs McKinnon.

Ruby carefully wrote out each of the invitations to the ball at Lady FitzDeane's writing desk, while Mrs McKinnon sat beside her in a straight-backed chair, with a list in one hand and her folded reading glasses in the other.

Lady Isobel had begun the task herself, but her concentration had waned and she had made many errors, so she handed the task to Ruby.

'You have a lovely hand, Ruby, would you mind continuing for me? Mrs McKinnon knows who is who. She will help.' Lady Isobel rose and offered Ruby her seat and as Ruby settled anxiously in the chair she added, 'I will take myself to bed for a sleep. I should try and build up my strength ready for the ball.'

Ruby accepted the task willingly, although she was very nervous, having never written anything as formal as an invitation before. Now she lifted the blotting paper away from the last gold-edged card and placing it in the envelope, said, 'There, done at last, my hand is about to drop off, so it is.'

'Oh, at last, Ruby,' Mrs McKinnon exclaimed, collapsing back into her seat with relief. 'I cannot tell you how relieved I am to have got that job done and so well, too. You made not one mistake. I am near exhausted myself, just from watching you.'

Mrs McKinnon laid her glasses down on the blotter and picked up the tidy pile of embossed envelopes.

'Right, let's just go through this list and tick off the envelopes against it. Then no one can accuse us of missing anyone. You do have a beautiful wee hand, Ruby.'

'It was the only thing the nuns taught me which I enjoyed,' said Ruby in response.

'The Lady Lydia Trevelyan, she's a one, if ever there was.' Mrs McKinnon sniffed and placed the envelope back on the top of the pile. 'If I didn't think it was the wrong thing to do, I would put that one straight on the fire, I would.'

'Why would you do that?' Ruby's eyes opened wide in alarm.

'Because she's a trollop, that's why. She would steal Lord FitzDeane and all he owned right out from under Lady Fitz-Deane's nose, if he let her, mind, which he wouldn't, as he has far more sense than that. But what tricks that woman hasn't pulled aren't worth talking about.'

'Why, what has she done, then?' Ruby leaned forward towards Mrs McKinnon and lowered her voice, encouraged by the semi-darkness and the glow from the fire.

Mrs McKinnon folded her own arms across her ample chest, then, with a quick glance at the door to check no one had opened it unawares, leaned forward.

'Well, I can't even begin to tell you how she dresses, because it would be most inappropriate, but let me just tell you this: what she has she flaunts and straight in Lady FitzDeane's face, too. And that one you just wrote out there...' Mrs McKinnon lifted the top invitation and jabbed her finger at the envelope underneath, addressed to another of their neighbours, '... he encourages her, so he does. If there was a name for a male equivalent of a trollop, he would wear it well.'

Ruby had no idea what a trollop was and she thought it best not to ask.

Mrs McKinnon continued. 'I only hope the lady is up to this ball. Oh, I know I encouraged it, on the doctor's advice, mind, but now I have seen this guest list, I don't mind telling you, I'm concerned. There are people I would have thought better of inviting. I had hoped Lord FitzDeane would have kept the list to the nice local lords and landowners, the people he grew up with as a boy, but our Lord FitzDeane, he makes friends wherever he goes, so he does.'

Ruby watched the older woman carefully as they went through the list. She had other thoughts on her mind. She was burning to ask Mrs McKinnon about the baby clothes hidden in the box in the linen room, but she realized that once she had spoken she could never take those words back. Something also told Ruby that if she asked that particular question, nothing at the castle would ever be the same again. She sensed a danger in being aware of the note and the contents of the box.

A small tap rattled the door, and Mrs McKinnon said to Ruby, 'Now, I'm trusting you, as a convent girl and a good Catholic, to understand that conversation you and I have just had, it's between us two. Not to be repeated.'

She rose from the chair and pulled and fastened the shutters. She knew she really had no need to ask for assurances of discretion. Ruby wasn't like the other servants and not only because she had been educated at the convent with the best reputation in Ireland. She carried a maturity like an invisible shawl wrapped around her and it made her appear so much older than her years.

Ruby smiled at Mrs McKinnon and the thought crossed Mrs McKinnon's mind that even Ruby's smiles appeared weary at times.

'Of course, it's our secret, although I have to say, I'm rather excited now about the trollop. It will be an education in itself to see how she behaves.'

Mrs McKinnon grinned. 'Aye, well that's as may be, just as long as she doesn't upset Lady FitzDeane.'

Ruby inclined her head towards the door. 'That'll be Jane,' she said.

'Aye, jealous, no doubt, that she isn't sat in here with us.' Then Mrs McKinnon shouted, 'Yes, come in,' and Jane immediately popped her head around the door.

'Come in, girl, what's up with you, has the cat got your tongue, or what?' Mrs McKinnon smiled kindly at Jane, she intended no rebuff knowing that Jane always appeared either cross or half scared to death.

Jane shot Ruby a look which only Ruby understood. It said, *Have you told her? Have you? Because if you have, I will hate you forever, Ruby Flynn.*

Jane had her story ready. She wasn't there. Ruby was a liar. She cannot read.

'Amy is calling for you, Mrs McKinnon and the nursery fire is nearly out, Ruby.'

'Run along Jane and tell Amy I am coming.'

'I am very grateful to you for this, Ruby,' Mrs McKinnon said, placing an elastic band around the invitations. 'We shall have to get these into the post tomorrow and then it's all systems go. We have to turn the luck of the castle. That's what it means to me and everyone here, Ruby – a night to turn our luck around and hope things will be sunnier from the morning after.'

Ruby said goodbye and then flew down the corridor after Jane.

'Don't run,' Mrs McKinnon shouted after them, but no one heard her.

Ruby turned the corner towards the nursery and Jane was waiting for her on the other side.

'God, you made me jump so you did,' said Ruby. 'And before you ask me, no, I didn't ask or tell her anything.'

'You are getting mighty cosy with Mrs McKinnon, though. The two of you together in there, writing out the fancy letters. Are ye after her place, Ruby? Do you think you want to be the next Mrs McKinnon?' Jane hissed.

'No, Jane, I am not, I was just doing what I was told, now stand out of my way while I see to the fire.'

'Well, just remember this, 'twas you what found it, you what read the note, not me. I wasn't there, I know nothing about it, I never wanted you to get that box down. Do you understand, Ruby?'

Ruby gave Jane a long, exasperated look.

'Jane I will never get you into trouble. Let's just forget I ever pulled the box down, shall we and I promise, I shan't ever ask anyone about it.'

Jane looked as if she would faint with relief. 'Thank God, Ruby, because Amy, she would kill me so she would and me mammy, she would take what was left and kill me again and I haven't even dared to think what me da would do to me, if I lost this job.'

'Well, think yerself lucky ye have a mammy and a da to worry about,' said Ruby, her voice softening slightly, as she brushed the ashes up from the fire.

Across on the other side of the landing, Lady Isobel sat on the edge of her bed. She took the letter Ruby had collected for her out of her bedside drawer and read it again, then she extracted a handwritten note from the back of the drawer, carefully concealed. The letter was from a private detective agency in Scotland Road, Liverpool, and it confirmed all of her worst fears. She had driven him away with her anger and her grief and she knew in her heart that was exactly what she had wanted to do. It had been her intention all along. She read the name and address. *Stella Manning, hairdresser,*

County Road, Liverpool. She felt a slight pang of guilt. She had pushed him to live another life so far away from the one he had loved at Ballyford.

She wished he had told her himself. But why the unsigned note left on her bedside table? She knew who had put it there. The words written in poison had stood guard as she slept. It had been the first thing she saw when she woke, propped up against her water glass. Mrs McKinnon didn't know, of that she was sure. Had he put her up to it? Was she as evil as the curse of Ballyford? Unable to help herself. Going about her business thinking nobody knew?

She slipped the letter and the note back into the drawer and then laid her head on the pillow and stared at the picture of them both in front of the fire, holding their firstborn. If the staff were conspiring against her, there was no one left to trust. 'It is over,' she whispered. 'It is all over and done.'

She had no tears left. They had all long since been spent.

Chapter seventeen

It was Sunday and Mrs McKinnon had given Ruby the day off as a reward for writing out the invitations.

'You won't get another now, until after we have cleared up from the ball, so make the most of it,' she said.

Ruby felt the eyes of the other staff members fix on her and felt the resentment rolling towards her in rising waves.

Ruby waited to see if Mrs McKinnon mentioned the bike, but it seemed that Lord FitzDeane had reneged on his promise. If he had ever remembered it at all. Mr or Mrs McKinnon would have mentioned it to her if he had and there had been nothing said. Even with the bike, Ruby had no idea how to reach Doohoma from the castle. She had memorized the road from the convent to the castle, so she knew enough to know that the convent was in entirely the wrong direction.

The previous evening, she had studied Amy and the McKinnons closely as they ate their supper around the large, scrubbed kitchen table. She was hoping that one of the stable boys would ask if she needed a horse, or that Amy might mention that Jack was stopping by and would offer her a lift on the cart to Belmullet, but no one spoke about her surprise day off and that was odd in itself. Mrs McKinnon had done Ruby no favours amongst her peers as Ruby, for the first time, felt their unspoken resentment.

'Don't mind them,' said Betsy as they undressed for bed. 'You are different from us, Ruby. You can read and write, you have had an education and none of us have. Oh sure, Amy and the McKinnons can read and write, but they aren't one of us, so it doesn't count. They are all just jealous.'

Ruby knew Betsy was trying her best, but none of what she had said made her feel any better. 'I almost wish I hadn't been given the day off, they were all so quiet and no one spoke a word to me.

'Come here while I tell ye,' said Betsy, pulling the blanket up to her neck and wriggling down under the cool covers. Despite the fire in the grate being lit before they went to supper, the damp penetrated any room in the castle that spent the day without a fire. 'Jimmy said to me that he had a feeling about you and not only Jimmy, Amy's mammy said you had something about your nature and that you wouldn't be anyone's servant for long.

Now Ruby was interested. She poked the fire and with one leap from the grate, jumped into her own bed. 'Go on then, what else did she say.'

'Well, she wouldn't tell me anything else, but she did say you had a wicked temper and that there was a man who was in your head and we would all know about it soon enough.' Ruby pushed her pillow into Betsy's face and the girls giggled. 'Did she have anything to say about Jimmy by any chance? Anyone would think you worked in the stables, not on the first floor, you spend so much time slipping out the back.' Their laughter could be heard along the staff corridor, but gradually the giggles subsided and minutes later both were fast asleep.

Now, it was the morning of her day off and feeling strangely deflated, Ruby was the first up to eat breakfast. As soon as she had finished she stood on the step and looked out into the courtyard from the back door. The rain of the previous day had finally stopped and a bright morning greeted her. She blinked up towards the scudding clouds; their progression across the bright blue sky lifted her spirits and blew away her low mood. Today, Ruby was a cloud. She might not have the bike she was promised, but she could roam the fields. She could be wild and random. Today, she was free.

As Ruby stepped out of the porch and into the courtyard, Amy placed her hand on her shoulder.

'Here you go,' she said. 'You won't be here for lunch, so you'll need food.' No one, from a tradesman to a beggar, left Amy's kitchen door without a drink and a bite.

The sun shone brightly and Ruby shaded her eyes with her hand in order to see Amy clearly. Her heart melted a little at her kindness. 'Amy, that's really kind.' Despite herself, a lump formed in Ruby's throat.

'Lord FitzDeane came into the kitchen at six and told me to make sure you were well provided for.'

'Did he?' Ruby was taken aback.

'Aye, shhh, keep your words in, make your way to the stables, Danny is waiting for ye. It was Lord FitzDeane who told Mrs McKinnon to give you the day off today, he said you needed to do something private.'

Amy grinned as Ruby gave her a hug. 'Stop, ye'll have me going soft. I'll be wanting to know, mind, why all the secrecy. I want to know where it is ye are off to, but that can wait till your business is done and never mind about Jane and the others, they are all as thick as pig shite and will have forgotten what irked them by the time ye get back.'

Danny was rubbing down Lord FitzDeane's horse with a fistful of straw as Ruby walked into the stables.

'Do you have something for me?' she said.

Danny grinned. 'I do. Lord FitzDeane said you were to have my bike for the day. The rest have all taken theirs over to the cottages. I'd have fed it and given it a rub down, if I had known ye was riding it out.' He grinned again, pleased with himself. 'Don't break it now, will ye, I'm away to see me mammy in Bangor Erris tomorrow and I can only go if I have the bike. She loves it that I can get home once a week now instead of twice a year. The bike has made a world of difference it has. Where will ye be for mass, then? Will ye call in somewhere on the way? The church at Bangor Erris is just on the bridge, by the river. You will be there in time, I'm thinking.'

Ruby didn't answer. She had no intention of spending any of her day in a church.

'Well, will ye take mass in Bangor Erris?' A look of alarm had crossed Danny's face. To miss mass on Sunday was the worst of all crimes.

'I won't be going to mass. Are you mad?' said Ruby, walking over to the stall to stroke the horse's nose.

Danny looked shocked. As shocked as if she had stripped

naked in front of him, as he had so often dreamed that she might.

Ruby placed the palm of her hand over the chestnut mare's warm muzzle and planted a kiss on the velvet cushioned nose, breathing in the earthy smell of sweet hay and sleepy horse.

'I shall ask for forgiveness when I attend next week and that, Danny, is the beauty of confession. The priest cannot say no,' she said as she closed her eyes and inhaled the smell. 'I will be forgiven and all will be well. Do you know where Doohoma is, Danny?' she asked, changing the subject. Ruby felt slightly stupid and cross with herself for feeling impatient with Danny.

'I do. Turn left out of the drive, head for Belmullet and then turn right. It'll take ye two hours if ye pedal fast. It's one road in Doohoma, all the way to the head. If ye go any further, ye will drown as the ocean is all there is, all the way to America and that's where I'll be heading, one day, when I'm finished here.'

'America? How will you get there?' Ruby was genuinely interested. She had no idea Danny had any ambition beyond mucking out Lord FitzDeane's horses.

'I don't know yet, but me brother, he's there in Chicago and he said when he gets settled he'll send for me.'

'Does he write often?' She pulled strands of hay from the manger and fed them to the horse from her hand.

Danny hooted with laughter, but a troubled look also crossed his face and his cheeks flushed.

'Write, none of us write, we don't know how. But he said he would find someone to write a letter for him.'

'When did you last hear from him, then?'

Danny had wheeled a shiny black bike out of the next loose box and now he looked embarrassed.

'I haven't heard from him yet. He's only been gone a year, but I will, as soon as he is settled.'

Ruby had learned to ride a bike at the convent. They had one with a huge basket on the front, which the girls took in turns to use for errands in the village. Ruby remembered the painful cuts and scratches she collected whilst learning to ride a contraption twice her weight.

She smiled at Danny, sorry now for pressing him to talk about his brother. He needed to hold on to his dreams, his hopes for the future, just as she did herself. His brother was gone and there would be no letter. She knew that. In his heart, Danny knew it too. It would just take some time before acceptance found a place to slip in. Before he could move from speaking of the brother who was waiting for him, to the brother who once was.

'Thanks Danny, that's grand,' she said kindly, as she took the handlebars. 'I'll bring you some pebbles back from the beach.'

Ruby tucked her skirt into her knickers, threw one leg over the saddle and was away down the drive as fast as her legs would take her.

Danny's hands shielded the sun from his eyes and he lifted his cap and grinned as she pedalled furiously away.

Danny was not the only one who watched her as she went. On the first floor of the castle, Charles FitzDeane leaned against the stone mullions of his study window. He took his cigarette case out of his pocket, lit up and watched until Ruby rode out of sight around the corner of the drive.

Ruby whooped as she turned the corner and headed for the gates. She was as free as a bird, until sundown. If anyone had asked her at that moment she would have struggled to explain how she felt. Free was almost too short and inadequate a word to describe her emotion. Overjoyed came close. Overjoyed sat in the basket at the front of the bike and whooped with her as she rode along.

It was the first time, since the storm, that she had been entirely alone, with no one needing, instructing or wanting her. For the first time since she had been rescued from the storm, she had a whole day to herself and no one expected anything of her. She could do exactly as she pleased.

The sun rose in the east and she turned away from the glare, into the west. The smell of the wet pungent earth stung the inside of her nostrils, and she could hear every noise as though it were ten times louder than it actually was. The sound of the squeak on the front wheel as it went round and round, the crunch of the wheels as they met and churned the gravel in the rough road. The birds twittering, the river roaring and even the silence of the bog.

She shouted hello to every man and woman she passed on the roads and stopped whenever she was waved down to be handed a drink by women standing in front of their cottages who saw her ride by. Ruby knew it was the custom to make this gesture to all travellers on the road.

This was not Ruby's usual life. Today she was someone else. She was simply a girl on a bike out for the day, visiting the place she thought of as home.

The first hour flew by in a haze of joy. There were many conversations with strangers at gates, as they dipped metal cups into a rain barrel and handed her an oat biscuit, each wanting her to stop and give them news of wherever she had come from. They were all desperate for gossip. But Ruby had no time to chat, for long.

She called into the store at Bangor Erris and was directed on her way by the shopkeeper.

'My sister's boy works at the inn at Doohoma,' she shouted after Ruby, puzzled by her urgency. No one rushed anywhere in Mayo.

As she left Bangor Erris, her mood altered. Her feet pushed slower and her heart beat faster. Eventually, she drew up in front of a signpost which told her that she was entering Doohoma. She stared down the single-track road towards the place where she had lived and her family had died. The place she knew would call her back, forever.

A travellers' wagon, pulled by two piebalds, startled her as they cantered past. Sitting up on the front board was a woman with long grey hair and black teeth. As she passed Ruby, she spat out a plug of chewed tobacco that landed on the floor at Ruby's feet. Laughing as she cracked the reins and sped by. On the back board sat two boys. One of them threw something at Ruby. It was a stone.

'Oi, you eejits,' she shouted, as she felt a sharp pain and then saw the blood dribbling down her leg. She felt tears prickling at the back of her eyes. This was not how she had imagined returning to Doohoma to be.

Taking her handkerchief from her pocket, she spat on it

and began dabbing to stem the flow from her shin. This gave her a chance to pull her thoughts together. She knew where the house was and how to get there.

This is it Ruby, she said to herself, *you are back home girl.*

The sun was shining on Doohoma. She could no longer feel the memory of the cold. It had left her, along with the smell and the distress she had once felt. The helpless, crying, lonely, empty uselessness at not being able to do anything to help or save anyone, not even her beloved dog, Max.

The silence was suddenly pierced by the pealing of church bells, signalling the end of mass. People slowly began to file out from the church onto the street.

'Goodbye, Father.' 'Thank you, Father.' 'Stop by for a drink and a bite, would you, Father?'

Ruby watched from her secluded spot on the ground behind the post hidden by a long thick tuft of coarse grass and listened while people took their leave of the old priest. The front door of the inn swung back and forth as men left the confessional to worship at the altar of Guinness.

And then she saw a man and a woman with two young boys and she shrank further back into the long grass and the wild ladies' tresses, growing along the roadside. She recognized him instantly. She remembered the gratitude she'd felt as he carried her inside his coat. She could still feel the warmth of his body and recalled wanting to scream out in thankfulness, to sob with relief that someone was holding her, thawing her ice-cold bones. She could still smell the musty mixture of wet wool and tobacco on his scarf as he carried her down the cliff. The snow, blizzarding against the exposed nape of her neck and his gloved hand, as he pulled his coat up further over her head as though he knew. And she could still see the pity in his eyes, drowning her.

There he was with his wife, pregnant back then, but now clearly the mother of two young boys.

'Daddy, please you take the ball and kick it for me,' the little boy shouted, as the older one ran ahead and taunted him by shouting, 'I'm going to get to the ball before you.'

'Don't tease him, CJ,' shouted Susan. 'If you kick the ball Con, he will make you play with him all the way back without stopping.' She laughed and linked her arm through Con's.

They turned up the hill and there, waiting for them at the end of the church wall, having guarded the ball throughout the mass, was a dog with a coat as grey as iron.

'Max,' shouted the elder boy, 'you are a good dog guarding the ball, isn't he, Daddy?'

'Aye he is that. Come on Max, good boy,' said Con as they progressed up the hill. 'Let's be home for dinner now.'

Ruby sat quite still on the verge. She was afraid to move in case her heart broke in two with the effort. The puppy who had slept on her bed when she was a girl, the only other living being who had shared her past. Knew the call of her family, the whistle of her da, the sound of her mother's laugh and the shouts from her brother. He was feet away from her. Old, with arthritic bones he hobbled up the road and she wanted to run after him and throw her arms around his neck. He was hers. She had thought he might be dead. But Con and his wife had cared for him for the past six years and now she had found him, she couldn't move. She sat stock still, as their voices faded along with the sound of the boys kicking the leather ball.

Ruby looked around at the sun-drenched road, the epitome of normality on a rare hot day in a coastal Irish village. Wild flowers ran riot and bloomed in the fields, unknowing or uncaring of past tragedy. The ocean breeze was as warm as she had ever known as it brushed against her cheeks. She thought of the winter in '47. It was impossible to believe that she was now standing almost at the place where her kin had died. Life here today appeared so normal, with children playing and priests running into the pub for the first drink of the day. It was as though the worst tragedy in the world had never occurred.

The congregation had completely dispersed. Ruby felt a gnawing inside her. She was hungry. Straightening the bike, she checked that her lunch was still intact in the basket and then rode through the village without stopping, just as her mother had done so many times before.

She saw the deserted cottage up on the cliff and began to walk towards it. Her heart was beating faster and she knew it was not from the exertion of the uphill walk, but from the anticipation of being in the place she had shared with her family. She would walk on the same turf, retrace her parents' steps and gaze out on the same view they had on countless occasions. She could feel the weight of that knowledge and of the anticipation weighing her down, slowing her steps.

As she neared the cottage, she held her breath. The door she had opened and closed a thousand times stood in front of her; would it be open? She hesitated as she extended her hand. Someone had fixed a bolt on the door that hadn't been there before. Had someone else moved in? It was impossible. The place was so obviously deserted. Her heart warmed at the sight of the rain butt and the washing line. These were her things and they made her heart soar with a sense of belonging. She half expected the bolt to be stuck, but with no effort at all it yielded to her hand and the house creaked a welcome as the door swung back on its hinges.

The black void of her past stood before her and she was afraid to step inside. The light from the open door scattered the sleeping shadows from their resting places as they made way for her to enter.

She whispered to herself, 'Move in, you eejit.' She needed to hear a real voice cut through the whispers, even if it was only her own. Her voice sounded strange. 'Hello, I'm back, I'm home,' she said in a voice, choked with tears and half smiled to herself. Drawing on all her reserves of bravery, she took one step into the house and was immediately swamped by so many long-forgotten memories jostling and competing for her attention, for space in her thoughts. And the noise of the voices, the laughter, the talking, the singing and the reading out loud, they were all there, waiting for someone to open the door and hear them. Ruby could not help herself, she stood on the threshold of her past and listened and watched as they came to life around her and a river of tears flooded her eyes.

As she slowly walked around the single large room, she saw the books that she and her mother had read together were still on the shelf on the wall above the range. They were damp from the ocean air and the lack of warmth in the house and they crumbled a little as she reached up to take them down. She opened one of the books and held it, barely able to read the words for the tears in her eyes. Pages slipped out and fell to the floor and as she bent down to retrieve them, a stamp on the inside cover startled her. Ballyford. The book had the same stamp as those in the castle library. It was there as plain as day. She looked inside the covers of all the other books on the shelf. They were all the same. Each one had once belonged to Ballyford Castle library.

'How? How did books from Ballyford library get here?'

She spoke out loud to the undulating shadows and looked around the room as if expecting an answer, but of course, there was none, only the familiar and eternal roar of the waves crashing against the shore at the bottom of the cliff.

Chapter eighteen

Ruby returned the bike to the stables and rested it against the tack room wall. She hid the books under the hay and would return for them early in the morning. She wanted to take them into the castle when the others were not around. There was no sign of Danny or any of the grooms or garden boys. She wondered should she put the bike back in the loose box, but she knew a litter of puppies had been born a few days before and were nestled in the straw. The staff would all be in the kitchen eating supper and Ruby, feeling hungry herself, hoped Amy would have saved her some.

As she passed the stable door the chestnut mare lifted her head from the manger and, with her ears pricked, snorted a greeting to Ruby.

'Are you still filling your belly?' laughed Ruby, kissing the mare's warm, velvet muzzle once again. Ending her day where it had begun. 'If Amy hasn't kept me any food, I'll be in here to join you.'

As Ruby gently stroked the white blaze on the mare's brow, she became aware that she was not alone. Someone was watching her and listening.

Feeling self-conscious her back stiffened and she turned to see if it was Danny, returning to the stable. Maybe he had heard her and wanted to put the precious bike away himself. Check that she hadn't caused any damage. But as the shadow moved away from the darkness of the kitchen garden wall opposite the stable, she saw that it wasn't Danny. It was Lord Charles.

'I'm sorry,' he said quickly, to reassure her. 'I didn't want to frighten you. I was in my study and I saw you cycle up the drive.'

He dropped his gaze and put his hands in his pockets. He looked uncomfortable. Ruby realized that he was waiting for her to speak.

'It is nearly dark,' she whispered, although no one would hear her. She hadn't whispered deliberately, her voice had failed her.

'Yes, it is. You are lucky to have made it. You took a risk there.' He lifted his head and smiled at her. The effect on her was so strong she thought she would faint. The air was filled with the heady smell of ocean night air and sweet hay, and she took a deep breath to steady her voice.

'I know, I'm sorry. I took longer than I thought I would.'

'Did you see the clerk? Did you knock on his door?' he asked her. 'I telephoned to let him know that you might.'

Ruby could hardly believe what she was hearing. He had done that for her? He had given her the bike, a day off and even telephoned Con? She was wholly unused to such acts of kindness. Her reaction to his words, her feelings of pleasure and gratitude for an act of kindness were familiar, like long lost friends returning.

'I saw them leaving church, before I went up to the house. I didn't know what to say to them. I wasn't sure if I would be welcome...'

Her voice trailed off. She felt ridiculous. He had gone to all that trouble and she hadn't been brave enough to introduce herself.

'Well, that's not a problem, is it? As long as you saw them. Maybe next time you could say hello. How was the house? I wondered how you would manage, with it having been empty for so long.'

Ruby leaned against the stable wall. She needed something to support and steady her. Lord Charles, a grown man, appeared to want to talk to her but Ruby was unused to talking to someone to whom her words mattered. She had to be careful now, every word she spoke was important because it would create an impression and she desperately wanted that impression to be a good one. She wanted him to like her.

He was older than she was and yet he also appeared so young. She studied his hair. It was thick, golden and fell across his forehead as he kicked the earth with the toe of his boot. He smiled at her again. 'I half thought you might not come back. That you would have some crazy idea to stay in Doohoma.'

Ruby felt her cheeks burn. How did he know? She was aware that they both shared something many others did not. They knew the deep pain of loss and they both also knew how it set them apart, made them different from others. Ruby knew it formed the basis of her relationship with Lady Isobel, even though the lady was from a very different upbringing.

'Was everything inside the house as you expected?' He

spoke again and she knew that she had been staring at him and dragged her eyes away.

'There was never much in there,' she half laughed. 'It was more, well, I suppose the memories.' She looked back at him sheepishly and then at the floor. She had no idea what the boundaries of this conversation might be. Was she expected to answer honestly, or to just listen and reply with single word answers? Was this a master–servant conversation or did Lord Charles really want to talk to her?

'It is the memories which are the worst,' he murmured.

'Yes, you are right. I will be honest with you, it wasn't my plan to return to Ballyford tonight,' she said boldly. 'I had intended to run away. But I would have returned the bike...' Her voice trailed away. Her words sounded ridiculous even to herself.

'Ah, but if I'm not mistaken, it's here that you belong, that's how you feel, isn't it Ruby? What changed your mind?'

His heart beat rapidly while he waited for her reply. He knew it was beyond comprehension, but he wanted her answer to include him. For him to have been a reason, or even part of a reason, for Ruby's return.

'I couldn't pedal back fast enough,' she said looking down at her hands, which she clasped and held in front of her. 'I felt driven away by the memories. They were too much for me. They all came at once and they, they...' Her voice trailed off again as she searched for the words.

'They swamped you,' he said. 'They swamped you and then you wanted to run away, to a different life and for you, the different life was here, at Ballyford.'

Ruby's jaw fell open. That was exactly what had happened. Words, at first slow and hesitant, now began to pour out. He had sought her out and spoken to her about her deepest, most personal secrets. She would speak to him as though she were his equal. She could tell that it was what he wanted.

'I could hear my mammy's voice, I even half expected to smell the dinner cooking in the pot hanging over the fire. It sounds insane, I know, but it was all there, everything, and I realized I didn't really want to be there. I wanted to come back, because being there meant facing it all over again and I didn't want to do that, really. At least here at Ballyford there's lots to distract me. Work to do and people who don't ask me awkward questions. People who know nothing, and you know in that there is some comfort, peace even. I can hide away.'

She lifted her head, boldly, to look directly at him, and to her dismay she thought she saw tears in his eyes. She couldn't be sure. The only light came from the library window above them, but she was almost certain.

'I know how that feels, Ruby,' he said quietly, 'wanting to run away from the place which holds the best and the worst of memories. I know just how that feels.'

Ruby felt an overwhelming longing to comfort him. To stretch out her arms and cradle him to her, to kiss the lines from his troubled brow. She breathed in deeply. It was an urge she had to suppress. His wife was her mistress, waiting for her in the nursery. It was her she had to return to, not him. She suddenly felt sick with guilt, disloyalty even, and yet all she had done was talk. It was the feelings she had towards him that made her feel troubled though she didn't even know what they truly were.

'I have to get back to Lady Isobel,' she said reluctantly.

'Yes, of course, off you go,' he replied, as though dismissing her somewhat impatiently.

She counted to three in her head. She had to walk normally. Pushing herself away from the stable wall, she stood upright. 'It's getting cold out here, are you coming inside yourself?' she said.

'I will in a moment, I will just stay and chat to the mare for a while. Sometimes she speaks more sense than I do.'

Then, for one fleeting moment, he reached out and lifted her hand. He placed his palm against hers and pressed, fusing the two together, and then he let her hand drop as though it had scorched him. They both stood for a moment, framed still in the glare of the moonlight, before she turned away from him and ran into the castle.

Chapter nineteen

'Is there any possibility that I might be fed anytime soon? Before I starve to death?'

Mr McKinnon had been good humoured to begin with, but as the preparations for the ball gathered momentum, he grew more and more exasperated by the disruption to the quiet and steady routine he had become used to during the barren and miserable years which followed the deaths of the Ballyford heirs.

'I had forgotten what all this ball malarkey was like,' he confessed to Amy one evening.

'Well, I for one am enjoying it,' Amy replied. 'What's all this space for, kitchen maids and pots and pans, the new range the size of Jack's cart and the like, if all I was using them for was to make the staff dinner? It was madness, Mr McKinnon, and you know it.'

Mr McKinnon carried the decanter of port from the dining table into the kitchen, carefully removed the stopper and laid it on a linen napkin. 'This won't keep, I think we had better not waste it, don't you?' he said.

Amy grinned and held out her glass.

'Aye, I do agree with you, Amy, it went on for a bit too long, the sadness and all. I remember Mrs McKinnon saying that if the curtains remained closed for much longer, we would all be blinded by the daylight when they were drawn back. All the same, I hope you're ready for it all to calm down again, once Lord FitzDeane returns to Liverpool. He's asked Mrs McKinnon to travel with him after the ball is over and to stay for a week or two, to staff up the Sefton Park town house and make sure they run it to Ballyford standards. He's a man of business. He needs more than the castle and the farm. It's shipping he's into. He tells me Liverpool looks to America for inspiration and that's what will secure the future of Ballyford. Personally, I think there is much more to it than that.'

Mrs McKinnon appeared back in the kitchen, after dealing with a spat between two of the garden boys, and dragged her chair closer to the fire to sit with them.

'Aye, it's true,' she said, 'nothing will turn him away from Liverpool, there's something dragging him there all right and it's more powerful than anything any one of us might say to him. He's asked me to find staff for the house and I was thinking, I might just go back to the convent where we found Ruby and take two of the girls from there. Two will be enough, if one of them can cook.'

Mr McKinnon filled a glass for his wife, while she pushed the chair cushion behind her.

'God, my back is giving me gyp this week. I know it's because of all the extra work.'

Amy passed Mrs McKinnon an extra cushion from her own chair. 'I don't suppose either of you are going to tell me what the notion is that's troubling Ruby, are you?' she said. 'I'm not daft, you know. I've known from the day she arrived that something is going on there. Since when have we had a servant who wasn't from one of our own tenants' cottages? God knows, there's enough to choose from, and since when have we needed someone who could read and write and with such a pretty hand for writing too? No, I know, you two are keeping secrets from me.'

Mr McKinnon inspected some imaginary mud on his shoe. He took the handkerchief out of his pocket and wetting the end with his tongue, bent down to wipe it off.

'You've mud all over your shoes,' Mrs McKinnon reprimanded her husband, bending down to take a look.

'I knew it,' Amy exclaimed, not taken in by their diversionary tactics. 'Ye shifty pair. Well, I'm waiting, if ye would be so good as to tell me one day, in your own time, mind. In the meantime I've enough to be going on with.'

Knowing when she was beaten, Amy changed the subject. 'I'm baking a cake, the shape of Lord FitzDeane's new ship it is, and I am icing it from the postcard Mr McKinnon brought me back from Liverpool. Would you both like to see it?'

'I've seen it just now in the cool room. I peeped in on my way back from the stables.' Mrs McKinnon laughed. ''Tis the best cake I have ever laid my eyes upon. How in God's name you managed to make it all so perfectly shaped, I have no idea. Lord Charles will be thrilled.'

'Yes,' Mr McKinnon said, 'that's his pride and joy now. He's very excited about her first voyage from Liverpool, but he is more sorry not to be there. Apparently things are moving much faster than he thought they would. He's been spending a great deal of time on the telephone to Rory Doyle who will stand in for him at the launch. Our Lord Charles is feeling a little miffed about that, I can tell.'

'Maybe he's learning sense then,' said Mrs McKinnon. 'There's nothing I would trust that Rory Doyle with.'

'Oh, I don't think it's trust that's the issue, Mrs McKinnon, more a general unhappiness that he won't be there to play his part. I'm most sorry to have to disappoint you on that score. He's actually looking forward to Rory Doyle's arrival.'

Mrs McKinnon groaned as Amy's eyes lit up, but only before a familiar look of pain slipped across her face.

'That shifty little blighter?' said Mrs McKinnon. 'Lord Charles is so soft, sometimes I want to knock his block off. How is it we can tell that Rory Doyle is a con man and Lord Charles can't?'

'My job is to watch Lord Charles's back, even though he doesn't realize it,' said Mr McKinnon. 'If there is anything untoward with Rory, rest assured, I shall surely spot it.'

'God, you two, you don't give up do you?' said Amy as she tipped back her head and downed her drink.

'Do you think maybe Ruby should go to Liverpool?' asked Mrs McKinnon, after Amy had gone to bed. 'I've noticed Jane has been awful shifty around Ruby. No one is as happy as they once were, not since she arrived.'

'Taking Ruby to Liverpool to run the house is the best idea you have had all day, Mrs Mack, although Lady Isobel will miss her.'

'I think it will be the perfect answer to our problem. Ruby may as well travel to Liverpool with us after the ball and whatever new girl we take from the convent school can go with her. Ruby will enjoy the responsibility.'

'Well, let's drink to that, Mrs McKinnon,' said her husband, his thoughts wandering to the comfort of their bed and the warming pan nestling between the sheets. 'I'll give you a head start,' he grinned, 'before I chase you up those stairs.'

'As if!' Mrs McKinnon put the empty glasses on the tray. 'It's been a long time since you chased me up any stairs.'

'Would you like me to?' Mr McKinnon placed the stopper back in the decanter and folded the napkin.

'No, I wouldn't, not at all,' she said. 'I like things just as they are.' And, with a smile born of a love which had begun in childhood and looked set to last into the final years of old age, they walked towards the stairs, holding hands.

Chapter twenty

Jane scowled when Ruby asked her to light the big fire in the library. But Ruby refused to be cowed.

'Shall I do it Jane? I'm not asking for myself, you know. The lady is so thin, she feels every draught.'

They both knew Jane would be in trouble if Mrs McKinnon found Lady Isobel alone, with Ruby lighting the library fire.

'No, you won't. The library fire is my job, keep out.'

Breakfast was over and as was usual on a Friday Dr Moynahan marched up the stairs. Ruby knew his visits irritated Lady Isobel. She never said so, but when he arrived she retreated into herself and her eyes became flat and lifeless. Sometimes she stood at the window and watched his car slowly retreat down the drive, having refused to stand up in his presence.

'Excellent!' Dr Moynahan announced with a flourish after he had examined Lady Isobel.

'I will have a word now with Lord FitzDeane, if that's possible,' he said to Ruby, folding up his stethoscope and putting it back in his Gladstone bag.

Ruby hesitated, rubbing her hands together nervously.

Lady Isobel turned to look at Ruby. She rarely spoke and when she did it was clear that it took a great deal of effort.

'Could you fetch Lord FitzDeane, please?'

Ruby went out through the nursery door and collided almost at once with Lord Charles, who had spotted the doctor's car from the breakfast room window.

'Whoa,' he said, taking hold of Ruby's arms. 'Are you all right?'

Ruby nodded towards the doctor.

'Good morning, Doctor,' said Lord FitzDeane, taking the doctor's hand in his own and shaking it warmly. 'How is Lady FitzDeane this morning? How do you feel, Isobel?'

Ruby noted that he always spoke to her as though she were a child who was slightly hard of hearing. She knew this sprang from concern, not malice, but she often thought how irritating she would find it and that if she were Lady Isobel she would tell him so.

'Well now, I would say Lady Isobel was much improved,' Dr Moynahan enthused. 'Ruby here tells me she has eaten well this morning and has even developed an appetite and that she's fighting fit.'

Ruby's mouth opened and closed, but she did not speak. That was not quite what she had said. She had merely told the doctor that Lady Isobel had eaten the meals she had prepared for her.

'She has improved so much,' the doctor went on. 'Her heart sounds so much stronger. I think it is time to take you off the night-time sedation, Lady FitzDeane. We can also accelerate your improvement if we move into the morning

228

room completely now and abandon the nursery. It is my opinion that being in this room, surrounded by all of this...' he waved his hands at the photographs of their precious sons, '... is having a detrimental effect and will impede your recovery. I would also like to recommend a brisk walk around the park for thirty minutes one way and then thirty minutes back along the other side each morning.'

Ruby found it difficult to keep an expression of doubt from her face. Her instincts told her that Lady Isobel's heart was not much stronger. It was true that Lady Isobel looked and sounded better, and had put on a few pounds, but she was still thin and frail. Ruby knew Lady Isobel could not possibly manage such a strenuous routine. The doctor was truly mad.

'What excellent news, don't you think so, Isobel?'

Charles looked down at his passive and unresponsive wife. Only Ruby knew that Lady Isobel was absorbing what she had heard and it would be another thirty seconds or so before she replied, if at all.

If Ruby hadn't been in the room, Charles would have addressed his wife as darling, but while Ruby was present he felt inhibited. She was watching him and the words stuck in his throat. He swallowed hard.

Bumping into Ruby had been a difficult moment for him. Only he knew that an hour earlier, alone in his bed, he had dreamt of her. He thought of her before he had even opened his eyes. It seemed to him that the more he tried to stop thinking about her, the more she invaded his thoughts. Being at Ballyford was becoming more difficult by the day. He was alone. He had no one to share his life with at Ballyford and now there was Ruby. His feelings for her were growing and consuming him, adding to his torment.

Isobel nodded, slowly, two reluctant half nods. She had not the energy this morning to walk, or even to argue. Ruby thought she looked as though she were thinking about something else entirely.

'How about trying the walk today, Isobel. Do you think that's a good idea, Ruby?' said Lord Charles.

'I think that is an excellent idea,' said Dr Moynahan, ignoring the fact that it was Ruby who had been asked. 'Let's start right away.'

Ruby avoided looking at either Lord Charles or the doctor. Instead, she looked straight at Lady Isobel. 'I shall fetch your outdoor clothes and shoes shall I, m'lady?' She was giving Lady Isobel the opportunity to say no. *Tell them to get lost and take a walk themselves*, thought Ruby.

Instead, Lady Isobel smiled at her. Her new breezy, devil-may-care smile. One that Ruby could tell, had taken some effort. 'Let's try shall we,' she replied obligingly and Ruby wanted to slap the doctor as she saw the self-satisfied smile spread across his face.

Lord FitzDeane walked the doctor to the top of the stairs.

'It is a relief that the anger has disappeared,' he said. 'I don't mind telling you that sometimes I feared for my own safety.'

'Well, you could have had her committed to the asylum. I'm not sure that wouldn't have been the best thing. They are trying a great new treatment using electric shocks, administered through a metal plate attached to the skull and apparently the results are quite impressive. They are using it in America and England, though 'tis not used so much here in Ireland yet.'

'I want to do the best for my wife, but I know her delicate nature would never withstand conditions in the asylum. Far better we deal with things here and keep it within the family. It's the way we do things, Dr Moynahan.'

'Indeed, but you must keep your mind open, much progress is being made since the war, things are altering faster than I can keep up with.'

Charles nodded thoughtfully and added politely, 'I hope you and your good wife will be able to accept the invitation and join us at the Ballyford Ball?'

The doctor beamed. Failure to be included on the guest list would have meant a month of misery at home with his wife. Everyone in Mayo knew that he looked after Lady Isobel. Not to be invited would suggest that the FitzDeanes were less than happy with his ministrations.

After the doctor had left, Charles wondered if he should help Ruby to walk Isobel and then realized that for entirely equal and opposing reasons he didn't want to be near either woman.

He had to return to Liverpool. He felt an overwhelming urge to flee. To return to his false life and his business. Plans for the ball were underway, he could be spared for a few days and return in plenty of time. Anyway, he felt uneasy about not being present to watch the arrival and delivery of the ship. Rory had not sounded himself on the telephone and it bothered him. He also wanted to place some distance between himself and his confused feelings for Ruby.

Half an hour later, he summoned McKinnon to his study. Charles was cramming papers into his case haphazardly and pushing the lid down in an attempt to force it closed when Mr McKinnon tapped on the door.

'Come in, McKinnon. Can you bring the car round to the front and take me to the station to catch the train to Dublin? I have to return home for the launch of the *Marianna*. Rory Doyle has been going great guns. But don't worry, I will be back in plenty of time for the ball, way ahead of any guests arriving.'

'Well, Mrs McKinnon will be pleased to hear that you will be back and there isn't anything we can't do in your absence. Between Mrs McKinnon and Amy, most of the preparation has already been done.'

'Good man, McKinnon. All the clothes I need are in Liverpool. I only have this case.'

Ruby had painstakingly taken every step with Lady Isobel. They had been outdoors for almost an hour and the rain was beginning to soak right through to Ruby's undergarments. Her outdoor coat was nowhere near as warm as Lady Isobel's and despite her determination to complete the task set by Dr Moynahan, she knew that Mrs McKinnon would skin her alive if she made herself or the mistress unwell for the ball. Ruby was needed to work, Lady Isobel to shine.

Suddenly she heard the car motoring towards them along the drive. It came to a halt and Lord Charles jumped out of the passenger side and sprinted across the lawn to them both.

'I have to leave for Liverpool on business, but I will be back in plenty of time for the ball. Keep safe won't you and if you need anything, as always, McKinnon has all the numbers.'

Mr McKinnon was using the back of his gloved hand to wipe the condensation from the inside of the windscreen. He dipped his head so that he could see Ruby more clearly through the open passenger door and raised his hand to her in greeting. Ruby thought she saw a look of pity cross his face. The rain had become much heavier over the last five minutes.

'For goodness sake, make haste indoors, both of you,' said Charles. 'You look soaked through and you'll catch your death in this weather.'

Ruby knew that he had been looking straight at her. She wanted to reply, 'It's the cold that brings your death, not a bit of rain,' but instead, as the car engine started up, she linked arms with Lady Isobel once more and led her towards the house.

The horn sounded as the car approached the bend in the drive and Ruby turned around. The rain was now torrential and every part of her was soaked. Her hair hung around her face and blinded her. Miserably, she lifted her hand to push the hair away from her eyes and looked down the drive. She could just make out Lord Charles's face, his hand wiping the back window, his eyes fixed upon them and Ruby could tell, even from that distance, it was her his eyes were fixed on, not Lady Isobel.

Seconds later, Mrs McKinnon was fussing around them both.

'For goodness sake, get to your room and take those clothes off. Jane, see to Lady Isobel. Put her coat on a hanger and bring it down to the boot room to dry. Danny, light a fire in there now. What madness possessed you to stay out in the rain this long?'

Ruby had no answer. She had felt wretched and lost in her own thoughts and hadn't even noticed the deluge, until it was too late. Lady Isobel had made no objection, but then, she never would. She probably hadn't even noticed.

In half an hour, with her hair towelled dry and wearing fresh clothes, Ruby stood in front of the fire in the kitchen. Amy handed her a mug of soup.

'Is Lady Isobel all right?' she asked Amy, anxiously.

'Of course she is. She was wearing a waterproof mackintosh and a hat. Her hair was wet, mind, but not as wet as yours and do you think she has asked after you? Not a bit of it. Betsy has looked after her and she's sat as warm as toast in front of the nursery fire.'

Ruby felt irked. Didn't Amy realize?

'I imagine she's as concerned about me as she can be, Amy,' said Ruby. 'Don't be too harsh on her.'

'For a feisty madam, you are too soft for your own good, sometimes.'

'I need to get back upstairs, I'll take her lunch with me.'

As Ruby pushed the trolley into the nursery, Lady Isobel suddenly spoke in a very clear and strong voice, so strong that it stopped Ruby and the trolley in their tracks.

'When the doctor comes next week, Ruby, tell him I won't receive him and don't allow him into my room. No more visits from the doctor, thank you and will you tell Mrs McKinnon that I said so?'

'I will, Lady Isobel, but what about the ball?'

'I shall still go to the ball. It's too late for me to do anything about that, Ruby. Mrs McKinnon tells me the invitations have been posted already. Maybe she's right anyway, she is a good woman.'

Exhausted by the effort of the walk, Lady Isobel closed her eyes, lay her head back on the cushion and, once again, slept.

Chapter twenty-one

Jack couldn't read very well, and when Amy handed him a list for the supplies she needed from Dublin, he was desperate for her not to discover his weakness. Amy's writing was bold and distinctive and Jack recognised the square heavy letters, he just couldn't string them together to make any sense.

'Sure, well, that all looks easy enough now,' he said, the list in one hand and a mug of tea in the other, as he sat at the kitchen table.

'Make sure they pack plenty of ice around those,' said Amy, jabbing her finger at a line on the paper. 'We don't want anyone being sick. I have plenty arriving on the day, but this is all I need for the preparation.'

Betsy was sat next to Jack and leant over to look at the list. Both she and Jack knew neither of them could read, it was all guesswork. 'Two heads are better than one though,' Betsy whispered to Jack, with a wink.

'Will ye take me with you Jack?' Mary ran to the side of the table and jumped up and down. 'Please, I've never been to Galway in me life, sure I would love to go.' Poor Mary said the same thing every time someone left the castle.

'Don't be daft, Mary,' said Betsy. 'How many times do we have to tell you? Mrs McKinnon would be scared stiff to let you out in Galway, she would be worried someone would steal you. The tinkers, they do that you know. You have lovely blue eyes and gorgeous hair.' Betsy grinned at Mary.

Mary was so thrilled with the compliment that she almost cried. 'Do I, Betsy?' she said, her eyes beginning to water. 'Do I really?'

'Yes, ye do, now go away and stop bothering Jack. I've told you, there's no way they will let ye go. Besides, Amy loves ye so much, she would never stop crying and the ball would be cancelled and everyone would be so sad.' Betsy didn't dare tell Mary yet that both she and Ruby were planning that one day they would somehow get Mary to Galway.

Amy came up behind Mary and whipped her across the back of the legs with the tea towel. 'You are a dozy dote, Mary. Get the rest of the bread out while I go through the list with Jack.'

Even Amy's reprimand could not wipe the look of pleasure from Mary's face. Betsy had said she had lovely blue eyes and that Amy really loved her. Such words would carry her through her chores all day.

Betsy returned to the list. 'We have a load of ice in the icehouse, Jack. We should ask Jimmy to start sawing some of it up into lumps. We need a heap of it to stop the food going off and people being sick.'

'God in heaven, no, we don't want that, of course, lots of ice,' said Jack, screwing his eyes up and trying to see if he could recognize any of the letters on the list. There was one thing of which he was sure: he had never seen most of the words before.

'Here, give the list to me,' said Mrs McKinnon as she walked over to the table, snatching it out of his hand and scribbling something along the bottom with a pen.

Jack's brow furrowed. Mrs McKinnon's sharp eyes diagnosed the problem at once. She knew instantly what to do.

'Do you know, Jack, I reckon there is a lot on this list and you might need a woman's opinion on some of it. Those quail's eggs for instance...' She pointed to the same item Amy had shown him a moment earlier. 'And the silver sugar balls and the gelatine for the trifles, I'm not even sure you will be able to find them. Why don't I send one of the girls with you?'

A look of relief crossed Jack's face.

'Do you want me to go Mrs McKinnon?' Betsy's face lit up and Mrs McKinnon's heart sank. What was the point of sending Betsy, she couldn't read either.

'No, sadly not you, Betsy, not on this occasion.'

Betsy appeared to shrink into the chair as disappointment crossed her face.

'For pity's sake, you're not thinking I have the time to spend a day travelling to Dublin and back are you?' said Amy. Her voice was pitched high in alarm. 'Even in Jack's new van I don't have that time to spare. Everything would fall apart if I left the kitchen, so close to the ball.'

'No, of course not,' said Mrs McKinnon, who was helping herself to a warm biscuit from the plate Amy had just put on the table. 'I was thinking of Ruby, maybe? What do you think?'

Just at that moment, Jane walked in through the door.

'Ruby what? Why in God's name is everyone always talking about Ruby?' Jane flounced onto one of the stools and picked up an oat biscuit from the plate without asking first and before she bit into it, scowled at everyone around her. Even Amy didn't feel like taking on Jane this morning.

'Well, I'm going to be spending much of tomorrow with Lady Isobel,' said Mrs McKinnon, ignoring Jane. 'Mrs Barrett, the tailor's wife, is calling up to the castle in the morning from Bangor Erris to alter one of her gowns. We've almost finished everything I put on the cleaning list, and we can easily spare Ruby and she's good at maths, she can add up well too.'

Amy took little persuasion. Her worst nightmare, with only days left until the ball, would be Jack returning without one of her main ingredients.

'I agree,' she said.

Jack nodded enthusiastically. 'Sounds like a grand idea to me,' he said. 'I would be a little nervous leaving some of these things in the van whilst I went in and out of the shops on me own. God, ye have no idea how bad it is in Galway. It's getting as bad as Dublin now. Sin runs mad through those streets, with no shame. The worst kind of people, tinkers, thieves and beggars, you can't turn your back for a minute. Rob the coat off yer back they would. A man just isn't safe in Galway, 'tis a terrible place.'

Mrs McKinnon wondered what Jack would make of Edinburgh, the city of her birth, or Liverpool or London even. It always amused her how those in the west of Ireland regarded

Galway and Dublin as places to fear, when she found Galway to be the friendliest city on earth.

'Well, if we are all agreed, I shall inform Ruby of the plans for the morning, then.'

Jane sat down at the table. Her resentment had been building by the day. 'What do you need to tell Ruby and not me? She's the newest here and it's all Ruby, Ruby, Ruby. No one has ever had anything to talk to me about. I think I would like to have been the one looking after Lady Isobel, seems like an easy job to me. Why wasn't I asked, Mrs McKinnon?'

'Ruby's coming with me to Galway, Jane,' said Jack. 'To help me with Amy's shopping list for the ball – it's her brains I'm needing. Now, if it was jolly company I was looking for, tis you I would have taken, for sure.'

'Really? But why her and not me?' Jane looked at Mrs McKinnon. How could she reply, *Because you can't read either, Jane, and would be no use to Jack*?

'Well, there is good reason, Jane,' said Mrs McKinnon, pausing while she racked her brains for an explanation that would not offend.

Amy beat her to it.

'Because you are as thick as the muck heap at the back of the stable and would bring back all the wrong things and then I would have to kill you with my bare hands.'

'Slightly less tactful than I would have liked, thank you, Amy,' said Mrs McKinnon, frowning sharply.

As Mrs McKinnon climbed the stairs, she thought that it might be a relief to shift Jane off to Liverpool instead of Ruby. Jane was becoming increasingly surly and difficult to handle and she would miss Ruby badly if she left. 'Never mind,' she sighed to herself. 'Another week and we will all be back to normal.'

Ruby had just finished giving Lady Isobel her breakfast when Mrs McKinnon walked in to the nursery.

'Morning, Lady Isobel,' Mrs McKinnon said brightly. 'We have the tailor's wife calling in tomorrow from Bangor Erris. They are to alter the gown we chose for the ball and she and her husband will stay here until the job is done. If it is all right with you, I'm going to send Ruby here into Galway with Jack.'

Lady Isobel smiled wanly, a smile that gave Mrs McKinnon an inordinate amount of pleasure.

'That will be a fun day,' said Ruby to Mrs McKinnon. 'Well, I'm glad it's Mrs Barrett and not her husband. He would drive us mad with talk of the football. He runs the boys' club in Bangor Erris and they say there are only two things he can talk about: the price of a suit and the results from the weekend.'

Lady Isobel gave one of her rare laughs and rose from the sofa. 'Well, I'm also relieved in that case,' she said, as she left the room.

'She's doing so well, isn't she?' said Mrs McKinnon barely keeping the glee from her voice as she plumped up the sofa cushions and Ruby cleared the breakfast things onto the tray.

'She is, yes,' said Ruby, although there was an element of hesitation in her voice. Ruby wanted to tell Mrs McKinnon that she simply didn't believe in this new, perkier Lady Isobel. How could she say, her mouth talks but her eyes cry? No, Ruby did not believe this was a genuine improvement. It was an illusion brought about by an enormous effort. It was false, of that she was sure, but she did not quite know why.

Downstairs, Amy had divided the kitchen into three areas of preparation and had taken on four girls from the tenant farms to help. A haze of flour and the smell of almond paste hung permanently in the air and shrouded the kitchen in a grey mist. Everything was ready for the moment when the maids of honour and apple charlottes needed to be loaded into the oven for baking.

Jane, Danny and the remaining servants had left to go about their duties and the four kitchen girls were in the scullery cleaning the copper pans and china for the table, while two boys, specially hired for the occasion, were cleaning the silver, a chore that would take them the entire week to complete.

Jack was deliberately slow with his tea, as Amy busied around the table clearing away the staff plates and mugs. He took his own mug and stood next to her.

'Oh, Jesus, you crept up on me, there.' Amy jumped.

'With feet my size, that's not something I do very often,' said Jack, placing his mug on the wooden drainer. 'Amy, you know what I want, don't you? I think it would work well, me and you. We would make a grand couple altogether. What do you think, would you consider it? Go on, would ye?'

Amy looked at him. 'I'm not who you think I am, Jack,' she whispered. 'I am no virgin, to be sure. I'm a broiler, not a roaster.'

Jack didn't look in the least shocked. 'Well, I am no virgin, either, so we would be the same there. At least we would know what we was doing. Have you been to confession?'

Amy slapped him playfully on the arm with the dishcloth. 'Of course I have, the following morning, every time.'

Jack was now genuinely shocked. 'What, ye've done it more than once? Jesus, you need to be married quick woman, to save ye from yerself!' He grinned at her and then added, 'Go on Amy, I know all about Rory Doyle, but Jesus, that was a long time ago and he's long gone and anyway, ye were just a girl. Let me, simple Jack, look after you. I have a very nice house and a new van, 'tis the best around here and I'm thinking of getting my own cow.'

Amy almost laughed, but she could see that Jack was deadly serious.

'Merciful Mother, Jack. Have I waited all this time to be proposed to wearing an apron up to me elbows in soapy water in the sink with a promise of a cow? Get out of my kitchen, go on.'

'Not until you give me an answer,' said Jack.

Amy moved a big pan around in the sink, shook the water off her arms and picked up a towel to dry her hands.

'I'll promise you this,' she said, smiling up at him. 'I will give you me answer after the ball is over, when I've had a bit of time to think. 'Tis a big question you have asked me, Jack, and I don't want to give ye the wrong answer. We can't rush into this. Marry in haste, repent at leisure, isn't that what they say?'

Jack couldn't conceal his disappointment and knowing he was potentially only days away from rejection, he took the audacious move of taking a step closer to Amy and kissing her on the lips.

'That was a bit of a liberty!' said Amy, when at last he pulled away, but at that very moment Danny burst in through the back door.

'The salmon, they're jumping,' he shouted.

'Well, thank God for that,' said Amy. 'My prayers are answered. I need twenty for the table.'

Amy and Jack stood at the back door and watched as the stable boys all ran together towards the river, laughing, shouting and throwing their caps in the air.

'There's no better place to live than here ye know, Amy,' said Jack. 'We all spend our lives looking into the distance, thinking we've missed something, wondering if being somewhere else entirely would make us happier than we are today and do you know what I think makes us happy?'

Amy put her hands into her apron pocket and looked at Jack. 'I can't know, Jack, because I don't think I've been happy for a very long time.'

'Well, I might be able to help you there. Knowing where you belong, and who you belong with, that helps. Looking at what is around you and realizing how lucky you are and appreciating everything you do have and not feeling sad about what you don't. There isn't one person at Ballyford who doesn't think there is something better lying beyond the river for them. Even Lord Charles, look at him, with his new shipping empire, when all along, he has the best in the world right here on his own doorstep. I know I'm not as grand as those paintings on the wall in the castle and I don't have a fortune or a big ship, but I'm here, in the place where you belong and I'm waiting for your answer, Amy, I'm waiting for you, for me to make you happy. When I stand at those pearly gates, me and the Lord and anyone else, we will all be stood there just the same, wearing and carrying what we came into the world with, which was nothing and all that will have mattered was who we spent our time with.'

Amy blushed. 'Go on, get going, ye daft lump. I need ye here early tomorrow to collect Ruby and get going to Galway.'

Jack wandered to the saddlestone, lifted his reins and climbed up onto his cart.

'Well, I've waited for years. A week won't hurt,' he said to his cob, as he trotted her on towards the gate to collect the milk churns and begin his day's work.

Chapter twenty-two

Liverpool

Charles woke and for a brief moment he was confused. He forced his mind to focus on his whereabouts before he opened his eyes. He heard the noise of the horse-drawn milk float trundling down the cobbled street. The sound of the glass bottles jangling sounded much louder than they actually were and pierced through his beer-fuddled brain and he sat up quickly. He had arrived back in Liverpool last night, changed almost immediately and was out on the town within the hour.

Now, a feeling of guilt flooded in and his first thought was of Ruby.

'Aggh, Ruby, Ruby, Ruby, Ruby,' he said to himself in anguish. 'Why did I ever go looking for you?'

He wondered how Ruby felt about him, a man in his thirties. She probably found him repulsive. He doubted there were many women like Stella.

'I far prefer older men, much more stable and reliable,' she had told him. 'I've moved out of me ma's, but she 'as her spies everywhere, she'd kill me if she knew what we was up to.'

She would indeed, he thought as feeling of self-loathing swamped him.

Charles wondered how what had what seemed so exciting in the evening could feel so sordid in the cold light of day. His dalliance with Stella had failed to heal him in the usual way. It had not cleared his mind or made him forget. He let his thoughts wander to their journey up the stairs and her enthusiasm to remove as many of his clothes as fast as possible, and his own to do the same with hers.

Once it was all over, Charles felt around on the floor, located his trousers and his cigarettes and matches. He always left his silver lighter at home on his away nights. He lit two cigarettes and passed one over to Stella. As he exhaled, he realized he had forgotten nothing. It was all still there persistent and nagging. Ballyford, the ball and Ruby.

'What'ya like at smoke rings then? Bet I can do a better one than you,' said Stella, interrupting his thoughts.

Charles had no idea what Stella was talking about.

'Me record is eight on one drag, what's yours?'

'Eight sounds a bit excessive,' said Charles.

'Oh my giddy aunt, where d'ya learn to talk with big words like that?' She leant up on one elbow, shyly pulling the pink candlewick bedspread up to cover the breasts he had almost eaten, only moments before.

Charles pulled deeply on his cigarette. 'Just 'avin' a laugh,' he said, grinning at her. 'Go on then, show me your best effort.'

She lay flat on her back. 'Don't breathe near me, you'll blow them off,' she warned, giving him a very stern and serious look, before exhaling eight perfect smoke rings.

Grinning and proud of her achievement, she sat up in bed cross-legged and flicked the ash away from Charles. 'Go on then, show me yours.'

'I will,' said Charles, 'with the next one. Is there an ashtray?'

'Yeah, down 'ere on the floor by my side of the bed.' Charles handed her his cigarette so that she could extinguish it.

The only light came from the glow of the Victorian street lamp directly outside the window. Charles could make out a sink in the corner of the room, and a Formica-topped table nearby, which appeared to be covered in dishes and food. A loaf of bread stood exposed on a board, with a bread knife lying next to it, while a hard-backed chair stood near the window with what looked like a small pile of clothes, folded on the seat. There was an unlit fire hearth in the corner, which smelt acrid. There was very little else. The room was cold and his breath formed white clouds that mingled with the smoke. Charles thought that the girls in service at Ballyford lived in better conditions than this.

'Where d'ya work, then?' Stella asked him, breaking into his thoughts. 'What's yer wage?'

Charles thought hard. Liverpool girls did not surprise him. Their forthright openness used to take him by surprise, but not any longer. He had recently agreed a wage with Kimble, who ran his office. He had an answer.

'Ten pounds and eight shillings a week.'

'Do yer?' She had turned to look at him with eyes wide. 'No wonder you were flashin' the cash in the pub, that's smashin' that. That's better than at Plessey's on nights. Who d'ya work for?'

Another question. She had no notion of social boundaries, but then neither did any of the girls he had met. He could talk to Liverpool girls for hours and never be bored.

He thought of the following day and the publicity that had been arranged for the launch of the ship. He said the first thing that crossed his mind.

'The *Echo*,' he replied. I work for the *Echo*.'

'Oh, go'way, do yer? My cousin, Tommy, he works for the *Echo*. A photographer he is. Really good. Does all the family occasions, weddings, christenings and the like. If me and you get married, he can do ours.'

Charles knew that there was only one way to distract her from this train of thought, so he flipped her onto her back and disappeared under the bedspread, reminding her to keep quiet as he did so.

'In case yer mam's spies hear you,' he said, in his pseudo-scouse accent.

'Oh my God, what'yer doin', where are you goin'? I've never 'eard of that before, you dirty beggar. Can I get caught like that?' They were her last coherent words for the next half an hour.

When he finally slipped from her bed, she begged him to stay.

'I can't,' he replied gently. 'Tell you what though, Stella, I'll meet you back in the pub soon, eh? Keep an eye out for me.'

'Promise,' she whispered back sleepily. '"Cause if I'm pregnant, you'll wanna know won't you. I can tell you're the kind of fella who will wanna do the right thing. Won't you?'

'Course I would love, see you soon,' he replied, before he was away and back out onto the street, looking for a cab.

Later, back in his own bed, Charles heard the grandfather clock in the hallway chime eight o'clock and it suddenly dawned on him that he was due at the dockside in half an hour.

Today was a big day. The *Marianna* was due to sail out of Liverpool and they were holding a press and launch party in the Liverpool Swan building, two hours before the bore took her back down the Mersey, and out onto the Irish Sea, on the first step of her journey across the Atlantic to America.

Mrs Bat stood at the bottom of the stairs outside the morning room door, like a sentinel guarding the gates of hell. Her bony shoulders quivered like the black nubs of wings as she looked up at him in disapproval. She always dressed in black, dour and foreboding. Once again he wondered if she slept in a bed or simply refreshed herself, hung upside down on the hallstand.

'You came home past midnight,' she said, disapprovingly. 'You didn't lock the front door properly and the hallway smelt of alcohol and sin. You can't pull the wool over my eyes.'

For a delicious moment, Charles wondered what she would think if he brought Stella back home for an evening. He pictured her suspender belt and stockings lying on the stairs to her flat and wondered what Mrs Bat would have said or done, if they had been here in the Sefton Park house instead.

'I heard you and checked and just as well I did, or we could have all been murdered in our beds.'

'I really would not be that lucky,' muttered Charles, as he removed the silver dome from his breakfast plate. Underneath were two nearly black slices of bacon and two rubbery eggs swimming in a puddle of almost solidified cold fat. In her interview, she had told him she was possibly the best cook in Liverpool. He shuddered at the thought of how bad the others must be.

He thought of Ballyford and the pork sausages made from his own pigs and the bacon which he could smell cooking each morning as the servants' door opened out onto the landing from the kitchen. The large brown eggs laid by his chickens in the stables were carried into the kitchen early each morning in a basket by Danny. As Charles buttered the cold, toasted bread, in his mind he smelt the fresh bread baked by Amy before anyone else had woken. He thought about the laughter he often heard coming from outside in the kitchen garden. The memory of Ruby's laughter broke through and his heart lurched. He was almost relieved when he heard the telephone ringing.

'Morning, m'lord, it's McKinnon here. The salmon are in.'

'Damn,' Charles exclaimed down the phone. It was always a moment of joy when he joined the staff and they ran to the river. He had thought this year that maybe the river was too low and they would have problems.

'That's fantastic news, McKinnon, and a relief to Amy I imagine. It is the launch today, but I'll be on the first boat back in the morning I'll net a few of those salmon myself. Will you meet me in Dublin?'

'I will that, Lord Charles. Everything is ready here.'

At Ballyford, McKinnon replaced the handset and sighed. It had been a long time since Lord Charles had sounded pleased to be coming home and it was the salmon that had done it.

'Have you told him?' Mrs McKinnon asked. She was polishing a brass table lamp in the hall. He couldn't see a mark anywhere and he was sure he had seen her doing exactly the same thing only a few days before.

'I have indeed and he said he cannot wait to return home. He was excited about the salmon. Perhaps he's also got the taste for Amy's cooking again. Maybe, just like you said, this ball is going to turn things around. I can already feel things slipping back into place. Slowly, mind, but if you think what it was like here six months ago and how everyone is today...'

Mrs McKinnon went on rubbing her lamp, thoughtfully.

'I hope you have your wish ready for when the genie appears,' said McKinnon, walking back through the baize door.

'Oh, I do that,' muttered Mrs McKinnon. 'I do that.'

On the dockside Charles spotted Rory Doyle immediately and shouted out a greeting.

'Rory, over here.'

They shook hands enthusiastically.

'There's a bit of a crowd gathering at the gate,' said Charles. 'The nationals are here, I met the man from *The Times* in the Grand and the *Liverpool Echo* are giving us a front page spread. They asked me did I think we could compete with *Cunard* and *White Star*. I thought it best to be humble and told them I hoped so.'

'They have all gone mad,' said Rory. 'The *Liverpool Echo* have written a full-page spread on the laundry, can you imagine that?'

'The laundry?' Charles looked surprised. 'Good Lord, why?'

'Well, the laundry for the ships in Liverpool is all serviced by the Chinese community. We have given them an extra seven thousand towels and they have washed and starched all the uniforms for the officers and crew.'

Charles was amazed by the number of people thronging around the Huskisson Dock gate entrance. The landing stage was heaving with a throng of passengers and luggage. Cab drivers were unloading car boots and piles of chests stood there, many of them labelled, *Wanted on voyage.*

The dock road was full of taxis delivering passengers from the hotels and last minute fresh provisions were being delivered to the ship's kitchen stores.

'Look at the balloons,' Charles shouted to Rory. 'Kimble, Miss Taylor and the staff have done a fantastic job. The best thing we did was to pinch them from our competitors. Now that you and Nathan have finished sorting all the legal documentation, you can concentrate on the operational side of the business. It is going to be hard work, but such fun, taking on the big boys like *Cunard* and *White Star.* I bet they are hopping mad that we're undercutting them on price. I have heard that they have almost two hundred free berths on their crossing on Saturday, thanks to ours leaving today.'

Rory felt no guilt about what he and Nathan had planned. He knew he was a cad. It was the survival of the fittest and anyway, wouldn't Kimble and Miss Taylor simply be taken back by the *White Star* or *Cunard*? Of course they would. All of the staff would be fine.

Apprehension sat in Rory's gut like stale vomit. His men had already left yesterday to head out to the place where they knew they would be most needed.

'Don't move in too quickly,' Rory had told the captain. 'We don't want anyone thinking you was waiting there. Nothing must go wrong. Wait until the last possible minute. Just make sure no other salvage boat gets there first. The captain of the *Marianna* is our man. He knows just what to do. You have no worries there. Take your time. He's expecting you.'

He said now, 'The first class passengers were allocated their cabins first thing this morning. Everyone is boarding now. We are breaking the mould, only having two classes, when the *White Star* has five. God knows where those in the lowest class sleep.' Then he added, 'You haven't used up all of Ballyford's money on this venture have you, Charles?'

A frown crossed Charles's face. He wasn't used to talking about money with anyone other than his accountant. Rory had been his friend since childhood, they had grown up together, but it still felt unnatural.

'I have used all my own capital, but what does it matter? Every cabin is sold for the next two months. At this rate, every penny will be paid back within two years and then the business will be in profit. Three years from now we'll have our own fleet, and in ten years we will be the dominant shipping line sailing out of Liverpool to America. It's all in the plan Rory, all in the plan.'

As they made their way into the building, the cameras began to flash and journalists started asking for quotes. Rory froze in horror. He had much to hide and many people to hide from. The last thing he wanted was for his picture to appear in either the national or local press. He now dropped back behind Kimble.

'Stop being shy,' laughed Charles. 'This is our big day, Rory.'

'No, not at all, this is all your baby, Charles.'

Charles was about to object, until Kimble turned to Rory.

'The captain of the ship is waiting to speak to you, Mr Doyle.'

Rory felt beads of cold perspiration gathering on his top lip. He knew his face had paled and his mouth was as dry as tinder. The stupid man, he thought, he has asked for me, now they can connect us. I cannot talk to the captain.

His heart was beating rapidly and his chest felt as tight as a drum.

'Yes, I've already spoken to him,' said Charles, 'I told him there were two owners and that you were on your way. It's the accepted thing to do, I believe. Makes the captain look important in front of the crew. After all, he's the man in charge of our assets from today onwards, so we'd better keep him happy.'

Rory felt himself begin to breathe again. The die was cast. Soon, he would be a very rich man and Charles would have lost everything.

'Turn to face the camera, please, Lord FitzDeane,' shouted the photographers.

The secretary, Miss Taylor stood primly at Charles side, frowning at the cameras. Suddenly she noticed a young woman at the very front of the crowd of bystanders behind the roped off area to the side of the customs hall. She was waving frantically at Lord Charles.

'Charlie, it's me, Stella,' she shouted. 'Hiya, it's me, Stella. Come and get me, the bastards won't let me through.'

As she jumped up and down on the spot, they were all blinded by the sudden popping of the flash.

Later, Charles sat with Stella in the Lyons tea rooms. He ordered her tea and handed her his pristine and folded handkerchief. He was trying his hardest to explain everything, but it was apparent that he would need to go through it all again. He beckoned the waitress over for a second pot of tea. Stella sniffed and cried and dabbed her eyes with his handkerchief. For a moment, he found himself comparing her with Ruby who, despite her start in life, or maybe because of it, appeared altogether more mature and robust.

'Look, it's not easy to explain, but I will try again. Do you think, if my sons had lived, I would be dressing up in pawnshop clothes and hanging out in spit and sawdust dockers' pubs? No, I wouldn't, Stella. I would be the proudest and happiest father alive. I would be happily occupied. My days would be spent riding across Ballyford land hunting, fishing and farming. I would have been planning trips abroad, employing tutors, worrying about their every waking moment. But fate robbed me of all that and it is a cross I have to bear.

'But you were not a cross to bear, Stella. You were fun and lovely and happy. I loved my time with you. If you had known who I was, you would never have trusted me. There are times when I have to escape, or I would go mad. My lovely uncomplicated Stella, you made everything easier. When I was with you, I was another person.'

Stella stared at him. 'Go on,' she said, her eyes widening at the sight of the cakes now arriving at the table.

Charles felt a sense of relief that Stella had calmed down.

'I can see a light now. Perhaps Isobel is even repairing.' He knew that was a lie. He knew it was Ruby who was bringing him to his senses. Ruby who had lifted the atmosphere at Ballyford and chased away the ghosts.

'Did she blame you? It can't have been all your fault. Takes two to tango, Charlie.'

'Well, I think she might be finding a way to live without the awful shroud of guilt. To keep the death of our boys somewhere to one side, so that she can function, up to a point at least. Do you understand?'

'Do I understand? I can't even understand half of what you're sayin', Charlie.' Stella remembered she was upset. 'I thought you loved me.' She sniffed into her handkerchief. 'It's a good job our Tommy was there, no one on our street would believe me if he hadn't been. I only went with him because it was me day off, to see the new ship like and now I find out it's your bloody ship an' I never even knew.'

As discreetly as possible, Charles removed his cheque book from the inside of his jacket.

'Stella, I want you to buy some nice furniture for your flat. You deserve to have nice things around you.'

He noticed her try to suppress a smile and Charles wondered what it must be like to find pleasure in something so simple.

Isobel found pleasure in nothing. She had chosen to withdraw and he would have sunk with her but he knew he needed to feel and experience life in order to survive, sometimes for just one day. It had been so much easier when it wasn't him at all but the man in the dockers' clothes and for that he owed Stella more than a few bits of furniture. As he placed the cap back on his fountain pen, he understood what a pathetic charade it had all been and he knew he would never be Charlie again. But how could he explain that to Stella?

Stella sniffed and studied Charles as he signed the cheque, while she tried to read the amount on the line above.

'D'you love yer wife?'

'I don't think I have ever loved Isobel and that is what makes it all so much worse. I was expected to take a wife and she was there.'

'I wish I had known you then, Charlie, we could have got married. I bet your family and the castle has loads of history, I love history, me.'

Charles almost laughed out loud. Stella's gift, to make him laugh.

'You would have hated my family, Stella, but you're right, there is a lot of history.'

Twenty minutes later, Charles was sitting on his own, and Stella had left with a cheque for two thousand pounds. For a moment, she was speechless. But she was a girl from Liverpool and so the moment passed quickly.

'God, I can buy me own hairdresser's shop with that,' she said. 'Ta-ra, Charlie. I will never forget yer you know. You were me first.' Stella said this much louder than Charles would have liked and he hoped he had imagined the smirk on the waitress's face.

He watched as Stella strutted away in her white strappy slingbacks and again he thought of Ruby in her sensible shoes and apron. The very thought of her pulled at his heart.

He knew that for the first time in his life he felt real love, but could never know its touch. He could not speak her name out loud. Her beauty blinded him. Her voice caused his heart to quicken. The sight of her brought feelings that he had never before experienced rushing to the surface. He wanted to protect her, hold her, love her. It dawned on him that he was in love, for the very first time, but he could have none of it.

As Charles pulled on his coat, he decided there and then that he would work day and night to grow the shipping business until it was a storming success. *McKinnon is right,* he thought. *I shall transform Ballyford into the biggest pig producing farm in all of Ireland. I will be dutiful in my care to my wife, stoic in my secret love and support of Ruby and I shall reform my ways.*

For the first time, he felt as though he could see a road ahead, where until now all he had seen was darkness. The oppressive weight had lifted from his shoulders. The future once again had a purpose, and for the first time in what felt like forever, he was alive.

Chapter twenty-three

Ballyford Castle

Ruby was so excited about her outing to Galway that she found it hard to think straight. Jimmy had polished her leather boots and Mr McKinnon had brushed off her coat and hung it in front of the range to warm overnight. Ruby and Jack were leaving at first light when the only people who would be in the kitchen were Amy and Mary, baking the first batch of bread. Mrs McKinnon had gone over the list the night before explaining every item in detail. Ruby had never seen a Dublin Bay prawn in her life and it took some explaining.

'They will be displayed with the salmon on the table. Amy has them peeled in dishes with a delicious sauce.'

'I can't wait to see that,' said Ruby.

Mrs McKinnon smiled. 'I wish you could have been here years ago, Ruby. We had a ball once a year, and dinner parties at least twice a month. No sooner had we recovered from one than Lord and Lady FitzDeane, they were planning another. But that was before. Before all the sadness.'

'Well, I know this much for sure,' Ruby said. 'Lady Isobel

ate her lunch in half the time today and asked me to show her the replies to the invitations to the ball.'

'Well, surely, if that isn't an improvement I don't know what is. Take care in Galway, Ruby, it's a rum old place. Remember, you are there as a member of staff from Ballyford. Don't forget that at any time. But most of all, don't forget the gelatine or Amy will skin you alive. She needs to bake the ox tongues in aspic tomorrow.'

Later that evening, despite the fact that she needed to be up early, Ruby and Betsy chattered in the darkness as had become their habit, over the sometimes deafening snores from Jane who, realising that she was missing out on the laughter, had moved back in.

'God, there is a sow in the pen sleeps quieter than Jane,' Betsy giggled.

Ruby slipped out of bed and pushed her rolled up dressing gown under Jane's head. The snoring stopped immediately.

'Bliss,' whispered Betsy. Ruby threw another block of turf onto the fire as she slipped back into bed. There was nothing she loved more than to fall asleep watching the flames, until her eyes stung and she could keep them open no more.

'Betsy, don't tell Jane or Mary, but tonight, when I left the lady's room and walked along the corridor, I thought I saw someone on the stairs. I thought it was the lady at first, but she was sleeping and it wasn't Amy or Mrs McKinnon and there's no one else who can be up here, is there?'

'Are you sure?' Betsy leant up on one elbow.

'I think so,' said Ruby, looking troubled.

'Well, that's not good news,' said Betsy as she crossed herself.

'They say she only appears before a death. Amy says she was on the stairs the night before each of the babies died. Go to mass tomorrow, will ye? When you're passing through Belmullet. Don't forget now and make sure Jack drives carefully.'

Ruby could tell Betsy was worried.

'I will. Now, I have to tell you, I've noticed the way Jimmy is all daft when you are around.' And with that, the atmosphere changed as Betsy moved onto her favourite subject, the thing that made getting up in the morning so much easier, her secret love for Jimmy.

Jack arrived as the cock crowed and found Amy sitting by the side of the range enjoying her first cup of tea of the day. 'I've already poured one for you,' she said, nodding towards the steaming cup.

As Jack removed his cap and sat down, he smiled at Amy. 'Well, the week will be up soon,' he said with a cheeky grin, filled with a nervous hopefulness.

'Jack, now I said a week, I know, but...'

Jack's heart sank and the smile slipped from his face. He thought he knew what she was about to say, but before he could stop her and ask her not to be so hasty in her decision, she continued.

'I have done some serious thinking. My life cannot go on as it has. I've done some things I'm not proud of, Jack.'

Jack didn't want Amy to see his face when she let him down, so he stood and wandered to the range where he heaped more sugar into his mug. 'Are ye sure ye don't want to wait the full week?' he said nervously.

'No, Jack, I don't need to, because my answer is yes. I will marry you.'

Jack almost dropped his tea.

When Ruby snuck down the stairs, being careful not to wake anyone from their last half an hour of sleep, she found Jack and Amy deep in an embrace. She coughed to let them know she was there.

'Here you go, both of you,' said Amy, bustling away from Jack and removing a pan containing their breakfast from the bottom of the range. 'That should keep you going until this evening.'

'Eat quick now, Ruby,' said Jack. 'We have to be at the port early to collect the fish and the flowers first. It will be nine o'clock before we arrive and that's if I push the pedal flat out all the way.'

Amy fussed around with tea and fried bread and then sat to join them.

'I will give Lady Isobel her breakfast today, Ruby. Don't you worry about anything here.'

Ruby grinned. 'That will be nice. She really is getting better, Amy.'

'Off now both of you and hurry yourselves. If those prawns are gone it will be a disaster.'

Amy held out Ruby's coat. 'If ye are late getting back, I will sit with her tonight. Don't you worry about the lady, I can take good care of her until ye return.'

Ruby was excited at the prospect of her day out. It was exciting to go out in the van with Jack. It reminded her of the trip she had taken with Con from his house to the convent. The seats with the dark brown stitches and the smell of leather and petrol. Jack's van was nothing like Con's car, but it shared that distinctive aroma. If she closed her eyes, she could be in either one.

She recognized Bangor Erris as they drove through and looked to see if she could spot the lady who gave her a mug of water and an oat biscuit on the day she cycled alone to Doohoma Head. She wondered to herself why she had hesitated and not spoken to Con that day. Was she scared of finding out who her parents were and having to leave Ballyford? What difference would it make anyway? Her life was as it was. Nothing would change that.

She still had the books from Doohoma in her room, stacked under her bed having retrieved them from the stable barn. She now tried to read a few pages of one each night before she fell asleep. She wanted to ask Mrs McKinnon if she knew why they would have been in her house at Doohoma, but each time she came near to broaching the subject she felt sick with apprehension and changed her mind. Maybe she just needed time.

Despite the early hour, the ocean breeze kept her awake. There were sights that were new to her, villages she had yet to pass through. As they left the ocean behind them and travelled inland, Mulranny felt familiar, but she didn't know why and from then on, all was a mystery. It was market day in Castlebar and the streets thronged with farm vehicles packed full of livestock, metal churns full of milk, wagons full of cabbages and potatoes. There were boxes of squawking chickens, hot pie stalls on the side of the road and children running everywhere. She could hear the auctioneer's voice shouting from the cattle pen and see the bars heaving with men through their open doors.

'Did you get back to Doohoma Head?' Jack asked suddenly. 'Did you find what it was you were looking for?'

Ruby folded her hands in her lap and looked down at them.

'I did, thank you, Jack. I'm not sure if I exactly found what I was looking for, but I did find the house.'

'Was it as you remembered it to be? You are very lucky having your own house, you know.'

Ruby sighed and looked out of the window. She didn't feel very lucky.

'Can you keep a secret?' asked Jack. 'If you can, I'll tell you one and then you can tell me one of yours.'

Ruby was intrigued. Jack didn't look like the sort of man who would have a secret.

'Go on then,' she said. 'It's a deal. You tell me yours and I'll tell you one of mine.'

Jack took his pipe off the dashboard and steered the wheel of the cabin with one hand and a knee whilst he lit up.

He's teasing me, making me wait, thought Ruby. Jack puffed away until Ruby could bear it no longer.

'Would you stop!' she squealed. 'Are you going to tell me a secret, or not?'

Jack gave her a lopsided grin, 'You mustn't tell the McKinnons,' he said, 'only I'm bursting to tell someone.'

Ruby pushed him playfully on the arm. 'Tell me,' she said again.

'Well, now, I am a man who has been in love with Amy for many a year and I finally plucked up the courage to ask her to marry me. She made me wait mind, but just now, before you came into the kitchen, she put me out of my misery and said yes, she will. How's that for a secret? She did say I wasn't to tell anyone until after the ball, but I know I can trust you, Ruby.'

Now Ruby stood up in the cab. 'Jack, that is the most fantastic news.' She was almost jumping up and down.

'Sit down,' laughed Jack. 'If I don't get you there in one piece she might change her mind.'

'Why does it have to be a secret?' asked Ruby.

'She wants to wait until after the ball is over and done and she said everything has to be back to normal because she wants a party and so do I. We will get the fiddler to come. I have waited long enough, so I have. Now tell me your secret.'

'Well, I have a mystery really, Jack. When I went home to Doohoma, I found that the books were still on the bookshelf, just as my ma had left them. They were damp and they fell apart in my hand, but the inside covers were still in one piece. They had been stacked tightly on the shelf and what I saw for the first time, and I cannot understand, is that the Ballyford library stamp was on the inside of each cover. I want to ask someone, but every time I go to ask Mrs McKinnon, something stops me.'

Jack took a long pull on his pipe. 'What do you know about your mammy and daddy, Ruby?' he said gently. 'What do you remember?'

He thought Ruby might not want to answer and he was ready to accept that. Jack was a man of few words himself and he recognized and respected it in others. It was the gentleness of his voice and the quiet manner in which he asked the question that helped her to open up in response.

'I remember all the nice memories. I remember my brother and fishing with my da. I remember that my mammy was a stickler for teaching us to read and write, but every time I try to think of the past, all that comes to mind is the last few days. My mammy told me I had family, but I couldn't make out what she was saying. She was very sick.

Jack glanced sideways at her as he changed gear. 'Well, if those books had the Ballyford stamp in, they came from the castle and the people who know everything about that are Mr and Mrs McKinnon. They've been here that long and their ancestors before them. If I were you, I would pluck up the courage and ask. What was your mammy's name, Ruby? Do you know?'

'Her name was Iona,' Ruby said.

Two young boys were running alongside the truck trying to hitch a lift on the running board. Ruby wound the window down. 'Get down. You will hurt yourself,' she shouted.

'Are they mad or what?' she asked Jack.

Jack didn't reply.

'What's up?' asked Ruby. 'Shouldn't I have shouted at them?'

'No, no, that's right. You tell them,' he said, changing gear and driving slightly faster. The crowd in the town had become thinner the further they drove away from the market and had finally entirely dispersed.

'So, Jack, that is one of my secrets and you're right. I know the day will soon come when I have the courage to ask Mrs McKinnon.'

'One of your secrets?' enquired Jack. 'You have more?'

'Oh yes, I do, but there is one secret I will never tell anyone.' Ruby blushed.

Jack recognized that blush. God knows, it had happened to him often over the years.

'Well, if you were to share it with me, I would tell you this. You could travel a long way to find a lad as nice as Danny, and the rooms he has above the stables, they could be made nice now so they could. Anyway, you don't have to answer me, I'm just saying. Everyone knows he's sweet on you.'

Ruby knew Danny had no notion of keeping his feelings private. She had even heard him asking Amy if she thought Ruby was sweet on him. There would be no harm in Jack thinking that Danny was her secret love.

'Shall I tell you something else?' said Jack, breaking into her thoughts. 'Your friend from Belmullet, who was at the convent with you, is coming from the pub with Amy's cousin to help at the ball. She will be staying for the night with the other casual staff.'

'Lottie? Why didn't Mrs McKinnon tell me?' Ruby couldn't keep the grin from her face.

'Well, now, I reckon they was wanting to make it a surprise. You could work on Amy and persuade her to let your friend stay over for a few days and help with the clearing up. Wouldn't that be grand?'

Ruby felt tears prickle behind her eyes. She had missed Lottie so much and she had such a desperate need to see her.

'Thank you, Jack,' she whispered, 'you are a really kind person. I'm glad Amy has said yes to you.'

Once in Galway, they loaded up with the fish and flowers, then parked the van in a garage that belonged to Jack's friend. They packed ice into the buckets of fish and then Jack and Ruby set off with the list. She was completely taken with the size and grandeur of Galway. At lunchtime, Jack even took her into a pub for a drink and a pie to sustain them both.

'No man or woman ever got a good day's work done on an empty stomach,' he told her.

He allowed her to dawdle outside the bookshop, the tailor and the dress shop. It was only when she spotted a sweet shop, she remembered she'd promised to bring some back for Mary, Betsy and Jane.

She bought eight ounces of sugar twist for Mary and Betsy, the same of mint humbugs for Mr and Mrs McKinnon, sour lemons for Jane and then a large mixed bag of misshapen sweets for the staff to share.

The light was fading as they left Galway, both happy that they had everything Amy had ordered. Ruby checked the quantity of gelatine over and over, so nervous was she of incurring Amy's wrath and being hit over the head with an ox's tongue.

Exhausted, but content, she slipped into the cab for the long journey home, while the street lights of Galway lit up the damp pavements and street sellers began to pack up the wares after a long day.

'They will be waiting up when we get back, wanting to hear all our news now.'

'They will and the fish will have to be put straight into the cold store as soon as we are back,' said Ruby. 'The ice in the back is such a big lump, it can't possibly melt for another day yet, and I would say that was a stroke of genius I had there, Jack, to lay the flowers on top of the ice.'

Jack laughed. 'Get you, one day in Galway and you are full of yerself.'

Ruby flopped back on the seat. The early start, the excitement of the day and the trudging along Galway's streets had taken its toll. Her head lolled back and her face changed from black to marmalade gold to black again as they passed beneath the gas lamps and headed for the outskirts of Galway and the long bumpy road back to Ballyford.

'I've been thinking about your books, Ruby. Now, what I'm about to say, ye must not tell another living soul.'

'Of course, Jack,' murmured Ruby, fighting to keep her eyes open. The motion of the wheels on the cobbles, the warmth of the cab, the dark of the night and her own exhaustion were carrying her away.

'I got the shock of me life when you said your mammy's name was Iona. 'Twas was all I could do to keep me face straight and the wheels from running off the road. I never thought I would hear that name again, so I didn't, and it has to be the same Iona, there cannot be another from round these parts.

'I doubt it,' murmured Ruby, sleepily.

Jack continued, 'From Belmullet to Kiltane, you will find plenty of Bridgets and Patricias, and in Bangor, Julia is a very exotic and popular name, but there is no family around here who has used the name Iona, that's for sure. I know where the name is from, 'tis from the island between us and Scotland, very popular there. It was Mrs McKinnon who chose her name when she arrived, but it was me they called to hand her to Rory Doyle, who took her away when the old Lord FitzDeane died and that is a day I have never forgot. And, God knows, for all this time, we thought she was dead and the old lord had ordered her killed and done away with and the feeling was so bad, Rory Doyle fled to England. Now, his running off like that made us think that maybe 'twas true.'

He kept his eyes firmly on the dark road ahead.

'She was only eight years old, was Iona, and she could read better than me. I can't read at all, to be honest, but the little princess, she was a clever one and a half now and everyone knew it. Oh, she ruled the servants at that castle, all right, so bold she was, you have never known a child as bold as she was. Had them all wrapped around her little finger and God, sure, they all loved her to bits. She would march into the kitchen and drag her own chair to the table and little Lord Charles, he was devoted to her he was, devoted. He did everything she told him and she mothered him something wicked. Someone needed to. His mother made an appearance on high days and holidays and that was it. You could have sunk a Belmullet trawler with the tears that were cried on the day Rory Doyle took her away. Jesus, some of them were nearly me own and I was just a young lad meself at the time.

'Now, here's the thing. She had turned up in the night when she was just a babby. Found in the stable she was, just like the baby Jesus. The stable boy discovered her when he came down in the morning. Danny's daddy it was, God rest his soul. She lay there with her big eyes looking at him and didn't cry at all at the strangeness of him, he said. All she had was the clothes she had been left in and a shawl wrapped around her. The old cook, God, she let out a roar, she did, when she saw her. She had grown up listening to the storyteller and that's why it was such a shock. It was like a prophecy that had come true. They reckon she was related to a mysterious girl who had lived in the apothecary's cottage with an ancestor of Miss McAndrew, back in the time of the famine. They say she had some connection with the Ballyford family. I don't know what was discussed, but that baby was put in the nursery and that was it, she never left until the day Lord Charles' grandaddy died and Rory Doyle did the bidding of his father and took his blood money and ran.

'God, that was a journey that night, that was. I had to drive the cart. You have never in your life heard a child give out like Iona did. Scratched Rory Doyle's face to bits, she did. God help us, one minute her and the young Lord Charles were playing on the nursery floor, the next, Mr McKinnon is scooping her up into his arms and Mrs McKinnon is throwing her belongings at me. I have never seen Mrs McKinnon in a state like she was on that day. Loved the girl she did. Rory Doyle was behind the front door. He didn't want Lord Charles to see him. Knew back then he did that he would wheedle his way into the young lord's life. His parents were never there and Rory Doyle knew that. Sharp as a razor he was and twice as shifty. Lord Charles followed him everywhere around the estate and Rory didn't want him to see him taking Iona away. I was upset at what we were doing, God, so I was. Taking a child away from what she knew was her home, but Rory Doyle, all he could see was the money in his palm the new lord had paid him to do his dirty work. Mrs McKinnon was in tears, desperate she was. Packed a bag and we were out of the room in less than half an hour.

'I said to her, "What are we doing? The granddaddy's just dead in his bed. You can't do this."

'"No, you are right, I can't," she said, "but his son can, and he is, so don't make this harder for me."

'She was talking about Lord Charles's father, so she was. He had been sat at his father's bedside and the moment the doctor pronounced he was dead, and the front door was shut on the doctor, he tore around the castle like a madman. He was different from the others. More like his mother, stiff as a board. I don't think he even knew my name, I was just a lad then, no more than fifteen, but I still don't think he knew my name on the day when he himself died years later.

'Mrs McKinnon, she threw the child's clothes in the bag and all the time, Lord Charles was pulling at Mr McKinnon's trousers and trying to pull the girl down out of his arms.

'"Who is going to stay with the wee lad?" I asked Mrs McKinnon, as she threw a coat at me to wrap around the child, but I had no sooner spoke than Mrs McKinnon held onto him by his shoulders and placed her hands over his ears.

'"'Tis a bad business," she said to me. "If you value your life, you won't repeat anything about this to anyone."

'"God, sure, of course I won't, never, not a word will pass me lips," I told her and then, just as we were ready to leave,

Mrs McKinnon shouted, "Wait!" She ran to a bookcase and took the whole top row of books and squashed them onto the top of the big bag. "God help her. She loves her books," she said and when I looked at her, the tears were pouring down her own cheeks, just pouring they were.

'The child had stopped crying now, there were just these big, terrible sobs which came every few seconds. God in heaven, it kills me even telling you this. Every sob was like a pain in me own chest, she was so confused.

'"Get downstairs," Mrs McKinnon said to me. "He's waiting outside the front door."

'I looked at Mr McKinnon for help, because I no more wanted to carry that child away from little Lord Charles than have the hot poker stuck in me eye. "He can't do this can he?" I asked him. But no one answered me, no one.

'It was dark, about the time it is just now. Night had fallen when we left in the old landau. I drove the horses and Rory Doyle sat the child in between us. 'Geesala,' he said and even though I had known him all of me life, that was the only word he would speak to me. I turned the horses out towards the Geesala road and we made the journey hardly speaking another word. He was never one to talk, always shifty. He put one face on for Lord Charles and another for the rest of us.

'Along the roads we went at a fast trot. 'Twas a full moon and I remember how it shone on Blacksod Bay and reflected off the water, lit the road like daylight, it did. The horses and I, we could see the way all right and the only noise was the hooves and the wheels of the cart crunching against the gravel road. It was as if we could be heard for miles around. And I thought to meself, someone is watching us. Someone is seeing and listening and I can tell, whoever it is, they are not happy. The hair on my arms and my neck, they stood up. The horses, they was jittery and almost spooked and yet they was used to being out at night. I often took out four in the old days, for the trip to Dublin when I took Lord FitzDeane for the morning crossing. I shivered and yet the night, it was warm. I blessed myself and I said to Rory, "Have you the rosaries with you?" He didn't answer, but moments later I heard the clicking of the beads. He was a wicked man doing an evil deed and he was praying. Explain that to me, if you can. And that was it, the wheels crunching on the road, the horses' hooves and the click of the rosaries as they slipped through his fingers was the sound that carried all the way and I know that like me, as big as he thought he was, Rory Doyle couldn't get there quick enough.

'We stopped on the road out of Bangor Erris and he pointed up a track on the left where I had to stop the cart. The forest became too dense for the horses and the ground too muddy for the landau. I knew there was a house up there. Just a small cottage, up in the trees and an old lady lived there, alone. We weren't going to Geesala at all and never had been. He had Iona whisked down before the wheels had fully stopped turning. She didn't cry, she just stood in the light of the lantern and looked at me with her big eyes and I have never forgot them, or her. I truly thought that something quite wicked had happened to the child and so did everyone else. That was why Rory Doyle had to flee. Oh, aye, there was a lot of anger directed towards Rory Doyle.

His poor mammy, she had no idea. Not a soul had told her what a wicked son she had given birth to.

'And so, now I know what happened to Iona. She died in the storm of '47 not when Rory Doyle took her away and she was yer mammy, of that I'm sure. So what have ye to say to that?'

Jack turned to look at Ruby. She was fast asleep. Her breathing was deep and sonorous, her head lolling from side to side. He doubted she had heard a word. He reached for his pipe on the dashboard and balanced the steering wheel with his knees once again as he lit up.

'Well, maybe just as well,' he muttered. He had guessed she was asleep from her lack of response, but had continued in the knowledge that he had at least tried to unburden his secret. 'Let sleeping dogs lie,' he said, as she turned onto her side to face him and noisily sucked her thumb. Jack smiled to himself. In her waking hours she was as independent as any woman he had ever met and yet, looking at her as she slept, she could have been but a child. 'Let Ballyford's secret lie,' he said, as he pulled on his pipe and drove onto the unlit road home.

Chapter twenty-four

Mulranny

Ruby woke with a shiver as they passed through Mulranny.

'Ah, you've woken. Grand, I just need to stop.' Jack pulled the cab over outside a cottage, which fronted directly onto the road. No sooner had Jack stepped out of the cab than the cottage door was flung open and Ruby heard a man shout out to Jack in greeting. Ruby noticed that a fire burned brightly inside the room and behind him, in the light of the lamps, she could see children sitting around the fire.

Now it seemed that she and Jack were being invited to step inside for a bite. Ruby had learnt, from her day trip to Doohoma, that there was no point whatsoever in refusing. Hospitality reached out from every roadside home and no one was more welcome than a weary traveller.

Inside the warm cottage, Ruby quickly became the centre of attention as the mammy of them all, Mrs Kenney, pushed a plate of fried potatoes into her hand and the children began to ask her questions about the castle.

'Is it true the castle is haunted?' asked a little girl who had been sitting at the window.

'Not at all,' said Ruby. 'I have never seen a ghost,' she lied.

'There are a few stories about that place, I can tell you,' said Mrs Kenney. Ruby saw Jack wink at her and gently shake his head.

'Now, we'll have none of that talk,' said Mr Kenney, handing two glasses of a strange-smelling cloudy liquid to Ruby and Jack.

Jack downed his in one and thumped his chest with his clenched fist. 'Sure, that's the best I have tasted for some time.'

'The talk is there's to be a ball at the castle.' Mrs Kenney looked at Ruby.

'There is indeed. I think the whole of Ireland must know. We have been to fetch the provisions from Galway. The rest will be delivered from Dublin in a few days,' said Ruby.

'The van is loaded,' said Jack. 'I can feel every pebble on the road hitting my arse the cab is so low.'

'My grandmother used to tell a story of a witch who lived in this very cottage and who finished her days up at the castle,' said Mrs Kenney, sitting down in her rocker next to the fire, ready to step into the role of storyteller, the strongest of all Irish traditions.

'In the time of the famine, it was now. She said everyone who lived in this cottage died, except for a young witch and she was rescued by the lord, and that when he sent her to the poorhouse, she cast a spell on the FitzDeanes.'

'Hush your mouth, woman,' said her husband. 'People from the castle don't want to hear all that nonsense your granny came out with. Sure, she was only sober for the first hour of the day. She talked nonsense.'

'That is not so,' Mrs Kenney said indignantly. 'Told us some awful stories my granny did, God rest her soul. Three months later, the lord of Ballyford, he was dead. Him and his whole family. An awful accident. 'Tis no accident when a witch casts a curse. The story goes that Lord Owen fell in love with the witch. Eilinora her name was and they say she was the most beautiful woman ever to have been born in these parts. She was of such beauty she would take the eyes right out of a man's head, just to look at her. She had Lord Owen captured, so much so that when he heard news of the famine, he rushed back to Ireland from England, on some made up story of having to write a report, and despite the danger to himself he secretly rode out here to find the young witch. She was within minutes of her life when he saved her, scooped her up on his horse and carried her all the way back to Ballyford, but not without danger to his own life, 'twas not an easy ride so it wasn't. He was attacked by gangs of starving men on the journey back: men waving sticks and wanting food and his horse from under him, but he fought them off and carried her like the wind across the bog on his horse back to Ballyford. Some say the men fell to the ground in disbelief, because they saw his horse lift into the air and fly clean off the bog as she sat there in front of him. 'Twas like the horse had wings.'

'Woman, will ye stop!' Mr Kenney shouted.

'No, please don't stop there,' said Ruby, handing her empty plate to the eldest child. 'What happened to this Eilinora? Are her family still at Ballyford?' Ruby's curiosity was aroused.

Despite his every instinct pulling and telling him they should hurry and get a move on, back to the castle, Jack couldn't help himself. He, too, wanted to hear more. Jack had already heard the story a hundred times at wakes on the estate and it always attracted the largest crowd, but it didn't detract from the thrill of the telling again. He imagined it was him and his Amy. He would ride through a thousand bogs and battle a million men to save her and he would make his horse fly if it were him. He was sure every word of the myth was true.

Mrs Kenney needed little encouragement to carry on.

'He carried Eilinora into the castle and nursed her on a pallet in the kitchen. By now, he was completely under her spell and he visited her night and day and never left her side. The staff, they would see him slip into the kitchen after they had already taken to their beds for the night and one of the maids told of how she came early into the kitchen one morning and found the lord asleep on the kitchen chair where he had been watching over the half-dead girl in front of the fire.

'Now, someone got a sneaky word to his wife – 'twas the cook, everyone is convinced of that – and told her all that was happening. Lord Owen's wife, she laid down the law and wrote that the girl had to be sent to the poorhouse in Galway. Trouble was, by the time she got there, his child was sat in her belly. Eilinora was madly determined she was, she would bear a child of Ballyford whatever it took. His wife ordered he take the girl himself and to make sure the poorhouse took her and that was what he did. Lady Lydia wasn't having it any other way. He was a kind man, so he gave them sure enough money for her keep and she had a room of her own, to save her from the typhus. God, they were dropping like flies in the poorhouse, twenty a day. But, when the matron went to unlock the room they had put Eilinora in, she was gone. Disappeared into thin air, she had, until two weeks later when she turned up back at Ballyford at the old Mrs McAndrews cottage. Now, when that happened, even the agent was half scared out of his wits, but Mrs McAndrew she let no one near her or touch her. No one knew what became of her, or of the child she was carrying, but it was my grandaddy who found the bones of a little girl in a coffin in this house and took her to the priest to be buried. 'Twas the first child of Eilinora and the Lord Owen. He knew nothing of this dead babby when he came back to find Eilinora in the famine, nor of the next child he put in her belly. He never knew of that at all because of the accident: a train crash in England. Lord Charles's grandaddy, he inherited, not that he ever expected that to happen. A distant cousin of the family and a bit of a rogue, but he knew about the curse and he lived in fear of it. A different type altogether now, I would say.'

All the children gasped and so did Ruby.

'A curse?' she asked.

'Oh, aye, a curse. Have you not heard about the curse Eilinora put on Ballyford?'

Mrs Kenney looked down at the circle of eyes and open mouths, waiting for her to continue. Even her husband had abandoned any pretence at making her stop.

'Oh well now, listen while I tell ye. The curse was that every male heir to Ballyford would die, or suffer in waiting, until the first female descendant from the line of Eilinora took her rightful place at the head of Ballyford, and only when that happened would the male line continue. It was prophesised that when a girl child was born, she would be left in the stables to take her place. That is how it has been ever since. The girl child did turn up in the stables, but that's a different story for another day.'

Ruby felt a shiver run down her spine as the embers in the fire died and a chill passed over her. Jack began to feel uncomfortable and became impatient to make haste.

'Now the storyteller, he tells it differently from my granny. He says that the lord of the castle had been bewitched and that she had practised her black magic and visited him in his dreams, that he never really had a secret affair with her and that he never even knew her, never mind gave her a child.'

'Visited him in a dream my arse,' said Jack, as he emptied his second glass.

'Sure, 'tis possible, it has happened before. I know a man out at Kiltane, the same thing has happened to him on more than one occasion and a more holy man you could not meet,' replied Mr Kenney. 'He has made more than one girl pregnant that way. Never off his knees begging for forgiveness so he isn't.'

Ruby had never heard either story before and she sat and sipped her drink, under the spell. Like Jack, her instincts were fiercely pulling her back to Ballyford, but she was so warm and cosy in the cottage, she could have remained there all night.

'What they do agree on is that Eilinora's last words, when the lord left her at the poorhouse in Galway, were the terrible curse on the castle and they say her image can sometimes be seen on the stairs, but only when a disaster is about to strike. They say that Lady Isobel saw her ghost on the night before each one of her babies died.'

'Oh my Holy Lord.' Ruby's hand flew to her mouth, as Jack laughed. She remembered her own sighting of the ghost.

'Let me know when you see her, will ye, Ruby, I've had half a dozen different descriptions over the years.'

Ruby had confided in no one other than Betsy that she had seen her and that she knew the ghost was smiling.

As they took their leave, Jack whipped out a few of the flowers from the back of the van and handed them over to Mrs Kenney.

'It would be a disgrace indeed, not to cross the palm of a storyteller as good as yourself, now,' said Jack.

He then pressed a coin into the palm of every child in the cottage, before they jumped back into the van and set off home.

'How do you know those people?' Ruby asked.

'I don't,' said Jack. 'I mean, sure, I know who they are, everyone knows who everyone is, but that was the first time I have been into their home. If you live on the road you will always be busy seeing to people, but sure, they live on the road because they like to do that.'

'Fancy being tenants in the same cottage for three generations; I doubt they have much choice.'

Ruby thought long and hard about the story. It felt familiar to her, as though it was a story she had heard but could not quite remember. She thought that the west of Ireland must be a very special place in the world in the whole scheme of things.

'How long now?' she said to Jack.

'Not long at all,' Jack replied. 'You will see the castle soon enough, once the ocean is on your left.'

Five minute later, Ruby shouted out, 'I see it, I can see Blacksod Bay,' as the ocean came into sight.

The moon sat on the horizon like a huge watery balloon, guiding them home. Ruby noticed that it looked as though dawn was breaking in the sky ahead.

'Would you look at that sky?' she said to Jack. 'It's going to be a scorcher tomorrow.'

Jack looked up at the sky. 'Sure, I've never seen a sky like that spread right across the bay, so.'

The moon disappeared for a while as they climbed up the hill and swung around and the sections of red sky appeared intense against the stars in the midnight sky, but only to to the right of the hill. To the left, the clear sky remained a deep midnight blue and sparkled clearly with the stars, which felt to Ruby to be so close to the earth.

The same question occurred to them both, at the same time. They also saw a billowing haze of smoke obliterating the stars in the red sky and hovering on the hill top, like a smouldering Vesuvius.

Jack pushed his foot down hard on the accelerator, but the weight of the van, and the steep incline, rendered his effort useless and the engine screamed out in protest. Ruby felt her heart beating wildly and looked at Jack's profile, too scared to speak. His eyes were fixed on the road, as though he dared not look up at the sky.

'Could they be burning the field?' Ruby whispered, her voice barely audible above the screech of the van, yet filled with false hope. She had seen this happen at the convent farm.

Jack's reply was curt and strained. 'No, there has been no harvest yet, it's too early.'

The engine screeched louder, but not for one second did Jack ease the pressure on the accelerator of his precious new van. He leaned forward onto the steering wheel as though urging his dear old horse on. Ruby leaned forward herself. Her face was almost touching the windscreen. The moisture in her breath briefly clouded the glass.

'Jack?' Ruby's voice trembled. 'Jack,' she said again, her voice loaded with fear.

This time he answered. 'I don't know yet, Ruby. We won't, until we get to the top.'

A long and agonizing moment later, as they climbed towards the brow of the hill to begin the descent down to the castle, Jack stretched to look for the first view of the castle.

'Oh God, no.' His words were filled with anguish and made Ruby's mouth go dry with fear. He rammed the van into a lower gear, slammed his foot back down on the accelerator and took off down the hill as fast as he could.

The sight which greeted them left Ruby speechless. She found it impossible to breathe. Ballyford lay below them, in the valley. A beacon of flames lit their descent and fired up the night sky. Clouds of billowing smoke began to fill her lungs and made them both cough and splutter.

'Put yer scarf over yer mouth while we are high up,' shouted Jack. The smoke was stinging her eyes and burning her nostrils. She ripped her scarf from around her neck and handed it to Jack, then took the handkerchief from her pocket and held it across her own mouth.

Tears streamed down both of their faces. Jack took the corners at a breakneck speed. The goods they had so carefully loaded into the back of the van crashed and banged from one side to the other. For a second, Ruby pictured the flowers she had so carefully stacked upon the ice, broken and bruised, but the thought left her as quickly as it came. She didn't care. They were hurtling towards the inferno.

'God have mercy, Lord have mercy.' Jack blessed himself as he drove.

'It's the nursery wing, it's the nursery,' cried Ruby. 'It is the top floor, oh my goodness, no, no!'

'Who was with her today? Who is looking after her?' Jack almost screamed the words at Ruby.

Ruby froze, too terrified to tell Jack in case he ran the van off the road. Amy's word's came back to her, *I shall sit with her tonight*. He was already driving wildly, half the time missing the narrow road altogether and skidding along the grass.

'Ruby, who is with her? Tell me, now.' This time his voice was laced with panic. He knew, of course he knew, that was why Ruby wouldn't answer him, but there was a chance, just a chance, he was wrong.

Jack knew.

Amy had volunteered to sit with Lady Isobel in the evening, to give Mrs McKinnon a break.

'You will be behind, after spending your day with Mrs Barrett,' said Amy. 'I will come up and take over as soon as staff supper is served.'

Betsy had also offered but Amy was determined.

'You have too many jobs to be doing Betsy and anyway, I

cook her food, 'twill be nice for me to say hello and see how she's looking now.'

'Well, she's definitely putting on weight, that's for sure,' Betsy replied, backing down gracefully. 'You might like a change, spending a bit of time upstairs,' she added. 'I like getting down and into the kitchen.'

Ruby knew.

She fixed her gaze on the study window at the end of the corridor. The windows were aglow, but there was no sign of a fire directly behind them, not like in the nursery, where they could now see flames shooting out of the window and up towards the sky. The main bulk of the castle was in total darkness. Ruby could see a small light at the entrance to the front doors and a light on the driveway, at the bottom of the steps. The main castle windows were deep and black; reflecting the light of the flaming sky, they blinked down at the speeding van.

'It was Amy, Jack.' Ruby tore her gaze away from the castle and looked at Jack with an agonized expression of pity in her eyes. 'It was Amy, but she will be all right, they both will.'

The van screeched to a standstill at the top of the drive and Ruby and Jack were both out of the door before the engine had stopped and running towards where they could see Mr McKinnon directing the tenants, with soaking wet bales of hay and straw, into the castle. Betsy saw Ruby and, dropping her wet bale of straw, ran to her and the two friends threw their arms around each other.

'Thank God you are all right, is everyone out?' asked Ruby. Betsy shook her head woefully.

'Thank God you are here, 'tis awful. Mary went in after them, she was so brave, Ruby, you should have seen her. She wouldn't listen to Mr McKinnon shouting her and she wouldn't leave without Amy.'

Betsy was sobbing and Ruby could make little sense of what she was saying.

'Where is Amy?' Jack screamed at Mr McKinnon. 'Where's Amy?'

Barely able to speak, Mr McKinnon pointed towards the kitchen courtyard. Jack and Ruby now ran as fast as they could, with Betsy hot on their heels. Ruby was amazed at how, at the rear of the castle, all appeared to be still and quiet. Devoid of normal bustle, empty of people or dogs, the courtyard felt almost eerie.

The lights were off, the kitchen door stood open and the range fire was still lit, casting a red glow across the cavernous room. Mrs McKinnon was sat on the floor and alongside her was the priest. There was no Amy yelling for respect in her kitchen, or shouting at Jack about the mud on his shoes. No pans of broth bubbling on the stove. As he approached, Jack instinctively removed his cap and Mrs McKinnon put her hand up to grasp his. Mary lay across Mrs McKinnon's lap, black with smoke and coughing. Her tear-stained face was filled with distress and on the floor in front of her and the priest, side by side, lay Amy and Lady Isobel. They were both, very obviously, quite dead.

Chapter twenty-five

The sky wept.

Or that was how it appeared to Ruby as the dawn broke and the heavens opened, providing a timely downpour of the heaviest rain they had ever witnessed. The steaming kitchen was crowded with tenants and staff, who had worked throughout the night and fought with every ounce of their strength. Now they had stepped indoors to catch their breath, as God lifted the burden from their exhausted hands, drenched the roof and finally controlled the fire.

No one spoke. The obvious words hung between them but were too raw to speak out loud.

The kitchen smelt overpoweringly of smoke and ash, wet bodies and despair. Jane took the hot teapot from the range and poured scalding tea into mugs as Betsy, who could not stop herself from sobbing, passed them around. Someone had put a mattress on the floor where Mary lay shaking like a leaf, and the only sound in the room was that of her pitiful sobs.

'My throat burns,' she whispered to Ruby and Ruby could do no more than scoop her into her own arms and rock her. Loyal and faithful Mary had been the bravest of the brave.

She had risked her own life to try and save those of Amy and Lady Isobel.

One of the tenant farmers was the first to break the silence. His face and arms were covered in soot and his eyes shone brightly from his mask of charcoal. He had been one of last men to stop fighting the fire in the upper corridor.

"'Tis a bad fecking night,' he whispered.

No one answered. They had no way of expressing the horror they had just witnessed.

A piercing scream suddenly ripped through the air. Two of the boys had run to fetch Amy's mother from the farm and as a sign of respect, she had been taken through the front door of the castle to the downstairs hall, where the bodies had been laid.

The nursery wing was entirely inaccessible. Piles of soaking bales were stacked along the end of the landing. The carpets were sodden, and pictures were stood against the gallery rails having been hurriedly dismounted for safety and moved away from the most damaging effects of the smoke.

Mercifully, the men had contained the worst of the fire and the main section of the castle had escaped major damage. It had been saved by its own skin, the thick granite stone walls and the fact that the nursery wing had been added as an appendage to the castle. The sturdy, studded double oak door at the end of the corridor, originally built to ensure that the noise of children did not disturb those in the main body of the castle, was almost twelve inches thick and had been slammed shut as soon as the alarm had been raised. Boys had run up and down the central staircase all night long, pouring water onto the hay bales, which Mr McKinnon had ordered to be stacked up against the doors. Now, the water ran along the floorboards, soaked the carpets and even began to seep through the ceilings and down the walls.

Mr McKinnon had been in search of Amy when he met Betsy, screaming and running down the main staircase.

'What in heaven's name are you doing?' he shouted to Betsy, barely able to believe his eyes. Betsy wasted no time in telling him.

'There's a fire in the nursery and Mary has gone in.'

From that moment on, all hell broke loose.

'Get down the stairs, Betsy, and tell the boys to fetch the fire tender from the stables and tell Mrs McKinnon what's happening. I'm going to see what's to be done.'

Betsy didn't stay to argue with him as she flew down to the kitchen, screaming at the top of her voice as she ran, 'Fire, fire!'

With a wet rag tied across his face, and his eyes streaming with tears from the smoke, Mr McKinnon had locked every door on his way along the study corridor. He thought that if he could seal the nursery wing he could prevent the fire from spreading. As he followed the sound of Mary's shouts it seemed like only seconds before Jimmy and the rest of the lads were running behind him. But they were all too late.

On the ground floor, he organized the fire fighting effort with military efficiency.

'Keep going, keep going, more, more,' he shouted to every man, woman and child he saw with an empty bucket. The tenants had arrived at the castle, carrying their own metal pails. Children as young as seven stood at the well and the stable taps, filling pails and passing them along the line.

At the open end of the nursery wing, the tenants had entered through the orangery. The hose from the fire tender was connected to the carp pond outside the orangery and here Danny worked his own miracle. McKinnon told him to pile the bales of wet hay along the top of the steps outside the landing door. 'I will, Mr McKinnon,' shouted Danny, 'I will, don't you worry about me,' and then he soaked them repeatedly with the hose.

They had all been stunned by the bravery of little Mary, who had run into the burning room to rescue her Amy, and she had almost done it. She had dragged her along the floor with a strength she had never known she had, until Jimmy reached her.

In the kitchen, the screams had given way to sobbing and murmured prayer.

'That's Amy's mother,' whispered Mrs McKinnon, only just able to contain her own distress. 'Who is with her?' She felt dizzy with exhaustion. *I'm too old for this*, she thought to herself.

'Jack is,' said one of the maids, sadly. 'Jack and the priest.'

'God help us all,' said Mr McKinnon, walking into the kitchen. He was the last to return indoors from the calamity outside and was soaked through to the skin. 'It's raining stair rods,' he said. 'Whoever prayed for rain has been rewarded.'

It wasn't just any old rain, but beating, wind-driven, fire-extinguishing rain.

They all heard the car coming up the drive at the same time.

''Tis the Garda,' said a small boy, unable to comprehend the meaning of death and the need for stillness and reverence. He ran in noisily through the kitchen door. 'Give us a drink then, I'm gasping, me mouth tastes of smoke.'

He grabbed the mug from his older brother and looked around the kitchen. He had never before been in a room with so many people, where not one person was speaking. It was not the Irish way.

'How will you cope with all this, aren't you exhausted?' Mrs McKinnon asked her husband. He seemed to have aged ten years in as many hours.

Mr McKinnon squeezed her hand, his eyes on her face. 'I will, because I have to. But right now, I have to drive to the station to collect Lord Charles from the train.'

'Does he know?'

'No, he knows about the fire, but not about Lady Isobel. I'll tell him when I see him. That way he will have some time to gather his thoughts.'

Mrs McKinnon wanted to say to him, *You also are too old for this, this will break us, it is too much*, but now was not the time.

'Danny, Jimmy, come with me,' said Mr McKinnon. He had a list of jobs he needed done while he drove to the station, but with all his heart he wished he could stay and comfort his wife.

This is too much for her, he thought, watching her help Mary into the library with a tray of tea for Amy's mother and Jack. She would have to organize for Amy to return to the cottages, and Lady Isobel to the castle chapel. In Amy's cottage, two candles would be lit at the head of her bed and her room would be filled with the sound of women whispering, murmuring and grieving for their loss. For Lady Isobel, the cold castle chapel would be filled with the sound of silence.

Mrs McKinnon had sent one of the boys on a bike to Bangor Erris for Annie Shevlin to attend to the bodies.

Annie wore a long black skirt and shawl with a dark grey woollen scarf draped over her head like a judge's wig. She could not have been more than four feet eleven inches tall and had toothless, sunken cheeks and bright black, pinprick eyes.

'Ah, Annie.' Mrs McKinnon hesitated as they entered the kitchen. She wanted to say, 'It's good to see you,' but of course, it was anything but. 'We will move Amy back home now and the lady upstairs and then you can begin.'

Mrs Shevlin had laid out every corpse in Bangor Erris and its neighbourhood for the past fifty years. Everyone wondered who would do it for her when it came to her turn.

She lived on the five shillings she earned for each corpse she tended. There had been talk of an undertaker establishing himself in the area. A notion which had been rapidly rejected. Only Annie knew how the corpse had once looked when enjoying life. Torn up rags were stuffed in cheeks to create a youthful appearance which the body may not have enjoyed for many years. Skin was scrubbed clean, dried heather posies placed in hands and each corpse was dressed in its Sunday best. Candles were lit and there they lay, in their own beds. In the west of Ireland, people looked after their own.

Chapter twenty-six

'I'm thinking now that the fire was caused by a block of peat, which had fallen from the fire.' The officer from the Garda held out his notepad and squinted slightly. He looked very self-important. 'The coroner will be reaching the same conclusion on the basis of my thorough investigation.'

No one said a word in response, but Mrs McKinnon's gaze fell upon the fireside. The grate was four feet from the edge of the hearth. Peat often fell, but well within the perimeter of the outer hearth.

Isobel had kept candles burning for each of the children daily.

'It could possibly have been one of the candles, as well, I'm thinking that now,' the guard suggested as he caught Mrs McKinnon looking at a candle holder on the floor. 'Maybe it toppled over in the draught, whilst the ladies were sleeping. But for the coroner's report, I'm sticking with the peat.'

What was known was that Lady Isobel had been asleep on the chaise longue when Mary popped in and Amy, exhausted from the days of preparation in the kitchen, was fast asleep on the chair near the door, where she had been waiting for Lady Isobel to finish her meal.

'Where is the young girl who raised the alarm and the one who ran in?' asked the guard.

'Betsy? She is downstairs and goodness me, you can't speak to Mary. She has been beside herself with grief. Betsy was a hero, discovering the fire, raising the alarm and then Mary running into it to save Amy. She nearly lost her own life in the effort. We almost had three deaths, not two. What did you want to ask them? Would you like more tea, maybe another slice of cake?'

The guard had so far written his report with the aid of copious cups of tea. He took so long that Mrs McKinnon's patience began to shred and she wanted to scream at him, 'Get out, get out!' but instead, she smiled sweetly and summoned the various members of staff as requested, everyone except Mary. Her eyes were heavy, but not as heavy as her heart. She had to keep repeating to herself, *Hold on, hold on.*

Mrs McKinnon wanted the guard gone, but she also felt her heart beating like a trapped bird in her chest as she still tried to make sense of her own discovery, earlier that day.

Two days later, Mrs McKinnon took a while longer than usual to leave her bed in the morning. The forbidden sun brightened her room, sliding sideways in through a crack in the curtain. Every shutter and blind in the castle was closed tight and would remain so for the entire week, as was the custom.

'I feel as though we have organized more than our fair share of funerals,' she said to her husband, as she perched on the side of their bed and drank the cup of tea he had made for her. In all the years they had been married, she had never once told him how much she appreciated that morning cup of tea. She didn't have to. Some things just didn't need to be said, with a bond as strong as theirs. They knew each other's thoughts.

Mr McKinnon had dressed in his morning suit and sat on the bed next to his wife, fastening his cuffs.

'There is no one who would disagree with you,' he said. 'We have to attend to Lady Isobel today and then I think we need to have a little talk. Maybe it's time for us to return to Scotland and break the chains with this life. The wickedness, along with the flamin' ghost I refuse to confirm the existence of but, we both know it is here; lurking, waiting.'

Mrs McKinnon gently laid the cup and saucer on the table next to her and took an object out of her dressing gown pocket. Both her hands were tightly cupped around something and she stared down at her lap, deep in thought.

'What is it? What do you have there?'

McKinnon put out his own hand and lightly unfurled her fingers. Lying in the palms of her hands was a soot-stained, emerald green, ribbed medicine bottle.

'What is that?' he asked. 'Where is that from?'

'Oh, it's where I found it that matters, not where it's from,' replied Mrs McKinnon, her voice edged with anger and dismay. 'It has lived in my medicine cabinet in the scullery for years. I replace it each year, in case we need to use it quickly. It is for emergency use only. The doctor and I go through the medicine chest once a year and he replaces it with fresh.'

'Is it the morphine?' McKinnon asked.

Mrs McKinnon nodded.

'Aye, and the last time we used it was when young Liam caught his fingers in the scythe at last year's harvest, remember?'

'I do,' said McKinnon. 'But why is that bottle in your hands now?'

'It was on the nursery floor, by the side of Lady Isobel's chair. I saw it the day before yesterday, when I took the guard up to the room, and I slipped it into my apron pocket before he could see it.'

McKinnon began to pace up and down the room.

'Why do you think it was in there, who would have used it?'

Mrs McKinnon watched him carefully as the realization slowly dawned.

'You think Lady Isobel meant to kill herself?'

'I do. She had the key to the medicine chest in her pocket. I couldn't believe it when Annie Shevlin handed it to me, after she had laid them both out. Lady Isobel cannot have realized that Amy had fallen asleep on the chair watching over her. She killed them both.'

'But, why?' McKinnon asked. 'Why?'

'God only knows. All I know is that I have lost two people that I cared for very much and right at this moment, I have no idea how I am going to get through yet another funeral.'

'What do we do about this? Do we tell the Garda?'

'God in heaven, no we do not. We shall have no scandal. This is another secret. As big as the last one and as God is my judge, I shall take both with me to my grave when my turn comes.'

Meanwhile, Ruby had thought she would make the McKinnons some tea and take it to their room as a gesture of kindness. She would tell them both that the staff breakfast was well under way and they could take their time. Today was a sad day for them and she wanted to take as much responsibility away from them as she possibly could.

Ruby felt almost faint with relief at the arrival of Lottie. She had travelled with the staff from the inn in Belmullet and half of the residents from the town the previous day for Amy's funeral and she had slept with Ruby and Betsy and Jane the previous night. Ruby was amazed at the change that had overcome Jane. Her surliness dispatched, she had been helpfulness itself and was clearly struggling with her own grief.

Now Ruby lifted her hand to knock on the McKinnons door but stopped when she heard them both talking. She could just about hear what they said and quietly turned to make her way on tiptoe back to the castle kitchen, with the still fresh tea tray.

She couldn't understand what she had just heard, but she had grasped the facts. Lady Isobel had taken her own life and accidentally taken Amy with her. Ruby felt cold to her bones, realizing that if she hadn't been in Galway with Jack, it would very likely have been her funeral that people were attending.

'Whatever is the matter?' asked Lottie who was placing the risen loaves in the oven with Mary.

Ruby shook her head. 'Nothing,' she whispered and nodded towards Mary to let Lottie know that she would tell her later.

Jane was sat at the table with the usually rowdy Danny. Each one quiet and solemn. They had no words as nothing anyone said could express the loss they felt at how awful the once bustling and busy kitchen was without Amy.

I don't want to be in here, it doesn't seem right any more,' said Danny, who wiped his tears away with the back of his hand. 'I wish Amy were here now, just yelling at me or sending me out with the broom or throwing the tin cup down the yard after me like she used to.'

'Shh now,' said Jane. 'Amy will be going mad in heaven if she sees you crying so she will.' Ruby was almost open mouthed watching Jane comforting others.

''Tis a good way to get by,' said Betsy. 'To imagine Amy is watching us, that she can see what we are doing. What would she be saying now if she could see the sorry state of us all?'

The previous evening, Betsy and Ruby had chatted to Lottie in the bedroom while they waited for Jane to join them. Jane who had moved in and out of her own room, depending upon her mood of the day. The last thing she wanted now was to be isolated. They were all shadowing each other, even the boys. No one wanted to be alone with their grief.

'It seems a crisis was all that was needed to bring that Jane down to earth,' Betsy had confided to Ruby and Lottie.

'Aye, that's true,' said Ruby. I would never have believed the change in Jane if I wasn't seeing it with my own eyes. She is a different girl altogether. 'Tis Mary who has done it. Little Mary, she has made everyone think and put us all to shame. She has never had a bad word to say about anyone, Mary, and look at her. I shall never forget what she did.'

''Tis such a shock.' Lottie joined in. 'What a life you all live here. I had no idea Ruby and here's me living the life at the hotel in Belmullet having a grand time and you with all these problems and now this.'

'I know,' said Ruby. 'I don't think I could take another calamity.' The girls turned down their sheets, entirely unaware that as Ruby spoke, a further catastrophe, as unstoppable as an ocean wave, was heading towards them all.

Chapter twenty-seven

Mr McKinnon took Charles his breakfast and found him sitting at the study desk, staring out through the window towards the ocean. His heart sank. That was where he had left him the previous evening with the promise that he would take himself to bed shortly.

'Did you sleep in that chair?' he asked as he approached the desk.

The answer was so obvious, Lord Charles ignored the question answering instead, 'When I swore to myself that I would never carry another coffin, it hadn't occurred to me that I might have to carry my own wife's so soon.'

Charles's face was a mask, betraying no emotion. He would survive the day, doing what he knew he had to do.

Lady Isobel would be buried today, three days after the fire and one day after Amy. Even though the lady of the castle was not well known locally, the communities from Belmullet to Bangor and all the villages around filled the chapel. Some villagers had set out from their homes hours before. Some had arrived for Amy's funeral the previous day and decided to remain for Lady Isobel's. They found themselves sleeping in the homes of relatives so distant, it was a stretch to even describe them as such.

'Sorry for your troubles. Sorry for your troubles.' The whispered condolences from people normally too self-conscious or afraid to address a lord swept Charles into the chapel. He was grateful that the crypt could seat only a hundred visitors and that the tenants and the villagers could not see his face. He knew more than most how to conceal the emotion local people would expect from him. He would not and could not wail. He also knew they would find his composure difficult to understand. It was in his blood, a consequence of breeding, and as a result they would judge him to be cold-hearted.

He said all the right things to anyone who spoke to him.

'Thank you so much for your concern.' 'I am touched by your words.' 'My wife would be so terribly grateful.' 'Yes, it is utterly devastating, but we shall pull through, with your kind thoughts to sustain us.' Even as he spoke the words, he knew all too well, there was no 'we' or 'us'. He was truly alone.

He took his seat at the front of the church and looked around him.

He had asked for Jack to be seated next to him. Amy, Jack's wife-to-be, had died with his own. He owed that to the man. Charles had not attended Amy's funeral. It was not expected of him and would only have made the tenants uncomfortable.

Charles heard a shuffle at the back of the chapel and saw Ruby, guiding Jack down the aisle by the elbow. His heart constricted. He felt the blood rush to his face, as if saying to him, *You are not dead. You are still alive. Hallelujah.*

'Thank you, Ruby,' he whispered, as he took Jack's arm from her. The sunlight streamed in through the stained glass window and caught her in a pillar of light. Wisps of her often wayward hair crowned her in a halo of chestnut and gold. She glided away, conscious of eyes upon her. As she moved, Charles leaned towards her, as though hooked by an invisible thread. It snapped, and she was gone.

A depressing sense of loss overwhelmed him. Where had it come from? From the wife who had slipped away, slowly but completely, some time ago? Or from Ruby, who refused even to look at him?

'*Exaudi orationem meam.*' The priest began swinging the incense thurible from side to side, filling the air with holy smoke. The congregation fell to their knees and with heads bowed, began to pray.

Over fifty couples had travelled from London to Ballyford Castle and a similar number from Liverpool. Many had left before the news of the fire had reached them. They had packed their finery, ready to attend the Ballyford Ball. Instead they had to dress for a funeral. Some had to scour the Dublin stores for mourning black. By the time fifty ladies had finished, there was not a black mantilla to be found in all Dublin.

The conversations murmured behind lamps and in corners were very different from those spoken out loud.

'Awful business. I was very close to her. I shall miss her dreadfully' lied an old friend of Charles's aunt, to an even older friend of his mother.

'They say the castle is haunted,' whispered a banker friend

of Charles's from London, to a school friend of Isobel's.

The farm girls circled the room holding out plates of food and taking empty trays back downstairs to the kitchen.

'I don't know how we would have managed without Lottie,' Mrs McKinnon said to Ruby, as she sent two more girls back up the stairs with loaded trays to feed the guests. Ruby could see that Mrs McKinnon was only just about coping. The swarm of girls from the cottages who had arrived at the castle to help were almost as much work as the wake itself.

'I'm not surprised she's struggling,' whispered Lottie to Ruby while Mrs McKinnon issued the girls instructions in a voice that occasionally contained an uncharacteristic wobble. 'When I asked one of them to carry a fresh platter of prawns, she screamed and ran for the kitchen door. She had never seen anything like it before. Mind you, they are farm girls, so we can't expect too much from them.'

Ruby grinned. 'And we are convent girls from the best convent in all of Ireland and therefore we are so much more sophisticated.' But as both girls started to laugh, Ruby pulled herself up short. Today was not a day for laughter. Yesterday they had buried Amy and today it had been Lady Isobel's turn.

'Don't you worry about laughing, girls,' said Mrs McKinnon, turning her attention back to Ruby and Lottie. 'You are standing in Amy's kitchen and there was no one who enjoyed a laugh more than our Amy, isn't that right, Betsy?'

Betsy nodded. 'That's half of the problem, that's why we miss her so much.' Ruby had noticed that Betsy was permanently on the verge of tears. She had found the funeral especially difficult.

'Sit down, Mrs McKinnon,' said Ruby, worried by how diminished she looked. 'You look as white as a sheet, let us finish off. Most of the guests have left now and the drivers are outside in the yard. Some people are travelling all the way back to Dublin tonight and will be lucky to make it for midnight, if they don't leave soon.'

Mrs McKinnon sank into the chair.

'That Rory Doyle and his awful wife are just leaving. I cannot bear them. Did you ever hear a woman talk so much during a requiem mass? Irish women can talk and that no one can deny, but they know to shut up in the sight of God.'

Ruby frowned. It was clear that the arrival of Rory Doyle and his wife had irked Mrs McKinnon.

'Give me five minutes with that man, I would tell him a thing or two. Ruined Amy's life he did and he had the nerve to turn up at her funeral. Maybe 'tis his uncouth wife I should have the five minutes with. I would wipe the smile from her face and shut her up, I would.' Mrs McKinnon shook as she spoke and twisted her handkerchief around until it resembled a rope.

Ruby reached out and took her hand.

'Come on, Mrs McKinnon,' she said gently. 'I'm taking you to bed for a nap. Even if you only have an hour. It will make you feel much better. Come on.'

Mrs McKinnon tucked her handkerchief back into her pocket. A long sigh, followed by a dip in her shoulders told Ruby there would be no resistance to a suggestion that would have seemed ridiculous only a week ago.

'An hour would be lovely, just to get my breath back,' she said gratefully.

Minutes later, Jane almost fell into the kitchen, carrying a tray which was obviously far too heavy for her. She staggered to the table and laid it down with a crash. A week earlier, Amy would have yelled at her for doing such a thing. Adjusting her cap, Jane let rip with her opinion of the guests.

'Jesus, if you listened to them all, they knew her so well they could even tell ye what time she went to the fecking toilet every day. One of them didn't even know she had lost five boys, said it was four, arguing with the woman next to him he was. I've never seen one of their faces here before, ever, and I nearly said so.'

At that moment, Ruby returned from putting Mrs McKinnon to bed. 'You won't say anything to anyone, Jane. That is not our place. What you will do is make sure today goes without a hitch and stop swearing.' There was a coolness and determination in Ruby's voice, which had the desired effect on Jane.

She's worrying me sick,' Ruby confided, nodding towards the passageway that led to the McKinnons' rooms. 'If you had told me she would ever be like this, I would have laughed in your face. She is the strongest woman I know.'

Jane began to clear the tray she had carried into the sink without a grumble. In the face of despair and disaster, the balance of power had shifted. Ruby, without effort or compromise, had donned the mantle of responsibility.

Lottie stood at the sink, washing out the sherry glasses. 'Maisie at the pub said that happens to people as they get older. She said sometimes a death can make a person grow old overnight and that some people, those who are really in love and have been together a long time, they die, one after the other, in minutes.'

Betsy was the next to enter the room, backwards, carrying two trays, precariously balanced, one on top of the other. 'I've told the girls just to wait at the top of the stairs for now and Jimmy and Danny are carrying up two more trays of drinks from the butler's pantry. I hardly recognized Jimmy, he's scrubbed up so well. Where's Mrs McKinnon?' There was a hint of surprise in her voice as she looked around the kitchen.

'I've put her to bed,' Ruby replied and an expression of understanding passed between Betsy and Ruby. Betsy would have done just the same had she been in the kitchen at the time. 'It just got to her, Betsy,' Ruby said. 'I wish Amy was here, she would know what to do with Mrs McKinnon and how to help her.'

And that was when it hit her. Amy wasn't there and no matter how hard they prayed or wished for it, Amy never would be again. Ever. She wasn't in the next room, or down at the cottages visiting her mother. She wasn't to be found in the cool room, or counting the sacks of flour, stacked like a row of praying monks in the larder. She was nowhere. She was gone. Forever. Speaking Amy's name out loud, in the kitchen where she had spent all of her waking hours, was almost too much. They were interlopers in Amy's kitchen and Amy had gone. Ruby felt the floor shift and her world tumble. Without any warning, she found herself sobbing. Her heart physically hurt, so much that she put her hand up to her chest. It was a pain induced by grief and longing and yet she had known Amy for very little time compared to Jane and Betsy. As the four girls now hugged each other tight, Ruby wondered, *What is happening to us? We are all falling apart.*

'That's the last of them, Lord Charles,' said McKinnon, as they walked back up the steps. 'I think it can be said that despite the circumstances, we gave the lady a wonderful send off.'

Charles didn't reply, but stood and waved until the last car had turned the bend in the drive. It had not rained and the sun had shone. He was glad of it. His guests could return to England and not complain about the Irish weather at least. The smell of the earth, the food, the language the lack of heating and the infernal damp, yes, but on this occasion, not the rain. He turned to speak to McKinnon and realized, with some surprise, that he had already left and he was completely alone.

Desolate. There were times in Liverpool when he experienced a familiar sensation. That was when he stepped into second-hand clothes, and became someone else entirely. A man called Charlie. A man who dallied with a girl named Stella. A man for whom no one waited to return safely home. He felt lonely then, in Liverpool. But that was a different kind of loneliness, born of living with a pain he could not share with anyone.

He wondered now if anyone would notice or mind if he sat outside on the steps for a moment and then it struck him. Who was there left to care? His parents, his children, Isobel, all gone. The only people to show concern were those he employed and paid. Not a living soul cared for him. He housed and fed and paid for every kind word that would ever be spoken to him, in one way or another. He felt exhausted. Looking out across the lawn to the river, he could hear the water roaring as it gushed over boulders and pebbles. His gaze was immediately drawn to her, walking happily in the fading sunshine, his Isobel. They had never loved each other. Theirs had truly been a union of two lost souls seeking a life of stability and security, but the love they did create and share, the love of their children, could never be erased. It would always be there, within the ruined walls of Ballyford.

She moved across the mossy green lawn, carrying a laughing baby in one arm, snapping branches from the lilac tree with the other. She once carried them indoors and placed them in a vase in their bedroom and they both admired their scent and beauty. The smell of lilac came towards him now and filled his nostrils. It was pungent and overpowering, her parting gift to him. Now their sons, of varying ages, were running around her, laughing and jumping, trying to attract her attention. He could hear their voices shouting gleefully, 'Mummy, Mummy.' The sun dipped and they became black shapes against the light, framed in a halo of gold and then they turned towards him and he saw their smiling faces.

'Isobel,' he whispered hoarsely, his throat thick with tears. He yearned to be with their children. It was all Isobel had ever asked for and all she had wanted and in that moment, he knew, she had taken herself to them. It was as obvious as the day is long because it was what he had always wanted too. The realization dawned on him and made his heart beat faster. Isobel had killed herself to be with her boys, but Amy, she had taken Amy too. He had kept his true emotions deeply buried. Locked down by dalliances with Stella, buying ships and anything he could amuse himself with to distract his thoughts, but these things, they were not available for a woman such as Isobel. By running away from Ballyford. By involving himself in every time-consuming activity he could create, he had kept his real thoughts far away. Thoughts he had never allowed to surface and the words that ran around in his head, but remained unspoken, *I want to be with them too*. Isobel had, she always had. She was never afraid to utter the unspeakable. Words which terrified him, haunted him.

I want to die and be with my babies, Charles. They are cold, they need me. I have to be with them. He ran from her because he could not bear to hear those words spoken. Once he accepted those words as real, he would be lost. He had wanted to crumble and die and to be with the children too and now he knew that Isobel had killed herself and had taken poor Amy with her.

'Isobel?' he shouted across the lawn. The images of Isobel and his children, blurred through his tears. 'Isobel?'

But there was no Isobel. She was happy, united with her babies, doing in death what she had always dreamt of in life. A desolate and lonely Charles sobbed and shed the tears of a man who wished he was brave enough to join them.

Mr McKinnon opened the door slowly and saw his wife lying on top of the bedcovers, fully dressed, staring at the ceiling. He noticed that she was wearing her shoes. In all their years of marriage, he had never once been allowed to put his shoes on the bed. It was a sure sign, something was very wrong.

'How are you doing?' He spoke softly as he sat down on the edge of the bed and took her hand in his.

She turned her red-rimmed eyes towards him and they became washed with a fresh flow of tears.

'What a day, what a week.' She took her handkerchief from the bedside table and blew her nose and then pushed herself up on the pillows.

'Do you know, when I saw them both before me, laid out on the floor, they looked as though they were sleeping, taking a nap, but I knew really, they were already dead. I feel so guilty, there they were, dead, and the first words I could think of were, "At last, it must be all over."'

'Hush now, hush.' McKinnon put his arm around her shoulder. 'You have not a thing in this world to feel guilty about. No one could have looked out or cared for Lady Isobel as much as you did. You did everything you could, even bringing in Ruby to watch over her all day long.' Mrs McKinnon shook her head, as if to swat away his words.

'It was all she ever wanted, you know, to die, but she would never have wanted to take anyone with her. It was the awful thing we used to dread, wasn't it? The thing we ignored knowing that really, if we are honest with ourselves, we brought Ruby here not just because of who she was, but to keep her alive and watch over her for us. We knew she was a danger to herself.'

Mr McKinnon sighed and squeezed her hand.

'If we really are being honest with ourselves, then yes, I suppose it was. It was after the last one died, I think, that things became worse. When she knew that Lord Charles would not tolerate anymore. When he began to spend more time in Liverpool, I think she knew there was no hope of ever holding her own child again. I don't think she could bear that.'

'Aye, well there's more to it than that. Mrs Shevlin asked me to fetch her wedding ring, for the coffin. It has slipped off her finger during the past year, her fingers were so thin and I had put it in her bedside drawer. Look what I found in her drawer when I went to fetch it.' Mrs McKinnon opened her own bedside drawer and pulled out two letters, both addressed to Lady Isobel.

A frown crossed Mr McKinnon's face as he took the letters from his wife. 'God in heaven what next?' he muttered, opening the first letter. It was a folded sheet of rough paper, but the writing was clear and what was more, it was familiar. *I have information that your husband is up to no good when he is in Liverpool. I have taken the liberty of employing a private detective on your behalf and he will shortly write you a report. When you have this information, you should contact your solicitor immediately and protect yourself.*

The letter was unsigned. 'Who the hell do you think wrote this?'

'Well, look at the paper,' said Mrs McKinnon. 'Do you recognize the writing.

The colour slowly left Mr McKinnon's face. 'My God, it's Amy's handwriting,' he said, with alarm in his voice.

'Aye, it is. There is no denying, it is. I think it's all my fault.' Mrs McKinnon reached for her handkerchief as the tears began to flow once more.

'Amy wanted to leave once, you know, a few years back. She said to me, "God, I've seen nothing but this castle. I need to experience something of this world before I die." I knew in my heart as God was my judge, she wanted to head to Liverpool and look for Rory Doyle. I persuaded Amy to stay, in truth, because I could not face having to work with another cook I did not know and look what happened to her. She never found Rory Doyle, but he came back to her and I know, as God is my judge, he put her up to that, but I will never be able to prove it. All he has ever wanted to do since that night is hurt the FitzDeane family.'

Mr McKinnon opened the second letter. It was from the private detective, confirming who Stella was and her whereabouts. Along with full details and times of when Lord Charles had been in her company. Mr McKinnon slowly folded the letter and placed it back into the envelope.

'Aye, you can as good as smell him on the paper. Wicked words. Rory Doyle is behind this. There is no way Amy would have written that letter on her own. We know he came back a few weeks ago and that she saw him. We just chose to ignore it. He put her up to it. Dictated it, I would say. 'Tis all his fault. The man is a wicked menace and always has been, ever since that night the old lord got him to take Iona away, because he was scared to death of some stupid curse. None of this was your fault,' McKinnon whispered. 'We should remember only the nice times. It wasn't you who never paid Rory Doyle his full amount of blood money.'

'Aye, I know that, and we will. We will remember the good times. But we must face up to the fact, Lady Isobel probably meant to take Amy with her. She saw her chance when she was asleep in the chair. She and Amy had exchanged many notes over the years about the menu and food, in the days when we had the balls. In fact, didn't Amy send a note upstairs with Ruby, only the other day, with the menu plan for the ball? Lady Isobel would have known that the letter was put there by Amy, for whatever reason it was, and Amy was too stupid to realize that Lady Isobel would have recognized her handwriting in an instant. Too blinded by Rory Doyle to see the obvious in front of her very nose.'

Mrs McKinnon sounded almost angry as she squeezed her husband's hand.

'I cannot tell Jack about any of this, or even about the bottle I found on the nursery floor. It is another dreadful secret Ballyford has heaped upon me. I keep asking myself, is this all my fault? Is it because of Iona?

'How can it be? You mustn't talk lie this. You are just upset.' Mr McKinnon would have said and done anything to make his wife feel better.

'I kept back the note and the clothes that Iona arrived in, you didn't know. I stored them away in a secret place where they could never be found. I thought that maybe one day they would be a clue as to where she came from and even who her mother may have been. I thought that Iona would find her way back here to us, to me, the only mother she had known and when she did, she would know that I had kept her in my heart and always held onto those precious clothes she arrived in.'

'I loved her too,' Mr McKinnon whispered. 'When the old lord banished her I kept strong for your sake, but it killed me inside too.'

'I knew that, I could tell. Now I'm asking myself, is it me who has brought all this bad luck upon us, having brought

Ruby here and keeping Iona's clothes? Is it my fault, for holding onto that box, is it cursed? They all whisper and talk about a curse on the castle, down in the cottages. God knows, every time one of the little ones died, they all started up again.'

Mr McKinnon shook his head. 'No, it is not your fault and it never, not in million years, could be. You did what you did out of love and grief and no bad can come from that. Don't let me hear you say that ever again. You must not look for ways to blame yourself.

'Lord Charles is a broken man,' he added. 'I shall not be telling him any of this. He will return to Liverpool, to his big ship and his smart new company and Ballyford will be forgotten. I have no idea what is to happen to the tenants, the farms, the pigs, or indeed, what is to happen to us all? The shipping company is his life now. It will be his salvation and we must ask ourselves, what will be ours?'

Chapter twenty-eight

The news broke on the BBC World Service.

The recently launched Liverpool to New York passenger liner, the *Marianna,* today developed an unexplained and severe list at 16.40 local time. The captain, Yannis Theopolis, displayed outstanding seamanship in taking the difficult and brave decision to send out a May Day signal to the *Cotopaxi,* which was sailing close behind. All passengers disembarked safely onto the passing ship. The crew have been commended for their swiftness and skill in coming to the aid of the troubled *Marianna.*

The captain was the last to leave his ship after ensuring that all passengers and crew had safely disembarked. The handling of the crisis has been described as exemplary.

Nicholas Nathan leaned across his desk and switched off the transistor radio. Picking up the receiver from the phone on his desk he made one brief call before leaving his office.

'Get a message to him, the deed is done.'

Then, lifting his bowler hat from the stand, he picked up his umbrella and brown leather case and headed out of the door to the Carlton Club, for his six o'clock gin and tonic. He wished Rory hadn't complained so much about attending both funerals. 'Standards, dear boy,' he had told him. 'Everything as normal. Get away as quickly as you can but you must keep up appearances until you hear otherwise.' Rory had pleaded every excuse under the book not to go. He claimed he was too upset. That his heart was breaking and the effort of keeping up appearances in front of his wife as his heart bled for woman he now claimed to have loved would kill him. That man really had no morals.

'Business as usual, business as usual,' he muttered to himself as he strode through St James's Park.

Mr McKinnon sat at the head of the table with Mrs McKinnon, Ruby, Jane, Betsy and Lottie and the remainder of the staff all sat around as he made his announcement. Lottie had wanted to remain at the castle, reluctant to leave Ruby and had been set free from her obligation to the hotel by Tony, who was delighted that she was stepping into Amy's shoes. Within hours, she had slipped seamlessly into the role.

'It would appear he has lost everything,' said Mr McKinnon in a sombre voice. 'The insurance company will pay the salvage company for the ship, but by the time it has all been accounted for, there will be heavy losses for Lord Charles. I am to collect the solicitor from Dublin in the morning, but apparently the company had been placed under the sole ownership of Rory Doyle. A great deal of money has gone missing. However, it appears that all the paperwork is in order and because there is no record of anyone other than Rory Doyle signing for the new ship, all the salvage money goes to him, one would imagine. He mysteriously handed the salvage company over to his wife and son when he joined Lord Charles. The bank account for the shipping company was even in his name. The police will investigate and I imagine that little thief Doyle will probably get away with it, because he always does. It stinks to high heaven.'

'Merciful God,' said Betsy. 'What will happen to our Lord Charles now? What will happen to Ballyford and all of us?'

'I have no idea, Betsy and until I do, we shall all carry on as normal. Lord Charles will need us now more than ever. Everyone should move about the castle in silence. Do not disturb him. He is a man who has much to think about.'

At that instruction, Ruby's heart sank. All she had thought about and wanted to do for days was to take him into her arms and soothe away some of the pain etched on his face. To ease the loneliness in his eyes and to let him know, they were all there for him. He was at the centre of their world and yet, she knew, he had no notion they even existed, so far had he sunk into the depths of his own despair.

Chapter twenty-nine

The flat-bottomed cumulus clouds were like excited ladies in crinolines, dancing across the freshly washed sky. Slate grey rocks jutted out from the shoreline, strewn in seaweed and kelp, like the discarded silk stockings of invisible bathers, until the tide returned to reclaim what it owned.

He had left Ballyford, walked out of the front door and down the steps and had continued walking until the waves, lapping at his feet, forced him to stop.

This was where he wanted to be and yet he knew that he did not possess the courage to walk into the ocean and disappear.

He looked out across the bay.

'God in heaven, help me,' he cried.

He looked up to the sky, as though searching for an answer, for anything, but all he found was a lone white seagull, circling overhead.

The conversation with his solicitor had been worse than any nightmare, worse than anything he could have ever predicted.

'It would appear there is nothing legally we can do,' his father's lawyer in Dublin had told him. 'Unless Rory Doyle decides to make a gesture as an act of goodwill.'

Charles's head spun. He had been duped by a man he had known all his life. A man he had regarded as a brother. The insurance company would hold their own investigation but under a threat of legal action from Rory Doyle, they would pay out without too much delay. The captain of the ship had acted in an exemplary manner. The entire rescue had been faultless. No one could have done more to ensure that the lives of the passengers were always put first.

'No one even wants to consider the liability, if lives had been lost,' Nathan had said to him. 'We all remember the *Titanic*. It wasn't that long ago.'

For Charles it was as if people were speaking in a foreign language and he was unable to comprehend a single word.

The facts were impatiently tapping at his brain, demanding entry, but his mind had entered a state of self-preservation.

Your wife is dead. Your children are dead. Your cook is dead. The man you thought was your friend was your jealous enemy. You have lost your integrity, credibility and all of your money. You are not who you once thought yourself to be. You may even have lost Ballyford. You are a fool. You are not the person anyone believes you to be.

One at a time, his brain allowed the facts to be absorbed as Charles struggled to accept the abuse of his trust. One thought however, consumed him. It was a thought he now allowed some room. It would be better to be dead than to face it all.

A watery grave, a cold dark depth in which to sleep, forever, that would be welcome. Icy water lapped at his bare feet and the shock of it felt like a chilled balm on sun-scorched skin.

He looked out across the silver shimmer of water, fixing his eyes on the frothing white breakers on the horizon. A bird dipped down then soared high with a catch wriggling in its beak. The gull screeched as the fish slipped and returned to the safe depths of the ocean.

'I can do that,' whispered Charles. 'If a fish can do it, so can I.'

The thought of Ruby came into his mind. He felt so far away from her. He knew nothing of her life and yet he felt as though he knew everything there was to know. She would be the only person who could understand his loss. The only person who had lost as much as he had.

He thought of Ruby and fell to his knees in the sand. Lost. When the tide came in, he would sit and let it take him too.

McKinnon ran into the kitchen.

'Has anyone seen Lord Charles?' he asked urgently. 'He's not in his study and I have to leave to collect the solicitor from the station at Galway.'

Mrs McKinnon was organizing the girls from the farms to help clear up the fire damage. A reformed and pleasant Jane was helping her, still displaying the gentle and caring side to her nature, never before seen. Lottie was baking and preparing lunch for when the solicitor and his clerk arrived. Mary, who had spoken very little since the night of the fire, was helping her and under Lottie's tender care was improving a little each day. Betsy was supervising Jimmy as they polished the silver cutlery together.

'We must keep up appearances,' Mrs McKinnon had said

at least a dozen times. 'Neither Amy nor Lady Isobel would want things to slip. Could you imagine?'

Ruby couldn't.

'No, no one has seen him down here.' Ruby's head had shot up. She had made excuse after excuse to wander up to the first floor to find him, to reassure herself that he was not in a bad way. She had known he was in his study, but she had no reason to enter. Only Betsy had access to his rooms and now that she had no need to be in the nursery, she spent her time helping Lottie downstairs in the kitchen.

'Go and look for him, will you, check that he has remembered the solicitor is coming. There is no saying where his head is these days,' Mr McKinnon said. 'I have to leave now, or I will be later than I meant to be.'

Ruby dried her hands on her apron as she untied the bow and threw it over the chair. She replaced it with Mrs McKinnon's shawl, which she wrapped around her shoulders before she ran out of the back door. Her steps were guided by instinct and her thoughts by despair. She knew exactly where he would be, even though she couldn't explain why, not even to herself, as she ran down the front lawn as fast as her feet would take her and out onto the road.

He didn't hear her footsteps in the sand, or her voice when she whispered his name. It was only when she put a hand on his shoulder that he looked up in surprise.

'Ruby, ah Ruby,' he said and then looked back out towards the ocean, drifting away to some place where she did not exist.

'What are you doing here?' she said, tucking her skirt in behind her knees and sitting down next to him.

He turned to face her. 'What am I doing?' He repeated the question. 'What am I doing? I don't know. I don't think I have ever known, Ruby. Everything I touch becomes a disaster. I have almost nothing left. I am no one. I am not the person I thought I was or who I am supposed to be. I am no one and someone who is no one, doesn't *do* anything.'

Ruby gazed at his profile. At the skin, stretched tight across his cheekbones, at the stubble, which made him look gaunt. She had no idea what to say and so she listened with patience while he continued.

'I am not the person anyone thought I was. The staff in Liverpool, they thought I was someone they could depend on, who was smart and careful, who would look after them. The solicitor from Liverpool is arriving today and I know he will tell me that the office has been closed down because I no longer have a company. Rory Doyle has already sold what I had out from under me and not even paid the staff their wages due, and that I find harder to bear than losing my own business, having let others down.'

Ruby watched as a tear slowly trickled down his face. She imagined the salty taste on her lips and she wanted to wipe the tear away and hug him to her.

The moment was surreal. She did not feel deferential. Ruby felt, and indeed had always felt, his equal.

She put her hand to her eyes and squinted. On the horizon, she saw a boat.

'It's a trawler, returning to Belmullet,' Charles said.

Ruby nodded. 'With the Dublin Bay prawns?'

'No, they come from Dublin.'

Ruby blushed. 'I'm an eejit, I am,' she said.

'No,' he replied. 'There is only one eejit at Ballyford and that's me.'

The sand beneath her was firm and her heart beat steadily in time to the gentle rhythm of the waves, but she felt the axis of her world shift when without any warning he asked, 'Would you like me to tell you about Iona, your mother?'

It took Charles two hours to tell the story, and he missed nothing out.

He told Ruby about the baby in the stable and the note, which tore his grandfather's heart in two.

'My father, you see, his son, he thought the castle was cursed. He had heard himself from the storyteller when he was just a boy, that as soon as a daughter was born in the line of descent from the famine girl, Eilinora, she would arrive in the stables at Ballyford. He also knew about the curse and and he wanted Ballyford purged. It was something to do with my ancestor Lord Owen. I didn't know this until recently. It was Miss McAndrew who told me the full story. She said that as Iona had been banished, there was nothing she could do to break a curse as old and as powerful as it was and so I decided on that day, there would be no more children born to Ballyford. The castle, it can crumble and die and me with it.

'I think I know that story,' said Ruby. 'A woman in one of the cottages on the Mulranny road, she told me something on the night of the fire.'

'Ah, yes. It is remarkable, is it not, that every family in every cottage knows more about my family history, than I do? But, that's the Irish for you.'

Ruby smiled. His demeanour had lightened as he spoke of Iona. The cares and woes etched in the lines on his face became smoother and lighter with each phase of the story he told. He felt as though he had been to confession. Holding Iona's story secret in his heart for so many years had been a heavier burden to carry than he had realized.

'Your mother, Iona, had a wonderful nature. The tenants still whisper about the famine girl, Eilinora. She was a witch, if you believe in that sort of thing. It was all a long time ago. Anyway, the direct line to Ballyford was broken by a train crash in England, so there is no one who really knows. Ballyford started all over again, if you like, after that. We were just distant cousins.'

'In the linen room, I found a box with the clothes of a baby in it. Were they my mother's?' asked Ruby.

'Ah, you found the box.' Charles looked hurt. 'I wondered what Mrs McKinnon had done with it. I never had the nerve to ask her. It was supposed to have been burnt, on my father's orders. Isobel also found it. You must have heard of the curse of Eilinora. I never believed the curse. Sadly, when Isobel found the box, she did believe it and began to blame me for the deaths of our sons. I looked for Iona you know, just as soon as my father died, but my son died and then another and finding Iona just slipped from my mind. I know you won't forgive me for that. By the time I did pull things back together and start the search again, I discovered she had died in the storm of '47. We still don't know where she was taken or how she arrived at Doohoma. It is some comfort to know that she met your father and that she had you and your brother. She knew love. She hid herself away and in that cottage, which made finding her so difficult. It feels as if nothing but bad has happened since the night Iona was taken. If only my father had known that it wouldn't take a young girl who everyone loved to destroy Ballyford, just his own idiot of a son.'

Ruby said, 'The books, at home, at Doohoma, the books had a Ballyford stamp in them, that is why? She took them with her?'

'Probably,' said Charles.

Ruby's hair lifted up into the wind and blew around her face.

'Is that why Mrs McKinnon came to find me?'

'As soon as we found out Iona was dead, we sent for you. It took the clerk six years to discover that Iona had once lived at Ballyford. He only found out by chance. He never gave up on you, Ruby. He told me that you never left his thoughts. And, thank God you didn't, because otherwise, you would not be here now.'

Later, when she looked back on that moment, Ruby didn't know how she found the courage to take his hand in hers. It was almost as if her hand had acted of its own will. She pressed their palms together, hers small and white, dwarfed by his. For a long, long moment they looked at each other, eyes locked in meaning and hearts beating in unison. His words, when they came, took him as much as Ruby by surprise.

'Since I first saw you on the steps, you have never left my thoughts. Yours is the first name to enter my mind each morning and the last to leave at night. You have bewitched me, Ruby. I must seem like a very old man to you, but right now there is only one person in my life I could be persuaded to live for, and that is you.'

Ruby's heart pounded in her chest. She found that she couldn't tear her eyes away from him.

'You and I, we're equals. We both have nothing and no one. We've both lost those we love and are both connected to Ballyford. Maybe this needed to happen, for things to be right, maybe this was where I needed to be.'

'I don't think we can count a fire and two deaths as benefits,' said Ruby. She had picked up a small twig from the beach with her free hand and was writing something in the sand.

'No, I wasn't saying that, Ruby. What I meant was that however it happened, here is where we are. I have nothing left and neither do you. All we have is what remains of Ballyford. It belongs to you as much as it does to me. It's ours Ruby, and my heart, that is all yours too.'

Charles placed his arm around Ruby as he spoke and pulled her towards him. Two hours ago, he wanted to drown in the ocean. Now, he was looking at Ruby and knew that he was going to kiss her. He felt as if he was soaring.

Ruby was greedy. She had never been kissed before and as his mouth closed over her own, she knew at once that she never wanted anyone but Charles to kiss her again.

They both yearned in the aftermath of death. They ached for a love which was life affirming and real. As she pulled

Charles towards her, eagerly, he whispered into the ear he was kissing, 'Are you sure this is what you want?'

'It is, it is,' she gasped back.

'Ruby, this won't be easy,' he said as his hands caressed her back and slid down her sides and along her thighs. He wanted to touch every part of her soft skin, to know all of her at once. As his thumbs circled her breasts and his teeth sank into her neck, he felt her rise and arch against him. She was urging him along, impatient for something she had never known. As he undid the buttons on the front of her dress, he felt the heat of her skin escape and for a moment, he looked down as she lay on the sand, trembling, afraid of what came next but imploring him with her eyes. Her head was giddy, he felt half drunk but his mouth, his teeth, they searched and aroused her further as she felt her abdomen tighten in response. Ruby's lips sought his eagerly. They clung to him, demanding and urging him on. As she held him to her, she saw the look of astonishment in his eyes and she smiled at the sound of his groan. She felt as though she were in a state of bliss, overwhelmed by a barrage of new sensations that assailed every part of her body. Her eyes closed and her lips parted as she moaned helplessly and as Charles looked down on her now naked body, he thought he had never seen a woman as beautiful. His own need consumed him as, unable to wait, he slowly entered her.

Her response was to arch against him as she shuddered violently and gasped as the tremors swamped her and left her unable to speak. Charles moved deeper into her and with the rhythm of the waves he lost himself, all he could hear was

Ruby sobbing with pleasure beneath him. Ruby felt as though she would die and climb to heaven. Never had she known such a deep intensity of emotion. As he cried out, she wrapped her arms around him. It felt as though he were falling, falling deeper into her, but she caught him, wanting him to know that she was still there, and always would be there, supporting him, forever more.

Charles was deep in thought as they walked back to the castle.

'What do we tell them? What will Mrs McKinnon say?' Ruby asked.

'We cannot tell them anything, or we will scandalize the entire Atlantic coast. We will have to wait a whole year Ruby and until then, it will have to remain our secret. Can you wait that long. Will you trust me, Ruby Flynn?'

As they walked hand in hand up the path to Ballyford, where they would have to part and live as near strangers, a master and his servant, the tide returned and washed the name, which Ruby had carved into the sand with her stick, clean away.

Eilinora had worked her magic. Taken by the tide, she had finally gone.

Epilogue

Ruby

I can hear them laughing down on the shore, Charles and the boys, and Lottie is with them, carrying her and Danny's new baby daughter in her arms.

I am in the study and their laughter drifts in through the open window. I can see fishing boats and the ocean. My view of the beach is blocked by the rhododendrons, but hearing their squeals of pleasure is enough to make me smile too.

But someone has to work. If Charles can sneak outdoors with our two boys, he will jump at the chance and so they are off, leaving me shouting after them, but it is no use. They outnumber me and besides, they know I am helpless when it comes to saying no, they have me wrapped around their little fingers, the three of them.

I can't say I really mind, 'tis a true joy, watching them, like now through the open window walking back up the drive.

The lorry collecting the last load of bottles of Ballyford spring water has just left for Cobh.

Oh, how everyone laughed at me when I suggested we could restore Ballyford's fortunes by selling bottled water. Especially

Lottie. It was something Charles had said when he offered me a glass of water in his study and it had played on my mind ever since. *I swear that the water from our streams has fabulous restorative properties. If I could, I would bottle it and sell it.*

'You can't sell the water God put into the mountain spring!' That's what everyone said.

And now, here we are, exporting over ten thousand bottles a year to New York and sure, the Americans can't get enough of it. I have new equipment being delivered from England soon, which will seal the bottles and save the lads having to do it by hand. When that happens, we can produce more and export more. The English aren't as keen yet, but they will follow. They say England is ten years behind America, I can wait. I designed the label on the bottle myself and even drew the picture of the castle and the words *Ballyford, Irish Spring Water* around it.

I have also had the nursery wing knocked down. There are thirty-six rooms in the castle. Why there needed to be a wing so far away that the children cannot be heard, I have no idea. I want to hear my children and I want others to hear them too.

When our first son, Owen, was born, I am sure Charles didn't sleep for six months. For the first three, the baby slept in our room and every time I woke, Charles was sitting up in bed, looking at him. By the time Eamonn arrived, he had relaxed. He carried Eamonn into Owen's bedroom and introduced him to his brand new baby brother. I have never seen a grown man shed so many tears.

We persuaded Mr and Mrs McKinnon to stay. They have their own house on the estate. Mr McKinnon's pigs won best of breed at Galway and we have orders for bacon pouring in. We can barely supply the demand from England fast enough. The McKinnons are like grandparents to the boys and we see them almost every day.

Rory Doyle is missing, a rich man. His mother finally died of a broken heart. We did the best we could for her. Charles had a soft spot for her kindness when he had been a boy and he would never have blamed her for the behaviour of her son. He shared her sorrow. Betrayal is a difficult pain to bear.

Lottie and I tracked down Maria who became the new cook and Lottie took over as housekeeper, once we had persuaded Mrs McKinnon that it was time for her to enjoy her retirement. I can tell you, giving birth to Owen and Eamonn was an easier job than that. Betsy and her Jimmy, they are expecting a new baby any day now and Mary, she is still in the kitchen, but she is special to us and we treat her as one of the family and she loves to do nothing more than accompany me to Galway when I get the chance to visit the shops. Jack is running the bottling and he now lives in the cottage next door to Amy's mother. We are happy. We have our roles and we know what they are. We have all been through enough together to enjoy every day to the full and not one of us wants to look back. Not ever. The past is behind us. We speak only of the future, even Jack.

Tomorrow, Charles and I are leaving the boys with Lottie and we are driving out to Doohoma.

We will walk up the cliff to my parents' house and picnic on the rock, facing Blacksod Bay, then we will walk down to visit Con and Susan and their boys and Sister Francis will join us for the day. I will have told Charles the news by then as we look out over the deep water my father and brother fished on. I shall do it when we are sitting on the rock where I myself spent hours as a girl. I will tell Charles. I think our daughter is on her way and we shall name her Iona.

Acknowledgements

I would like to say a special thank you to my editor, Rosie de Courcy and to Amanda Ridout, CEO at Head of Zeus. Both women, in addition to being top of their profession, are inspirational and passionate about books, writers and the world of publishing. I owe every word I have written to their faith and belief in my ability to deliver.

I would also like to say thank you to the entire Head of Zeus family who work as a highly focused and ambitious team, earning them the digital publisher of the year award for 2015. A remarkable achievement for such a young and innovative publishing house. I would like to thank my agent Piers Blofeld, yes, that's right. He is related to the great giant of cricket commentary and yes, Ian Fleming did use his family name.

Having Rosie, Piers and Amanda in my life means I do not suffer from the renowned writers affliction of loneliness. They are always there and they absolutely understand every idea I bore them with, before bringing me back down to earth. But more than that, they let me be. They never push or guide me or tell me what they would prefer me to write and for that, I am eternally grateful.